SANTA

YNEZ

SANTA YNEZ

A Novel

DENNIS ROY PATRICK

DOEG HILL PUBLISHING
Santa Ynez, California

Santa Ynez
by Dennis Roy Patrick

Published by
Doeg Hill Publishing
P.O. Box 670
Buellton, CA 93427

ISBN: 979-8-9864791-0-1

Library of Congress Control Number: 2022911613

Publisher's Cataloging-in-Publication
(Provided by Cassidy Cataloguing Services, Inc.)

Names: Patrick, Dennis Roy, 1951- author.
Title: Santa Ynez : a novel / Dennis Roy Patrick.
Description: Santa Ynez, California : Doeg Hill Publishing, [2023]
Identifiers: ISBN: 979-8-9864791-0-1 (paperback) | 979-8-9864791-1-8
  (ebook) | LCCN: 2022911613
Subjects: LCSH: Cowboys--California--Santa Ynez--Fiction. |
  Ranches--California--Santa Ynez--Fiction. | Deaths--California-
  -Santa Ynez--Fiction. | Family-owned business enterprises--Cali-
  fornia-- Santa Ynez--Fiction. | Self-realization--Fiction. | Secrecy--
  Fiction. | Santa Ynez (Calif.)-- Fiction. | LCGFT: Western fiction.
Classification: LCC: PS3616.A8694 S36 2023 | DDC: 813/.6--dc23

Copy Editor: Isabella Piestrzynska

Proofreader: Cindy Conger

Cover and Interior Design: theBookDesigners

Book Production Coordinated by Gail M Kearns, TP&B
(www.topressandbeyond.com)

Printed in USA

For June Erva who loved this story

Author's Disclaimer Regarding
Fictional Names and Events

This book is a work of the author's imagination, and all events, businesses, names and other identifying characteristics are invented with the exception of public figures, whose names are used fictionally, and the characters named Carlos and Billy who kindly gave me permission to use their names. Otherwise, any resemblance to actual events, businesses, and persons, living or dead, is purely coincidental.

Santa Ynez is a small agricultural community on California's Central Coast. On a map, it's about ninety miles north of Los Angeles.

SANTA YNEZ

"When you are on the wrong road, sometimes the most progressive man is the one who goes backward first. As long as there are such people, hope lies in our future."

—RICHARD WEAVER

PART ONE

"Ruin, eldest daughter of Zeus, she blinds us all, that fatal madness—she, with those delicate feet, never touching the earth, gliding over the heads of men to trap us all. She entangles one man, now another."

—HOMER, *THE ILIAD*

1

---◇---

Exotic fish of all colors swirled beneath the stem of his martini glass. Presumably they were after the pimento-stuffed olive. The transparent "aquarium bar" at the newly remodeled Coral Casino was quite the rage when first installed. Cole sipped his martini and stared out at the Santa Barbara Channel where less pampered fish swam.

He felt her hand on his shoulder and turned. Jessica looked as she always did, perfect for the occasion. White linen, blond hair lightly touching tan shoulders.

"Congratulations, Dr. Clay." She kissed him on the cheek. "Our table's ready."

They took seats at a table on the patio beneath the blue-and-white-striped canvas awning. Jessica had already ordered a bottle of Sauvignon blanc, which sat chilling in a silver bowl at the center of the table. She poured herself a glass and tipped it toward her husband before taking a sip.

"It's been a long road. We should celebrate."

"This is a nice surprise. Thank you," he said.

Cole finished his martini and poured himself a glass of the wine. He looked up the coast. "You can almost see ground zero from here."

Jessica looked toward Isla Vista several miles to the

3

north. She could just make out the buildings of the University of California, Santa Barbara, where they had met as undergraduates. "Feels like a hundred years ago."

"It was eight. This month, in fact."

"Ever the historian."

"Pretty easy. End of our sophomore year. The party on Campus Point."

Jessica smiled. "Who would have thought? A sophisticated Angelino falling for a yahoo from the Santa Ynez Valley."

"Former yahoo."

"So now what? What does a former yahoo with a doctorate in intellectual history from Stanford do now?"

Cole reached for a twisted parmesan bread stick. "Presumably what all historians do. Think great thoughts, write books that slow man's march toward the abyss," Cole replied. "What does a former debutante do with a law degree from USC?"

Jessica flashed a coy smile, the way she did when she had news. Cole knew then she had been holding back, that the celebratory lunch had as much to do with what she was about to say as his completing his doctorate.

"As a matter of fact, I have news on that front. I got the offer."

"The offer?"

"Yes!"

"From?"

"Sterling, Davis and Platt. My number one pick. One of the best entertainment practices in LA, beautiful offices on the west side, great comp. The whole deal."

"So it's LA, I guess."

"Of course," Jessica said. "We stay here, I'll be doing

trusts and estates for rich geezers in Montecito, and you'll be teaching high school history."

Their food arrived. Jessica had preordered herself a chilled lobster salad; Cole a club sandwich. Cole leaned forward and spoke in a whisper. "Be careful. We're surrounded by the geezers."

"Right. Sorry."

"I have applications in at UCLA, the Claremont colleges, and Occidental. They all have history department vacancies. Hopefully, something will come through." He looked at the ocean; a light chop dimpled the channel. He shook his head.

"What?" she asked.

"Sometimes I wonder if we really want to raise our kids in Los Angeles. The epicenter of self. Where a celebrity's latest stint in rehab bumps a story on world hunger."

Jessica waved her hand dismissively. "Oh, please. Like the size of Oprah's house in Montecito doesn't get equal attention up here?" She picked at a piece of lobster. "It's more than that. LA's just more sophisticated— there's more *happening*."

Cole surveyed the elegant dining room of the Coral Casino. Perfectly beautiful people looking perfectly bored. "No doubt. Whether any of it is 'good' is a different issue."

"What's 'good'?" she asked. "Matter of opinion, isn't it?"

"Actually, *that's* a matter of opinion," he replied.

Jessica took another sip of her wine and extracted a tiny piece of lobster shell from her teeth with a freshly manicured fingernail. "That's what I said."

"No, you were saying the opposite—that what is 'good' is subjective, a matter of opinion. I meant that philosophers disagree on whether that's true. Many believe there exists an objective, absolute standard of good, of right and wrong. Others contend it is relative, situational."

"And you?"

"I believe in objective good," Cole said. "The trick is knowing what it is."

"Well, that's confusing. What good is an objective truth if we have to debate what it is?" Jessica asked.

"It makes a difference to believe that it exists. Otherwise, what is the point of seeking it out?"

Jessica shook her head and smiled. "You debated these issues with Elliot growing up?"

"No. Those conversations were more about beef prices and the likelihood of rain. But that's why I miss the ranch. No complex ambiguities."

"That's for sure. More like a feudal manor from ancient times. Your brother trades firewood for farrier services."

"Barter is very efficient."

"You'd be bored senseless up there. You've moved on, Cole; we both have. Besides, we stay here, Dustin'll end up a cowboy."

"There are worse things."

"Like?"

Cole considered the issue. "Investment banker, lawyer..."

Jessica smiled. "Well played."

"You know it's a big part of my DNA, that ranch. My mother's people, five generations," Cole added, now serious.

"Yeah, and your grandfather is a Connecticut Yankee,

a centimillionaire telecom exec. I'd say your DNA is a mixed bag."

"Was," Cole corrected.

"Huh?"

"Prescott. He *was* a centimillionaire exec. He's now a poor rancher, ironically."

Jessica finished her lunch. "We need to think about the house."

"I assume we sell it and pay off your parents."

"Yeah, and it's appreciated significantly."

She poured more wine into their glasses. "The issue is, what are you going to do with yourself in the interim, before we get resettled down there?"

Cole looked to the ocean and back. "The ranch has got some challenges."

"Really? That's a shock," she said, the sarcasm thick.

He ignored her. "I need to spend some time sorting through it. The trust expires in a little more than two years. After that, Travis and I will hold our interests directly and be in charge. Which means, for all intents and purposes, Travis. I want to clean things up before I hand him the keys. Only fair."

He folded his napkin and finished his wine. "In fact, I'm going up to see him ride in Salinas tomorrow. Taking the camper. You should come. Be fun, like old times. Maybe we can produce another heir for all the money we're going to make."

"Not a chance," she laughed.

"Which? Salinas or the heir?" Cole added playfully.

"Either. I don't do campers and it's too early for another heir. We have a lot to think about, Cole," she added, now serious.

"See you tonight counselor," he said smiling as they stood to leave.

Later that afternoon, Cole drove under the high wrought-iron gate framing the entrance to the Hope Hills neighborhood where they owned a home. The land that became Hope Hills had been settled by an Irish immigrant who ran sheep over its gentle slopes. There is no record of whether he and his family enjoyed the stunning view of the Pacific Ocean or the neighborhood's private secluded beach. But its current occupants did, when they weren't playing golf or tennis at their private Las Olas Country Club. Cole had a conflicted relationship with the club. His first visit had been cut short by a dress code violation helpfully flagged by a member—the local Episcopal priest who enjoyed his "bloodies" in the lounge on Sunday shortly after preaching to the already saved. Jeans violated the club's dress code. After the infraction, Cole had boycotted the club for a year, finally succumbing to Jessica's insistence that they join to meet the "right people."

As the road skirted the private lake past multimillion-dollar homes, Cole reflected on their own home—the one Jessica's parents had financed with a low-interest loan. The arrangement made him uncomfortable. Jessica had made it clear she would not live on Cole's family ranch, Arroyo de Zaca, some forty-five minutes inland from Santa Barbara. The loan from her parents was a way for them to get into the California real estate market while each pursued their graduate degrees.

When his car slid into the gravel driveway of that home, it felt unfamiliar. It was. Jessica and Cole had only lived there a short time before Cole began his PhD program at Stanford. For some time, Jessica split her time between Cole's apartment in Palo Alto and their Santa Barbara home. Three years into the arrangement, Jessica had moved back to Los Angeles to live in her parents' guest house while she attended law school, an arrangement that provided built-in babysitting for their young child. The house in Santa Barbara had been rented until recently when Jessica, law degree in hand, moved back.

Cole killed the engine and sat. The house looked smaller than the image he held in his mind's eye. He stared at it as if for the first time. The trellis that framed the entrance to the white stucco cottage was covered in bougainvillea vines. The front yard wrapped gently to the south, where it met a small barn and garden. Hope Hills was, ostensibly, an "equine community," but Jessica had insisted that Cole's horses stay at the ranch. Not unreasonable under the circumstances Cole thought, though he would have loved to ride on the beach that stretched for two miles just below the bluff on which their house rested.

He walked to the front door but found it locked. He had not brought his key. He knocked but there was no answer. In the backyard past the pool he found a spare key under the fake rock where he had put it. He wondered why burglars were not more adept at spotting fake rocks. He unlocked the back door and entered.

"Jessica?"

There was no answer.

The kitchen was cluttered with ordinary things. A newspaper spread on the dining table, yellow stickies spotting the refrigerator door. Cole walked down the hall that led from the kitchen to the bedroom wing. The hallway was filled with pictures of Jessica and Cole and their young son Dustin—riding on the ranch, family gatherings, picnics at the beach. One pulled him in. It was a shot of Jessica and Cole and their friends at UCSB the year they met. It was a picture of innocent joy, the unknowing anticipation of all that would follow. It reminded him of the lives that they had expected to live, of friends no longer part of their social circle; friends not, as Jessica put it, "on the same track." For reasons Cole did not understand, that picture, at that moment, broke like a cold wave over his shoulders.

He let it go. He walked to the door of their son's bedroom, knowing he was in Los Angeles with Jessica's parents. He opened it anyway. It was filled with the ordinary things of a child's life—a Star Wars Lightsaber, a baseball mitt, Lego pieces of every color scattered across the floor. A framed picture of his uncle Travis competing at the Calgary Stampede occupied the prize space over his bed.

Cole closed the door gently. Dustin had been born shortly after Jessica graduated from UCSB. Jessica once described him as the brightest star—and darkest cloud— in the firmament of their relationship. From the moment he slipped from her womb into Cole's hands, all red and wet and squalling, he had been the center of their universe. But Jessica never let Cole forget that his insistence they have the baby had, in her mind, clouded the bona fides of his proposal and their decision to marry.

Cole walked into their bedroom, the room dark. Jessica was asleep, or at least doing a good job of pretending to be. He couldn't tell. He undressed and slipped under the covers, pressing his body against her back and bare legs. She roused slightly and rolled over. Cole pulled her tee shirt over her head and they made love without speaking. As Cole rolled to his side his mind fired with the possibilities. He wanted to talk, to explore every avenue of the new life they planned. But, as he reached out to touch her shoulder, he heard the cadence of her breath, the tiny whistle in her throat, and he knew she was already deep in sleep.

2

---◇---

Cole awakened early the next morning, Jessica was still asleep at his side. He watched her sleep. First light flooded the room and gave shape to the objects within—Jessica's antique dresser, silver-framed pictures of Cole's and Jessica's parents, an ornate leather chair hand tooled by Cole's great-grandfather. He wanted to wake her, but he knew she would not appreciate the gesture. She was not a "morning person" and reminded him often.

As he rose to dress, he felt the distance between them as if it were an object, tangible and hard. He knew the time they had spent apart, pursuing degrees they hoped would fuel their aspirations, had taken a toll. He resolved to close the gap, to cover the distance between them.

But first, Salinas. He had promised his brother.

He left the house and drove north to Arroyo de Zaca. The Clay family ranch rested in the center of the Santa Ynez Valley, an easy drive north from Santa Barbara along the old "El Camino Real," now Highway 101. He parked near the barn and traded his car for a camper truck and continued north. With luck, he would be in Salinas in three hours. He smiled as he settled into the collapsed front seat of the truck, its rattle and smell familiar. He had logged a thousand miles in that truck, competing in high school rodeos all over the Southwest. He pushed an eight-track cassette into a player bracketed to the bottom of the dash. *Jerry Jeff Walker Live at Gruene Hall.* He marveled at the glorious antiquity—of both music and machine.

He arrived at the Salinas Valley Fairgrounds in late afternoon. Shadows spotted the gravel lot as a light breeze carried the smell of dust and dung. He parked and walked through a clutter of trucks and trailer rigs in an area reserved for contestants and the stockmen who supply "rough stock" bulls and broncs to the rodeo. The Clays were both. His younger brother Travis, now a highly ranked saddle bronc rider, was also manager of the family's rough stock business. Cole found Travis tending their prize bucking horse, Ragged Edge.

"Hey."

Travis turned. "Hey, big brother!" He stepped out of the pen, closed the gate and embraced him. "Didn't think you'd make it. Figured you'd be lecturing on Greek philosophy or something, putting the snowflakes on the straight and narrow."

"I'm pretty much unemployed at the moment. Thought I'd burn some time with the deplorables, for perspective."

"You've come to the right place, amigo. Most these guys consider their GED an advanced degree."

"You would, I guess," Cole smiled.

"Yes, sir. If I had one."

Ragged Edge reared and kicked the metal panels between them.

"Least she's still well behaved."

"She's a demon. Elliot said to Ace her."

"Acepromazine is a tranquilizer. Who tranquilizes a bucking horse?"

"Stockman who needs her to release proper. She's got a shot at the National Finals in Vegas but needs one more clean release in a sanctioned event to even be considered. If she fights the chute she could get bounced, then we're screwed. You know that, big brother."

"Not sure the cowboy'd appreciate us dulling down his draw."

"Hell, he might."

"Who is it?"

"Wade."

"Who'd you draw?"

"A dink. Be lucky to do ten points on him."

"You still in the running?"

"For the finals? In theory, big brother. Ain't holding my breath."

They walked back to the camper and unfolded two lawn chairs. Cole retrieved a cooler of beer and they fell into the easy banter they had always enjoyed. At twenty-four, Travis was four years Cole's junior. He was two inches shorter with an olive complexion and dark piercing eyes. Cole, by contrast, had his father's light brown hair and blue eyes, graced by the same olive complexion. The combination of their Mexican and Scotch-Irish heritage had proven beneficent for both. By any standard they were exceptionally handsome men, a fact their mother had warned them to ignore. "What matters is not what God made of your face," she said, "but what you make of your heart."

"Funny how things work out," Travis said. "When you won that national high school deal, I thought you were goin' to the finals for sure. You were my idol. The Lone Fuckin' Ranger."

Cole smiled and finished his first beer. "That all changed the first time Elliot put you on a bronc. You must'a been twelve or so. Remember that?"

"I remember, scared as shit. But I wasn't gonna get bucked in front of you."

There was a moment of silence as Travis reached into the blue Igloo cooler and rustled through the ice. He retrieved two more beers and handed one to Cole.

Cole pulled the cap. "Shit. Once I saw you sit that horse, I knew it was over. You, little brother, are the cowboy."

"Probably just as well, big brother."

"Why's that?"

"Weak chin. Man jus' don't look right in a cowboy hat when he's a little slight in the jaw. You got that kinda academic look, I guess. You look like you been readin' all day and are about to say something important. Man's gotta have a real square jaw to be a cowboy."

Cole nodded. "Guess it was all preordained."

"Yes, sir. But you've done okay. I mean, look at you, frickin' PhD, rich wife. You done good, big brother. You're kinda the Lone Ranger again, just a different deal. Me, I'm still Elliot's Tonto."

Cole shook his head. "You can't say things like that. It implies a subservient position for the Native American. You're stereotyping."

He thought about it. "Okay, I'm Elliot's Mexican."

"Half-Mexican."

Travis leaned back and smiled. "Couple no-account half-breeds all we are."

"Speak for yourself. My mixed heritage will bring diverse perspective to my teaching."

Travis laughed. Cole had always loved his younger brother's laugh. He laughed in a high pitch, unguarded and sincere, as if he could extract the joy from a moment, unconcerned by what others thought. Cole was jealous of his capacity for willful innocence.

Travis opened his beer and took a long pull. "You're 'bout as diverse as Mitch fucking McConnell. You're the 'waspy-est' guy I know."

"I don't think 'waspy-est' is a word, little brother... and what do you know about Mitch McConnell?"

"Hell, Cole. I read the papers."

"Really?"

Travis smiled and killed his beer. "No, but I saw him on Fox. No wonder the Republicans are getting their asses kicked."

"Weak chin," Cole added.

"No chin." Travis stood. "Never be a cowboy."

"You had to come back to that."

"Sorry, brother. I'm gonna rest up some in my rig. I ride in the first group. Should be about 7:00 p.m. If you flank me, you can help me run Ragged Edge down the chute and get Wade set."

"See you then."

At the appointed hour, Cole rapped on the door of the sleeping compartment that occupied the front quarter of Travis's horse trailer. Travis emerged, hat in hand. He pulled it tight so that his ears distended slightly on each side, then strapped on leather chaps. Transformed, he made his way through the graveled maze of trucks, trailers, and horses with Cole trailing closely behind.

As they walked in evening light toward the arena, the sound of summer rodeo rose up to greet them. Cheers from the arena, the voice of the rodeo announcer, and the chatter of cowboys all blended into a sort of white noise that folded over them like a familiar blanket. It was the sound of every summer of Cole's youth. It whispered tales of beer, cowgirls, and kisses stolen beneath the bleachers of some long-forgotten county fair and of glory...a silver buckle, the right to swagger, if only for a week until the next contest down the same summer road.

Cole smiled as they pushed through the Contestant's Gate toward the chutes. Travis did not. He hated to arrive early. It made him nervous. He rode by instinct. Too much time to think didn't help.

They waited for the buzzer signaling the end of the last ride.

"*Tough ride for Dancy Roth,*" cracked through the PA system. "*Our next rider, Travis Clay.*"

Travis climbed the rails of the bucking chute and lowered himself gently onto the back of a bay gelding. He grabbed the thick rein, paused for a beat, then nodded his head slightly. At that exact moment, Cole, on the ground behind the chute, pulled the flank strap on the bronc as a second cowboy in the arena pulled the gate open. Travis reentered a familiar space—eight seconds of sheer violence, of sweat and muscle and will juxtaposed: two thousand pounds of horse trying to remove one hundred and seventy pounds of cowboy equally determined to stay; the cowboy digging metal spurs into the neck and shoulders of the horse; the horse answering each insult with hooves sent skyward, snapping the head, neck, and shoulders of his provocateur forward and back in a raging, rhythmic arc—a ballet from hell.

The eight-second buzzer sounded and Travis reached for the pick-up man who had galloped to Travis's side, using him to slide off the bronc and onto the ground. Travis's score flashed on the arena scoreboard to scattered applause that he did not acknowledge. It had been an adequate performance by both horse and rider but nothing more. Disappointed, he walked straight to the gate that exited the arena floor, turning left as he did, returning to the bucking chutes where another rider prepared.

Wade Roy, in his rookie season, was barely twenty years of age. He wore a white western shirt over Wranglers topped by a black Resistol hat, its brim flat in the style of a bull rider. He didn't look like he could bench press a hundred pounds. The tongue of his belt passed four inches past the buckle, such was the narrow width of his waist. Cole wondered how it was possible this scrawny kid was among the top money winners so far this season.

"You ready?" Cole asked.

"I guess," Wade replied. "That bitch a' yours sure jacked up."

"She's a little fresh. She'll be fine," Cole said.

They both watched as Travis pushed the chestnut mare down an alley and into the bucking chute, the horse throwing her head and kicking every inch of the way. They were late to load, the quick push not helping the horse to calm.

The announcer came back: *"Okay, I think we're ready…. Up next is Wade Roy. Wade's having a banner rookie year, may even claim the last slot to compete in the National Finals Rodeo in Las Vegas."*

Travis slapped Wade on the back. "Let's go."

Travis and several cowboys crowded the catwalk as Wade lowered himself onto Ragged Edge, her back arched and taut. The mare reacted instantly. Constrained by the narrow confines of metal panels in the chute, she struggled in a vain effort to buck and threw her weight side to side. Momentarily, Wade's leg was pinned between the horse and the chute wall. He leaned forward to free his leg just as the bronc threw her head up, catching Wade square in the face. Wade's nose spurted blood as Travis quickly leaned in and pulled him off the horse and out of the chute.

"We're going to move on. Give this mare a chance to settle."

Travis handed Wade a bandana. "Walk it off." Wade climbed down and walked away, holding the bandana to his nose.

Travis passed Cole a canvas bag. "Like I said, Elliot said t'Ace her. He packed a syringe in the bag."

"Well, Elliot isn't here."

Travis looked away. "Son of a bitch's always here. I'll talk to Wade. Give you a minute."

Cole paused to look around him, then turned back to Ragged Edge, her back still coiled, eyes wide with rage. He pulled the zipper back on the bag. He waited as a cowboy climbed down from the adjacent chute and walked away. He retrieved the already-loaded syringe, then reached through the bucking chute cage. He pushed the syringe into an artery on Ragged Edge's neck, removed it and placed it back in the bag. Cole gently stroked the mare's neck. She began to settle.

Travis and Wade returned and, with Cole, they watched as the adjacent chute released another contestant. The eight-second buzzer sounded.

"No score…. Okay. Wade Roy's getting set for a second go on Ragged Edge."

Wade climbed the chute and slowly lowered himself onto the mare's back. Cole leaned down and reached into the chute, preparing to pull the flank strap.

"This horse's been a big bucker this year; might even earn her own trip to Vegas. But if she shies a second time, Wade'll get a reride on a different mount."

Ragged Edge reared again, momentarily throwing Wade off balance, then settled for an instant. Wade nodded, then disappeared as the chute opened and the crowd roared. After flanking the horse, Cole moved down the catwalk to see the arena. By the time he had a decent view, Ragged Edge was on her back, Wade trapped between the horse and the ground. The horse struggled to regain her footing, and, when she finally did, her rear hoof struck Wade's head. The horse galloped off. Wade remained still. Travis caught Cole's eye as the eight-second buzzer blew.

Moments later, red-and-yellow blinking lights bounced off metal panels in the staging area where Wade lay motionless on a stretcher. The ambulance transported Wade the short distance to an unused portion of the parking lot where a medevac helicopter sat waiting, its blades spinning slowly. It was the last image Cole saw before retreating behind the thin metal walls of his camper's shell.

At 2:00 a.m. the next morning, Cole still struggled to find sleep. He longed to push past the edge of his consciousness, to dive deep in mindless waters; deep enough to extinguish flickering images of Wade's wreck. But he couldn't. And he knew it was the bourbon. Like the wrong lover, it had delivered a jolt of euphoria but held peace just out of reach. He cursed the bourbon and opened his eyes, foggy. He hated the feeling; like his head was filled with cotton; like he had lost the ability to command that magnificent synaptic dance that leads inexorably to an answer, to clarity. He hated the feeling because Cole Clay, above all else, lived in his head. Surrendering to the anxiety that denied him sleep, he surveyed the books that cluttered the table in front of him: *Icarus Fallen* by Chantal Delsol, *Ideas Have Consequences* by Richard Weaver. He raised a dog-eared copy of Plato's *Republic* to his eyes. Its words fell in and out of focus until, finally, he fell into a deep sleep.

The next morning, he awakened slowly, the camper cluttered with empties. His cell phone vibrated. He answered and heard his brother's voice.

"Okay, give me two minutes," Cole rasped.

Cole pushed his legs over the edge of the bed, took a deep breath, and dragged himself to the camper's tiny bathroom. He turned on the faucet. It growled and produced a thin stream of brackish water. He splashed his face. Morning light pierced a faded newspaper taped over the window. An old headline and picture of a much younger Cole covered the page: "Local Wins Western Regional High School Championship." Cole ripped it off, wiped his face, and dropped the paper to the floor.

Outside, the contestant parking lot emptied as trucks pulling horse trailers rumbled toward the exit in no ascertainable pattern. A few rigs remained, their owners packing gear and loading horses. Cole walked the short distance to Travis's rig. The trailer was already loaded with their horses. Steamy breath blew through barred windows above stenciled words that were chipped and faded: "CLAY RANCH BUCKING HORSES."

"What'd you hear?" Cole asked.

"Nothing good. He's at Salinas Memorial."

Suddenly the stock trailer rocked as Ragged Edge kicked the trailer's siding. Cole smacked the side of the trailer with the open palm of his gloved hand.

"Quit!"

Travis climbed into the truck cab, its diesel engine rattling.

He cranked his driver side window up and smiled, still oblivious to the world of hurt about to descend.

Cole followed a few minutes later, driving south on Highway 101 to the exit for Salinas Valley Memorial Hospital. One mile from the exit, he spotted the sprawling cinder-block building, left the highway, and pulled his truck and trailer to the curb. He pushed through the hospital's glass doors. An elderly woman at reception greeted him with odd cheerfulness, as if it were a social call and not the last place on earth he would choose to be.

He was directed to Wade's room and traversed a long hospital corridor, its spotless floor reflecting bright florescent lighting above. He walked past a seated duty nurse. She eyed his progress with a vague look of disdain. He looked down at the dirt clinging to his boots and wished he had removed the spurs that clicked with each step as if to announce his intrusion.

Cole was relieved to see a group of cowboys outside a door he assumed was Wade's. He acknowledged several, shaking their hands quietly. He tipped his hat at one he did not recognize, an older man in a western-cut sports coat and a silver belly Stetson. The stranger extended his hand.

"Mr. Clay, my name is Clive Westgate. I'm with the Rodeo Association. Assume you're here to check on Wade. I'm wondering if we might have a word?"

"Sure, give me a minute. Wanna check on him first if I can."

Clive stepped to the side.

Cole was not prepared for what he saw upon entering the room. Wade was unconscious, tubes penetrating his nose and mouth. His head had been shaved and was wrapped in thick gauze. His pulse and blood pressure were monitored on screens casting a green glow over an otherwise dark room. The room was silent but for the hiss of a ventilator and the intermittent beeps of a pulse monitor.

He did not notice her until she tried to speak. "You were..." her voice cracked. She tried again. "You were there, weren't you?" Wade's young wife sat in the shadowed corner opposite his bed.

"Yes, ma'am, I was. I'm Cole Clay. I'm a friend of Wade's," Cole replied.

A nurse entered. "Sir, you are not supposed to be in here. You will have to leave."

"Of course." Cole turned to Wade's wife. "If there is anything I can..." He trailed off when she raised her hand for him to stop and shook her head. She began to weep and buried her face in tiny hands, the thin bones of her unadorned fingers visible.

As Cole exited the room, he glanced down the hall to see Clive Westgate at the coffee machine, his back to Cole. Cole hesitated, then turned and left the hospital. The last person he wanted to talk to was someone with the Professional Rodeo Cowboy Association. The PRCA held jurisdiction over all sanctioned rodeo events.

He knew then they would be investigating the accident. But he wasn't ready. He had to think. He had too many questions himself to start answering them.

Cole continued south lost in his thoughts and oblivious to the beauty of the passing hills. Approaching Paso Robles, he exited the highway near a ramshackle country market and a Chevron gas station. He pulled his rig between the pumps and filled up, then walked into the dark market. Its pine-plank floor bowed slightly as he walked between half-empty shelves. An elderly Mexican man stood behind the counter. His face was a dark mahogany, his hair and whiskers white. Deep lines in his cheeks spoke to a hard history. He did not speak.

Cole placed a six-pack of beer on the counter and pointed to the bourbon on shelves behind the cash register. The clerk turned and pulled a pint bottle down.

"*No. Dame el completo,*" Cole demanded. The clerk pulled a full handle then smiled a toothless grin.

Back on the highway, Cole drove through the hills and oak-lined canyons of California's Central Coast. The wild wheat and rye had turned gold and beige, their coat of color broken by tight green canopies of live oak spotting every hill. Cole thought of his college classmates from the East, sons of privilege who summered in Maine in white clapboard houses nestled in rocky coves among evergreen pine. Before they left school each spring, to summer with families who had owned those retreats for generations, they never failed to deride California's hot summers and the brown hills that announced its coming. To Cole there was nothing prettier, his affection for their color exceeded only by his love of the smell—the dry scent of sage, oak, and dirt.

Cole rolled down the window of his truck and breathed in the air. He tried not to think. He pulled the six-pack of beer from his back seat and opened one, happy to be somewhere between where he'd been and where he was going. He wished he could stay.

Somewhere south of Santa Maria the topography began to change and Cole saw it as if for the first time. The open grazing land of his youth was now interrupted by acres of tightly manicured rows of grape vine. To Cole's mind, the vineyards were as unnatural as the feral pigs that also blighted the hillsides of his home county. Grapes and pigs, two nonnative invaders who had found the weather and soil of the Central Coast an irresistibly beneficent environment in which to propagate.

Like almost everyone else in California, the pigs were immigrants. Their forefathers had arrived involuntarily in the hulls of Spanish galleons to be turned loose along the coast to provide fresh meat for return voyages. Now they rutted the pastures of every ranch in the Santa Ynez Valley, their numbers growing exponentially with the average sow delivering eight to ten babies twice a year.

It wasn't the Spanish, but Hollywood, that brought the vintners. Owing in part to the success of the film *Sideways* in 2004, the California wine industry pushed its footprint south from Napa and Sonoma into the Central Coast. Every multimillionaire with too much money and nowhere to put it decided to plant a boutique vineyard—you can only have so many Teslas. The result, locals believed, had been devastating to the Santa Ynez Valley and, in particular, to Cole's hometown of Los Olivos.

Cole remembered riding his horse into Los Olivos as a boy to visit the quirky local shops that lined the single main drag. Side's Hardware and Shoes had been his favorite; Homer Side presiding from his rocker just inside the door, directing customers to a particular nail or washer in an irritated tone that suggested selling his wares was more a bother than his only source of income. Cole had once asked him where the shoes were. Old man Side had barked back: "This is a hardware store, son. Why in hell would I stock shoes?" "Side's" was now a chic eatery featuring twenty-two-dollar hamburgers and truffle fries. Still no shoes.

Most of the original establishments had been replaced by wine "tasting rooms." Forty of them. As a result, every weekend the town's resident population of about one thousand sought refuge from a roving mass of visitors who had come to sample some of the one hundred and twenty locally grown varietals. As a general rule, they sampled too liberally.

He passed another ranch, this one transformed not by grapes, but marijuana. Land Cole had ridden on horseback as a child was now covered in white plastic canopies warming the leaves of the plant California had recently legalized for recreational use. The skunk-like odor along that stretch of highway was so heavy Cole wasn't sure if it was the beer, or the air, sustaining his buzz.

The push to legalize cannabis in California had united the pro-pot left with the libertarian right under the banner of "personal freedom." They had argued pot was a "personal life-style issue" affecting only the user. Most knew better. Greenlighting pot farming had plenty of "external effects." The terpenes vaporized by the cannabis plant had a chemical composition similar to turpentine. Their adverse impact on other crops—especially wine grapes—was well known. The visual blight of plastic canopies was now everywhere. And there was Travis's perspective: "Having to wade through a gaggle of half-baked hipsters sporting tiny fedoras every weekend is enough to kill the deal for me." But Santa Barbara County's Board of Supervisors had seen it differently. Some wondered how politicians who could dictate your barn paint in the name of environmental sensitivity had been so fast to roll over for the pot lobby. But Cole knew the answer: Pot was a cash business, and the marijuana lobby had spread it widely. In any case, between the vineyards and the pot farms, it was clear that cattle grazing was getting squeezed. It was just a matter of time before every square inch of the Santa Ynez Valley would rest beneath plastic tarps or trellised vines owned by corporations whose names he did not recognize.

Cole opened a second can of beer and recalled the classical economic theorists he had read at Stanford. They would applaud the "consolidation" of land in Santa Ynez as the movement of assets to their "highest and best use." Efficiency was the lord god of market theorists. The family farm be damned. It was hard to argue with the logic of Adam Smith and his progeny. After all, wasn't the transformation of Santa Ynez not only inevitable but desirable? Progress?

As Cole pondered the question, a black Range Rover pulled alongside his truck. Its female occupants, twenty-something and carefree, were doubtless up from LA for the weekend. From their demeanor, Cole assumed they had been sampling at least one of the Valley's new products, maybe both. The brunette on the passenger side lowered her window. Cole reciprocated, expecting they needed directions.

"Hey, are you a *real* cowboy?" she screamed into the wind in Cole's direction.

Laughing, she rolled up her window and they sped off, leaving Cole to contemplate her inadvertently existential question. Was he a "real cowboy?"

Cole was born on their cattle ranch, Arroyo de Zaca. It had been a cow-calf operation as long as anyone could remember. It still was. As a boy, Cole had learned to cowboy at the side of his father Elliot and their ranch hand Carlos. His grandfather Prescott had his own ranch, and, for a while, they combined their cattle operations to achieve the scale necessary to make a go of ranching on the Central Coast. In time, Cole's younger brother Travis joined them in the saddle. Those days were some of the happiest of Cole's life. At the time, Cole could imagine no higher accolade than an old timer calling him "a pretty good hand."

Cole perfected his craft. He learned to ride and rope and doctor cattle. He became an expert horseman and, like his father, he rodeoed. But, unlike Travis, Cole had an unexpected conflict: He was an excellent student and academics competed for the time he might have spent on a horse. How he might divide his time between ranching and school became a source of conflict between Elliot and Cole's mother Valentia. It was her wish that he go to college and pursue his interest in history and philosophy. In the end, she won.

Cole graduated second in his class from Santa Ynez High and matriculated at the University of California at

Santa Barbara. He dove into his academics and discovered a passion for history, intellectual history in particular. Starting with the ancient Greeks, he worked his way through the ideas that had animated the Renaissance and the Enlightenment, then on to the great European philosophers and political and economic theorists.

He and Jessica planned a life, a life that saw them securing graduate degrees and enjoying careers unbounded by the parochialism of Santa Barbara County.

But their plans were interrupted by tragedy. Soon after Cole and Jessica began their graduate programs at Stanford and USC respectively, Cole's mother was killed in an automobile accident. Cole was forced to face realities he had suspected, but suppressed, as if ignoring a bad dream would make it not so. Elliot's alcoholism had consumed his life; worse, his mismanagement of the ranch and its operations had ushered in the very real prospect of losing property that had been in their family for generations. Travis quit high school at seventeen to help full time. Cole drove south to the ranch most weekends, less often farther south to see his wife and child in Los Angeles. That fact planted seeds of resentment in Jessica; an equal measure of guilt in Cole. Now, graduate degrees in hand, they were ready to move on, to purge those memories and build a life.

With all that in mind, Cole reflected on the question: Was he still a cowboy? What did that even mean? Did it matter?

He had studied man's journey through the long sweep of history. He now believed that while "agriculture" had allowed nomadic people to settle, to form communities from which came much good, the great leaps of human progress had been fueled not by farmers, but by industrialization and science and religion; *by ideas*. In particular, ideas regarding governance of the "polis," the rules of engagement for the grand compromise by which humans traded their ostensible freedom in a "state of nature" for the efficiency and safety of living in concert with others.

From Cole's new perspective, the idea of spending his life *ranching* seemed somehow too small. He found his sustenance now in history and ideas—ideas with scale and scope; ideas that impacted the world. He was also tired of being "land rich and cash poor." He now had a glimpse of Jessica's world and he wanted it to be his own.

With these thoughts, still jumbled and unformed, Cole made a sweeping left turn off the highway and came to a stop between two wooden columns. They framed the entrance to Arroyo de Zaca, the place where he had learned to cowboy and to love the land.

He stopped to admire their simplicity. He had built the columns himself many years before. The reclaimed fence board that skinned the columns looked good, better for years of weather. And they looked right, like they belonged. He was glad he had talked Elliot out of the ornate stucco columns of stone and wrought iron he had proposed. If you want an Italian villa, build it in Tuscany. This was "old California"—Mexico until the United States stole it in settlement of the Mexican-American War. It should look like it.

Cole considered the rain-worn letters on the fence board to the left of the gate. "Arroyo de Zaca." Zaca ranch took its name from a creek that flowed along the eastern perimeter of the ranch. "Zaca" was said to be a

Chumash word, but nobody knew what it meant. For many years it had meant everything to Cole.

He punched the combination into the gate and watched it open slowly, its solar batteries laboring to push the weighty barriers back. He followed the serpentine flow of the gravel ranch road up a mild grade toward the residence. He passed through towering white oaks, some over three hundred years old, lining each side of the road. Trees like these, seedlings when the first Europeans arrived, were being cleared from neighboring ranches to make room for vineyards or pot farms. To date, the Clays had been unwilling to trade three centuries of history for improved economics. How long they might stand astride the rising tide of modernity was anybody's guess.

As the road crested, he pulled to one side and took in the view. From there he could see two-thirds of the ranch's roughly two thousand acres. The view never ceased to amaze. Rolling hills transected by deep canyons; patches of grey and brown sage; lichen dripping from the branches of valley oak; the black dots of Angus dotting every pasture. It was a beautiful piece of earth, all the more surprising for its proximity to LA about two hours south. Cole marveled at the incongruity of a cowboy culture thriving so close to LA. How much longer that culture could survive was an open question.

Cole parked near the barn and walked up the steps and into his childhood home. Wooden planks on the front porch creaked, announcing his homecoming. He pushed through the heavy oak door and stepped inside. The smell of wood and leather met him. More than the familiar surroundings, it was that rich scent that told him he was home.

He hung his hat on a peg in the foyer and entered the "great room." It was dark and full of noise. Cole had protested the addition when first proposed: a sleek, flat-screen television oxymoronically bolted into a cedar plank wall that dated to the *hacienda*'s construction in 1923, more than a decade before a farm boy named Philo Farnsworth would invent a technology called "Tele-Vision." Cole objected less to the technology than the programming it had spawned. Like an electronic annelid worm, television had birthed multiple generations of its own young without, it would seem, any cross-fertilization with intelligent life. The result now met Cole full force: Sean Hannity agreeing with a crony guest who was agreeing with "all the experts" who agree immigration is a "huge" problem. More specifically, Mexicans on our southern border.

Cole's stepmother Victoria owned the couch, cigarette in hand. She was riveted. She loved Sean. Indeed, she often said she had divorced her ex because he was a "liberal tool." Cole suspected more to the story. Custody of Victoria's twins, Leaf and Summer, had been awarded to their father amid allegations of extra-marital affairs and alcoholism. Cole had no interest in the details. She and Elliot married eleven months after Cole's mother died. Victoria exercised her "visitation rights" by inviting the twins to stay at the ranch for two weeks each summer. So far as Cole knew, Leaf was male and Summer female but both preferred "nonbinary" gender pronouns like "ver" and "verself." Their visits to the ranch were always an occasion for linguistic gymnastics.

Victoria, on the other hand, wore her sexuality like a beer logo light. Victoria's blouses invariably revealed

more of her ample breasts than most cared to see. She
was oblivious, unaware of her new reality. She had been
a stunning beauty in her twenties, but cigarettes and
alcohol had taken a toll, as had the sun. Her penchant
for Mexican food didn't help. Her mouth was pinched
and small as if perpetually reacting to the bitter pill life
had served.

"Well if it isn't Dr. Clay," she opened. She took a
long drag on her cigarette and exhaled slowly through
her nose. Cole thought of a dragon.

"Hey, Victoria," he replied moving toward the door
to the kitchen.

"Where you goin'?" Victoria objected. "I haven't seen
you in like, forever, and you blow through like it's nothing? Stay awhile." She patted space on the couch next to
her. "I never asked you: Where do you come out on this
immigration deal? I mean you might be a bit conflicted
with your mother's side and all."

Cole was a hawk on *illegal* immigration but would
staple his hand to the floor before admitting it to Victoria.
"My mother's people weren't immigrants. When they got
here, this *was* Mexico." Cole exited the great room and
pushed a swinging door into the kitchen.

The kitchen was small and cluttered, iron skillets
and pans covering an old-fashioned tile countertop. It
smelled of the coriander and garlic and chili powder
that crowded the red cabinets, which had been waxed
to a high gloss. The floor had been hand-hewn from
white oak retrieved from the ranch. To Cole's mind,
that floor, stained and scarred by generations of boots
and spurs and spilled red wine, traced the history of the
Clays better than any genealogist's report. The planking

dipped and buckled but to Cole it was stable ground, a place where he had retreated from the sharp voices of his mother and father, where he had made Mexican Christmas cookies with his *abuela*, who never betrayed the reason for his refuge.

She turned as he entered and Cole smiled. Marisa, his mother's mother, looked older than her years but carried herself with the dignity of her station among a generation of landed *patronas* whose grace and strength had grounded the social order of an earlier era in the history of Old California.

She stepped forward to embrace Cole, then pushed him back. "*Estás demasiado flaco.* Sit!"

Cole obliged, taking a seat in a square wooden chair that rocked slightly as he sat. He glanced at the splintered leg, its foot pad missing a half inch of pine. He smiled recalling his first dog, a red border collie named Pismo who had doubtless done the damage.

"You could replace this, you realize," Cole noted.

Marisa just smiled and handed Cole a plate of tortillas and chorizo. She took a seat with Cole at the small table and poured them black coffee that smelled of cinnamon.

"How are things?" Cole asked, fearing the answer.

"They are as God intends."

Cole smiled. "A theologic determinist. I should have known."

"I don't understand."

"A determinist believes things are predetermined, already decided."

Marisa nodded her head.

"But that presents a dilemma." Cole sipped coffee that smelled like his childhood.

"Why so?" she asked.

"Well, I assume the theology is Catholicism. Christianity assumes free will. There's some tension there—free will and Determinism. Sam Harris did a whole book on that."

"Who is this Sam Harris?"

"A really smart atheist."

"He doesn't count," she protested.

"Well, it doesn't really matter," Cole chided.

"Of course it does. You should not read words of a man who does not believe," she said, dipping a tortilla in salsa.

"Maybe, but whether it influences me is already determined." Cole raised both arms and smiled, the issue resolved.

"You trick your *abuelita* with fancy words. It does not mean you are right."

Cole stood then leaned down to kiss her cheek. "Where is he?"

Marisa pointed to the south. "*Jabali.*"

As Cole stepped toward the door, she spoke. "You think too much, Nieto. These paths of which you speak, not so different. We are free to seek God's will or to reject it. But God already knows our path. It is only we who struggle to see it."

Cole left the house shaking his head. His grandmother, with no formal education, had just reconciled Determinism with the idea of free will. He knew Stanford professors who would have crashed on that reef. He smiled as he pulled open the gate to the paddock where he kept his horse. The old timers say you only get one good horse in your life. If that was so, Cole had him in Slick. He had been Cole's "parade horse" during his high school rodeo days but did double duty as a ranch horse. Cole enjoyed cutting and sorting cattle as much as any sport. He dreaded the hours of golf he saw inevitably in his future. He was looking forward to getting back on Slick.

He haltered and saddled his horse, swung into the saddle, and walked him out. He knew where Elliot would be. The pigs loved the moist pasture around the stock pond near the center of the ranch.

After a short ride out, Cole spotted his father on horseback and pushed Slick into a lope to catch up. Elliot's horse was in a dead walk when Cole caught up and jigged nervously as Cole reigned up next to him.

Elliot did not turn to see who had joined. "Don't you know better than to lope up a rider's ass like that?"

"Good to see you, too, Elliot. I'm surprised to see you on horseback at all."

"Why's that?"

"Horses are dangerous for old guys," Cole answered.

"Yeah, well you're getting on yourself."

"Nowhere near as old as you."

"Yeah, you are. What was it your mother always said? Old soul," Elliot recalled. "Thought you'd be in Santa Barbara celebrating with the old lady."

Cole ignored the reference to his wife Jessica. Elliot was threatened by Jessica and her family and never used her proper name, as if his dismissiveness would ease his discomfort around her refinement.

"Had to get my horse. Bring'n him to Santa Barbara."

"For what?" Elliot asked.

"The Fiesta Parade. Travis signed us up. Have to promote the brand, right? You should ride with us."

"Fat chance," Elliot spat.

Elliot reigned up and they stopped near the top of a grassy hill overlooking the stock pond. Six feral pigs were busily routing the grass with sharp short tusks in an endless quest for anything edible. Elliot pulled a Winchester lever action .44 rifle from the sheath on his saddle. He handed it to Cole as he dismounted. Elliot pulled a pistol from his saddle bag.

They held the reins of their horses and walked to the edge of the hill. Elliot assumed his "shooting position"— feet spread wide, both hands on the pistol, arms fully extended.

Squinting down his pistol's barrel, Elliot instructed: "Take that grey sow on the left. I've got the razorback on the right. On my call."

Cole aimed his rifle and waited.

"Now."

Both men fired. Both missed. The pigs ran, not even fast, more annoyed than frightened. The horses were. They pulled back hard and bolted.

Cole and Elliot walked to retrieve the horses.

"You know I don't recall you ever hitting anything with that pistol," Cole observed.

Elliot looked down at the pistol in his hand. "This is an original Colt 45. Samuel Colt got the patent on the revolving chamber pistol in 1836. This one was manufactured in 1849."

"I'm sure the pigs appreciate you using vintage weapons," Cole noted as they reached the horses and stowed their weapons. "Might hit 'em with a modern one."

They retrieved the horses and saddled up. They walked them back to the barn in silence.

Finally, Elliot spoke: "What happened to the kid?"

"Well, if by 'kid' you mean Wade, I don't know exactly. He was down by the time I could see. Travis said Ragged Edge sun fished, then rolled. Nasty wreck."

"Dangerous sport," Elliot observed flatly.

Cole stared at the stoic man who was the father he had always known. Hard and detached, as if what happened to others was no part of his experience. In this case Cole knew better, and he wondered how he could be the product of this man's loins.

"What're they say'n?" Elliot asked.

"That he should have gotten a reride the first time the bitch shied."

Elliot considered as he pulled a tin of Copenhagen from the breast pocket of his shirt. He pinched a thick wad and packed the dip inside his lower lip.

"Damn good thing he didn't," he said finally. He let loose a thick stream of tobacco juice then wiped his mouth.

"And why's that, Elliot?" But Cole knew the answer. He wanted him to say it, if only to affirm the distance between them.

"She needs a few more releases to qualify," he said. "She may be going to Vegas."

"Well, Wade sure won't," Cole added.

As they unsaddled at the barn, Cole felt as bound to the events of the last several days as Elliot felt detached, as if they traveled through time and space as mirror images.

Back at the residence, Cole showered and prepared to leave for Santa Barbara, carefully avoiding the door that separated the main hallway from the dining room. He could hear Elliot and a voice he did not recognize. He was in no mood to socialize. He kept walking.

"Hey, Cole, is that you?" Elliot boomed from behind the door.

Reluctantly, Cole stepped in. Elliot, Victoria, and Travis were drinking with a man Cole did not recognize. About fifty, tan and handsome, he wore Rag & Bone jeans and a white shirt with the top two buttons strategically undone, the better to show some grey chest hair.

"Take a chair, son. Want you to meet somebody. Cole, this is Steven Smith, but everybody calls him Indigo. You've probably heard of his wines," Elliot slurred.

Cole touched the brim of his hat and extended his hand. Indigo stood and shook hands. His hand was soft, like the nap of his jeans, Cole thought.

"Nice to meet you, Mr. Smith," Cole said. He turned to Elliot. "I was just leaving to go home."

"You mean your in-laws' place?" Victoria interjected. Cole ignored her.

"Aw, shit. Have one glass with us," Elliot demanded.

Cole hesitated, then sat.

Indigo poured Cole a glass of red wine. "Try our pinot. This is an Indigo Estate wine. Of course, all of our wines are estate wines. I own six hundred acres in Napa." He poured himself a glass of the pinot and pushed his ample nose deep in the glass. After pausing for effect, eyes closed, he reviewed his wine as if a gold medal hung in the balance: "Just the right amount of tannin, light fruit, with a touch of lemon grass and citrus. Earthy and just aggressive enough, like a good woman."

Victoria blushed. Cole noticed. Elliot didn't. Elliot had apparently sampled several of the six open bottles on the table. Cole suspected Indigo had sampled more than the wine but let it go. No business of his.

Recovering, Victoria jumped in. "Indigo is looking to expand his operations into the Santa Ynez Valley."

Cole took a sip of his wine. He couldn't taste the lemon grass. It tasted like any light red to him. No upside in offering a review.

"I'm partial to beer and bourbon, Mr. Smith. I'm sure this is excellent."

"Ah, a man of the people," Indigo chortled.

"Yeah, that's my boy. A Stanford PhD man of the people," Elliot mumbled.

Indigo ignored Elliot, the better to press his own agenda. "I was just explaining to Elliot and your brother that my vineyards produce thousands of cases a year. But demand exceeds supply. If I'm going to expand my production capacity, I'd love to do it down here. I need more fruit."

Cole hesitated. He knew the ranch would be forced to adapt; that the economics of small cattle operations were not sustainable. At the same time, Indigo embodied everything he loathed about the "new economy" and destruction of the agrarian culture he grew up with. He couldn't help himself. He decided to go all Friedrich von Hayek on him.

"I'm not sure why supply should be a problem. Grapes are a commodity. If you meet the market price, you'll be awash in grapes. The leverage in your business is all about your vintner's skill and marketing, the demand for your product being a function of how many people believe all that happy horseshit about lemon grass and citrus."

Travis tried to hide his smile as Elliot's face grew tight and red, like a balloon attached to a helium canister with an open valve.

Cole waited for the pop, almost hoping.

But it was Indigo who responded, seemingly as cool as his Tommy Bahama loafers. "That's what a lot of folks think. Folks who don't really know anything about the art of winemaking. You see, son, great wine—the only wine I will put my name on—requires *great* fruit. And that's all about *terroir*, the sum total of a site's constants reflected in the fruit—chemical and nutrient composition, latitude, elevation, contour, sun exposure, and climate."

Travis shook his head. "Damn, I thought *terroir* meant 'dirt.'"

Indigo was undeterred. "Actually, Travis, dirt is what grows the weeds your cows eat. *Terroir* is what a skilled vintner needs to produce a great wine. They are quite different. I'm not sure which you have, but I'd love to find out."

"Well, I'm sorry, Mr. Smith, I think we're out of both. Any *terroir* we have is pretty much devoted to growing that shitty grass," Travis said.

"Great meeting you, Indigo." Cole stood, tipped his hat, and left.

Elliot, Victoria, and Travis held their breath. Indigo was angry and, for a moment, he flashed the blade usually hidden in the smooth folds of his carefully crafted charm. It wasn't what Cole had said, but how he had said it. As if he didn't understand Indigo's standing in the wine community, his expertise.

"Who runs this place?" Indigo snapped.

"It's complicated," Elliot explained. He quickly moved to pour Indigo another glass of pinot and hoped he would drop the subject. Too much information would not further Elliot's objectives. They desperately needed to improve ranch cash flow; wine was an obvious avenue. But ranch politics, and control, were complex.

Cole's mother Valentia had been the only child of Marisa and Cole's grandfather Diego Flores. Arroyo de Zaca had been in the Flores family for five generations. At Diego's death, the ranch went to his daughter Valentia. Valentia had, in turn, provided that the ranch would pass to her sons Cole and Travis; in the event they were minors at the time of her death, the ranch would be held in a trust that would expire when Cole, the elder son, reached the age of thirty. She also provided that her husband Elliot, should he survive her, would manage the affairs of the ranch until the trust dissolved and the boys assumed joint control.

Like all estate plans, Valentia's plan had been crafted at a moment in time—in this case, happier times in the marriage of Valentia and Elliot—when Valentia had been most concerned about not burdening her young sons with the legacy of her family's land before they could carry the weight; before Elliot's judgement had been clouded by the fog of alcohol; before he came to view every decision through the distorting lens of his own personal bitterness.

None of that mattered now. Valentia had died unexpectedly and the estate plan stood, as immutable as all the bad decisions we would take back in the hindsight of our lives. Cole and Travis owned the ranch but Elliot controlled it, and would until Cole reached thirty in just less than two years.

Elliot explained none of this to Indigo. Secretly, he loathed him, as he did everyone whose life had seemingly turned out better than his.

Elliot looked at his watch and stood. "It's late. Let's take this up again tomorrow. We don't want to bore Miss Vickie with all the details." Indigo was happy to oblige, assuming he would soon be privy to inside information Elliot had kept from his wife.

"Okay, let's talk soon." He waved his arm over the six mostly empty bottles of wine. "Just keep these," he said, as if this were an unusually magnanimous offer.

Victoria looked up and smiled as Indigo stood. "Thank you, Indigo. You're so generous."

Victoria walked Indigo to the door while Elliot retired to his bedroom. It was then, for the first time, that Elliot wondered how generous Indigo had been with his wine and his attentions. As his clouded head hit the pillow, he realized he didn't care.

Cole drove the familiar route from Zaca to Santa Barbara towing a horse trailer and Slick. The winding path of Highway 154 passed Cachuma Lake as it snaked through the Santa Ynez mountains before dropping into the city. The lake was low, testimony to California's perpetual drought. The slopes of the mountainsides were scarred by the latest wildfire. He suspected there was something to global warming but it was not anything Cole worried about. Man, he held, was on a more direct path to his demise. He wouldn't need the weather.

He glanced over his shoulder as he crested the mountain. It was just after sunset. The hills presented a near perfect palette of Central Coast twilight—purple, grey, and yellow, modeled in shadow and light.

It was dark by the time he reached the showgrounds. He quickly stalled Slick and drove the short remaining distance to Hope Hills. When he pulled into the driveway, he saw their bedroom light off. He retreated to the liquor cabinet just off the kitchen and poured a nightcap.

The next morning, he rose early and took an Uber downtown. Parking would be a mess. Santa Barbara's annual Fiesta Parade was the largest equestrian parade in the nation. The event was heavily influenced by the area's Mexican traditions, and the staging area was choked with horses, riders, and wagons festooned in traditional *vaquero* tack, saddles, and dress. A cacophony of silver and flashing silken color. Mostly red, white, and green. The colors of Mexico.

Cole was soon sequestered in a small park outside the throng, leaning against a horse trailer. His brother approached on horseback leading Slick.

"Thanks for getting him," Cole said.

"No problem, big brother. You look like dog shit, by the way."

"Thank you. I feel worse."

"Too much of that a'hole's pinot, perhaps?"

"You mean the fruit punch? Had a couple of night-caps. Tie 'em up. I need coffee."

They walked through the parade participants without speaking, making their way to a small coffee shop a block off the parade route. Sambo's was packed. Cole and Travis snagged two seats at the counter. A harried waitress poured them coffee. Cole took it black. Travis loaded his with two teaspoons of sugar and cream.

Cole, still groggy, watched. "Why don't you just drink the pancake syrup?" he asked.

"What's it to you, big brother?"

Cole looked around a room overflowing with tourists.

At least half the patrons were Mexican. The parade drew Mexican families from all over the county whose population was forty-two percent Hispanic.

"How weird is this?" Cole asked, starting to surface.

"What?"

"Look around."

The walls were still decorated with murals depicting the travails of a child who came to be known as "Little Black Sambo." Founded in 1957 by two Santa Barbara businessmen, the restaurant had capitalized on the popularity of a children's book by Scottish author Helen Bannerman. In the story she penned, a dark-skinned Indian boy had tricked four hungry tigers into chasing themselves in a circle until they turned to butter—butter now available to slather on pancakes, the restaurant's stock in trade. At its height, Sambo's was a national chain claiming one thousand, one hundred and seventeen restaurants in forty-seven states. But financial challenges and racial animus brought the chain to its demise.

Only one Sambo's remained—the one in which Cole and Travis were enjoying their coffee.

Travis looked up at the paintings. "Yeah, so?"

"What do you mean 'so'?" Cole asked. "How'd you like it if we were eating in 'little fat Pedro's'?"

"Depends."

"On what?" Cole pushed.

"How good the coffee was," Travis responded. "Anyway, you're misreading the story. The kid was a hero. He tricked the tigers. He won. Besides, I don't know what anybody else thinks. Hell, I'm not sure they do. I'm only certain of my view. And I like the coffee."

"I knew it. You're a solipsist."

"A what?"

"Someone who believes each person can only be certain of his or her own consciousness. Everything else is a theory."

Travis downed his coffee. "Sounds about right. Pay the check, big brother."

Cole placed cash on the counter and they left.

Back at the parade route, they reached the horses as the PA blared: *"Riders in section one mount up."*

Cole pulled himself into the saddle and gathered up Slick. "That's us. Let's get this over with."

Before Cole answered, they were approached by another rider. Jace Wyatt was about twenty years of age and full of piss.

"Amigos!" he greeted.

"Hey, Jace. How's it hang'n?" Travis said.

"Well it is, and that's the problem. Gonna correct that tonight, that's damn sure," Jace predicted.

"Don't be too friendly, Trav. He's got a shot at Vegas you know."

Jace laughed. "Well your little brother sure don't, professor."

"Why's that?"

"Cause while he was down here play'n on your fancy ranch, I been practicin' my craft all over these United States," explained Jace. He leaned down to pull the forelock of his horse through the head stall.

"We'll see," Cole said.

They waited to fall in line, the parade about to begin. Their plain dress stood in stark relief to the colorful wagons, silver-laden saddles, and costumed riders who had to come not just to ride, but to celebrate Santa Barbara's cultural history.

Two Andalusian stallions passed in high stepping gait, fighting every inch, their mouths dripping white foam as they chewed their oversized bits. *Vaquero* overlords pushed the horses forward with sharp silver spurs that left their mark in a pink smear of blood and sweat.

"Why don't they just walk? Look like they're going to war not a damn parade," Jace said, his disgust undisguised. He released a stream of tobacco. "Damn Mexicans. All show and no go."

Travis looked to his brother and waited. Half-Mexican themselves, both were sensitive to the subtle racism of many white "working" cowboys. From an early age, Valentia had urged them to ignore it. "The less secure a man, the more he needs to feel superior to someone." Cole had not always taken the advice. He once walked on a deal for the ranch truck they needed because the good ol' boy salesman had offered a chair to everyone in the room but Marisa. Cole had paused only a moment before standing to escort his grandmother out. "She's not the help, asshole" was all he had offered.

This time Cole just smiled and let it pass. And so they slipped onto State Street for a spectacle Cole hated.

Horses, riders, and wagons passed throngs of spectators standing six deep along the parade's route through downtown Santa Barbara. Cole watched the process as if a spectator himself—a matched pair of silver-grey Andalusians with flowing manes reaching halfway to the street; black Friesians straining to carry the weight of gleaming silver saddles; scores of horses and riders in all manner of dress; the horses jigging nervously as their riders waved in a slow mechanical arc, the two movements entirely disconnected, as if the horse and rider had been conjoined by Photoshop.

Cole, Travis, and Jace joined other rodeo cowboys behind a banner announcing "Fiesta Rodeo, Saturday-Sunday." They lagged behind the mule-drawn wagons preceding them. Horses hate a mule the way a dog hates a bath. Why mulers add bells to their rigs was beyond Cole. If mayhem was the goal, it was hardly necessary.

Tourists exploited the gap among parade entrants, darting across the wide street nervously, as if they expected a stampede, not the ragtag clutch of still-buzzed cowboys that approached. They passed the reviewing stand and an over-amplified parade announcer:

"Next up, some of our PRCA Rodeo Cowboys competing in our own Fiesta Rodeo and Stockmen's Show."

Several cowboys removed their hats and waved. Cole sank as low as he could. To no avail. The announcer continued:

"We also have a Fiesta Veteran with us. Say hello to our own Cole Clay, Western Regional High School Saddle Bronc Champ back in 2011."

There are times when death seems marginally preferable and, for Cole, this was one of them. He had a doctorate in intellectual history but he would always be a "high school rodeo champ" at home. It was his own fault for agreeing to ride in a cow town parade. Cole thought of Marcus Aurelius's admonition to "accept the things to which fate binds you."

But it wasn't fate that bound him to this agony. It was Dustin. He wanted to see his father ride with "Uncle Travis and the cowboys" and there was little within his power that Cole would deny his son.

They rounded a corner and the crowd thickened. Like a magnet pulling metal from sand, Cole's eyes spotted

Jessica in the sea of spectators. Dustin stood in front of his mother wearing his cowboy best. He smiled ear to ear when he saw his father and uncle approaching.

"Hey, cowboy!" Cole called. Travis edged his horse closer to the curb where Dustin stood. He spun his horse to the delight of his wide-eyed nephew.

As Cole passed, Jessica smiled. She did not wave. When he had passed, he turned and looked back. She was already threading Dustin through the crowd to go home. Neither the parade nor the cowboy culture it celebrated were of interest.

Mercifully, they reached the end of the parade route eight blocks later. Travis had managed to snag parking for their rig near the end. They pushed the horses into the trailer, still saddled, and got on the road.

"Where's your car?" Travis asked.

"At home. Figured you could take me back."

"Sure, but I gotta register first."

"For what?"

"Our home town rodeo, big brother."

Cole shook his head. "Registration has been open for three weeks. I'd a' thought you would have registered earlier, given the stakes."

Travis smiled and packed a wad of Copenhagen into his lower lip. "You're right about the stakes. Can't believe who goes to the finals in Vegas comes down to this dink-ass deal."

Travis rolled down the window and loosed a stream of tobacco.

"You know, I'm coming around to the generally accepted view that is a disgusting habit," Cole observed.

"That's cause you're a pussy, big brother," Travis

smiled as he rolled the window back up. "It'll only a take a second and you'll know half the guys. Can lord your degree and shit over 'em."

They parked outside the Earl Warren Equestrian Showgrounds and entered the makeshift registration office. Cowboys stood in line to pay their fees and choose their events. As a child, Cole cherished every moment with older cowboys. He now saw them in a different light. It was as if one entered some de-evolutionary vortex in which men are reduced to their essence, all testosterone and adrenalin, without any hint of frontal lobe filter. Men who had seen each other at a rodeo a week before would speak as if they'd just met a distant cousin from Wales. They traded lies and slapped backs. They competed in an undeclared contest to construct the most profane sentence.

Cole braced himself as he and Travis joined the queue to pay their fees. Jace stepped in line just behind him. Jace was a ringleader in this cowboy ritual.

"Hey, Cole, you son of a bitch!"

He slapped Cole's ass then moved both palms to his shoulders. He touched the nape of his neck. Cole thought of ritual allogrooming, a proclivity of all primates.

"Hey, Jace."

"Screw you, professor. We're enemies now. I need to win this deal," Jace barked. "Can't get beat by the little brother of some pussy professor of women's studies."

"It's history, actually."

"Same difference. But *I'm* about to make some history, I'll tell you what!" Jace turned to address the cowboys lining up behind him, all dutifully laughing in unspoken acknowledgement that Jace was winning the contest.

"Good thing I'm pitted against all these tiny dicked posers. Should be no problem," he bellowed.

Cole lost it. "Tone it down. There are kids in here."

"Sorry, bro. I'm a little jacked," Jace admitted under his breath.

A cowboy in the front of the line completed his registration and walked back. Several of the men standing in front of Cole and Travis reached out to shake his hand as he passed. Oliver "Olly" Davis wore black jeans, which, to a cowboy, is like wearing a nametag that says "asshole." But those black jeans set off his oversized gold-and-silver belt buckle. That buckle announced his status and explained why he never bothered to enter the machismo/moron contest. He didn't have to. He was the reigning World Champion Saddle Bronc rider.

Olly spotted Cole and Travis near the end of the line. "Hey, professor. I thought you succumbed to liver damage."

Cole smiled. "Not yet. What brings you to our little rodeo?"

"Easy money."

Travis jumped in. "Don't count on it."

Olly turned to Travis just as a young cowgirl interrupted them. "Mr. Davis, can I get your autograph?"

Olly's eyes stayed fixed on Cole. "Last time I got beat by a Clay, we were in high school."

"Yep. Last time a Clay tried," Travis said.

Olly just laughed as he signed a Fiesta Brochure for the girl.

As Olly moved through the throng, the waters parting as if for Moses, Travis shook his head. "What a jerk."

"He's just trying to get in your head."

Cole and Travis reached the front of the line. Travis

handed in his form. As Travis wrote out a check for the fees, Cole glanced behind the registration table through an open door. Clive Westbrook was talking to a rodeo official. Cole had not seen him since he ducked him at the hospital and was happy to escape, again, without contact.

Back on the road, they passed under the gate announcing Hope Hills. Travis took in the neighborhood as if for the first time. By any measure, it was beautiful—multimillion-dollar homes on multi-acre lots; oak-lined streets winding through gentle hills framed by a lake to the north and the Pacific Ocean to the south.

"I can't believe you live here, big brother."

"Why?"

"Too perfect. Gives me the creeps, like a Stepford wife gonna meet you at the door with a martini and a cyborg kiss or something."

"You're thinking of 'Moneycito.' That's where the perfect people live."

Travis pondered the comparison as he looked around again. "Yeah, I guess you're right. This is where you can live like a one percenter and pretend you're not. Hell, if this place had sidewalks it'd feel almost normal. Like a nicer version of a neighborhood in one of those fly-over states you all make fun of over brunch at the Four Seasons."

They came to a stop on the road in front of Cole's house.

"Thanks for the ride. And the biting social commentary."

"*No problema*, amigo."

Cole walked to the side yard. He had seen Jessica there from the road. She was seated on the knee-high garden boxes he had built from river rock. She wore her casual jeans, espadrilles, and a flannel shirt, all tied together nicely by a gardening apron, as if Martha Stewart had dressed her for the gardening cover story.

"Hey."

Cole sat on the stone planter wall. "Where's Dustin?"

"Playdate, dropped him after the parade." Jessica turned back to her work."

"What's the matter?"

Jessica put down the trowel, "Déjà vu. The bad kind."

"What's that mean?"

"Just seeing you in that parade. Knowing you're getting involved in the ranch again. Your father, Travis, the whole mess. We've seen this movie."

"They're family, Jess."

"So am I."

"I've got this summer to try to straighten things out. I owe that to Travis...and Marisa."

"You don't owe them a thing. That ranch is doomed. You should sell it to a vineyard or one of the cannabis kingpins. Your share would be a lot of money. We could use it to resettle in LA, maybe near the beach."

"Travis will never sell."

"That's because Travis never finished high school. It's all he can do."

Cole bristled but let it pass.

She picked up the trowel again and dug a small hole. She placed a basil plant in the hole and gently pushed the soil over its roots.

"Sometimes I think you watched too much John Wayne as a kid. You do realize that whole thing's over, don't you?" she said.

"What whole thing?"

"The cowboy thing, for heaven's sake."

Now it was Cole's turn. Déjà vu. He thought of his ride down the coast, the girl's question.

"Depends on what you mean by 'cowboy thing.'"

Jessica looked at him with a look that rested somewhere between confusion and exasperation. "I don't know what that means."

Cole stood. "No, you don't."

Jessica grabbed another basil plant and slipped it from the plastic sleeve. "Cole, if you're going to do this, give it the time it needs. Stay at the ranch. Get it done. I'm going to be spending some time with Mom and Dad in LA, anyway. Start looking at schools."

"Jess, we've been apart too much these last few years. We—"

"Yeah, and who's fault was that?" she interrupted.

"No one's."

Jessica shook her head. "You sure managed to visit Zaca enough."

She dropped the trowel and turned to Cole. "But you're right. We do need to be together. And I thought we would be. Going to LA, finding a school, looking at houses. This summer. Then you announce you need to spend more time on the damn ranch. Which is it?"

"It's both. I can't hand Travis a bucket of shit."

"Then figure it out. Get it done. Stay at the ranch. Take all the time you need."

"And Dustin?" he added quietly.

"I have him enrolled in a summer program at the John Thomas Dye school for a couple of weeks. Great school. If he attends, it may help him get in. After that, we'll be back. He can spend as much time on the ranch as you want."

"I would have appreciated being consulted on plans for Dustin."

"Well, I'm sorry. A slot came up and I took it. I think you were in Salinas."

Cole thought of all the things he could say. But he sensed it was not the time, that it would only get worse. He let it go.

"All right, then."

3

---◇---

The following weekend was Prescott's birthday, an annual event that united the clan in food and drink, if not common cause. Elliot hosted at the ranch. Elliot and Victoria assumed their posts at each end of the table. Marisa and Cole sat on one side; Travis and Prescott the other. Cole had made Jessica's excuse but wasn't sure anyone bought it. Her absence was noted. It only added to the instability of the mix, the good vibe unlikely to exceed the half-life of an unstable isotope.

For a while the conversation swirled around ranching and rodeo and the too-precious-by-half private school Dustin attended in Hope Hills. But the real issue swam just beneath the surface like a seal knifing through the Santa Barbara Channel. Victoria, heavily into Indigo's best pinot noir, threw the first harpoon and the tide turned crimson.

"Prescott, I'm curious," she said. "The ranch has got some challenges and we are thinking about pot."

No one knew exactly how to interrupt that. Prescott deflected. "Well, I'm sure that would relieve some of the anxiety."

Everyone chuckled except Elliot. He knew Prescott believed those "challenges" had been created by Elliot's mismanagement. That he had been, and was, a disappointment to his father was a wound that would never heal.

"We don't need to get into that now. It's grandpa's birthday," Cole interjected.

"No, I'm curious, Prescott. It's legal, no? And they say the price they pay for land is much more," Marisa offered.

Prescott sat back, sensing no escape. "Then do it."

"Ah!" Victoria chirped.

Elliot knew better. "I thought you were a conservative. Quite open-minded of you, Prescott."

"I'm not sure I'm a conservative in any meaningful sense," Prescott said.

"What do you mean?" Marisa asked.

Prescott waved it off. "It's complicated."

"Oh, that's rich. What? Too complicated for the farmers?" Elliot said.

"That's not what I mean," Prescott replied. "It's just that these labels—conservative, liberal, left, and right. They don't mean much anymore," Prescott started. "Strictly speaking, conservatism seeks to conserve something: a culture, ways of being, religion, a common heritage. I think we've lost a lot of that. We are a collection of very disparate groups with radically different perspectives, values even. What common understanding do we seek to conserve? I'm not sure anymore."

Victoria was now, inevitably, drunk. "What?" she slurred.

Marisa persisted. "Explain. Democracy, it's a good thing, no? These differences. We vote, work them out."

"Yes, but the mechanisms of democracy are about *process*, but process to what end?" Prescott asked.

Elliot turned to Cole. "What do you think, professor? This shit's right up your alley, ain't it?"

Elliot was baiting him and Cole knew it. He answered, anyway. "I think it's worse than that. Those mechanisms of democracy Prescott's talking about? They're biased in favor of change, which has the effect of driving us further and further away from a common center."

"Why? That makes no sense. You can vote to change stuff or keep it the same. Even go back," Elliot argued.

"Yes, in theory," Prescott said. "But it doesn't tend to work that way, at least in a liberal democracy biased in favor of the rights of the individual in relation to the community."

"Damn right. Keep the feds off our backs," added Elliot.

"Fair enough," continued Prescott. "The feds. A central and distant authority. But all those freedoms laid out in the Bill of Rights, and many more the Supreme Court just made up over the years, were applied to the states and communities. Even to individuals."

"Yeah, and that's a damn good thing," Elliot said.

"No?" Marisa asked, looking from Elliot to Cole.

"Yes, good in a way. But what gets lost is one's freedom to live in a community that reflects its values, values which may well involve *constraints* on individual freedoms," Cole said.

"Sounds shitty. Constraints aren't better because they're local," snapped Elliot.

"Depends on how you define freedom," Cole said.

Elliot rolled his eyes. "Oh, please."

"Maybe the guy who embodies the values of a community, its freedoms *and constraints*, is also the freest," Cole explained.

Travis entered the water: "Who thinks that?"

Cole just smiled, there was no point. Prescott came to his defense. "The ancients. That is how they defined virtue."

"Wait," Victoria slurred. "Who are 'the ancients'?"

"The Greeks mostly," explained Prescott. "But we are getting far afield. Right now, I'd like the freedom to enjoy my birthday cake. I assume we have one?"

"I don't understand. There aren't twenty Greeks in Santa Ynez," Victoria correctly observed.

Elliot laughed out loud. "That's right, sweetheart. Screw the Greeks, the old ones and the new ones."

Cole knew he should let it rest but balked at giving Elliot the last word. "Maybe. But there have been a lot of people over a lot of years who took the idea seriously, that you can be as much a prisoner to your vices as a slave to government; that we aren't freer because we can access porn twenty-four-seven."

"Oh, I don't know about that," Travis smiled.

Marisa gave him a cold stare.

"Just say'n. Not my view of course."

"Of course you're freer! This is such bullshit. Doesn't mean everything's always the right choice," Elliot said as he refilled his wine glass.

"Fair enough. But the whole community is affected by your choices. So you get back to square one: Would a community be freer if it could define its own rules, the sort of place they wanted to live, even if some of the rules limited individual freedom?" Cole asked.

"Guess it depends on who's makin' the rules. I can see some holy rollers around here defining 'virtue' a little too narrowly," Elliot said, his voice now indistinct.

"Then you move to a different community," Cole said.

"If you can," Marisa observed.

"Fair enough. There are tradeoffs."

"So if you are not a conservative, what are you, Dad?" Elliot asked Prescott.

"A liberal, in the classical sense, but that term has taken on a wholly new meaning. As I say, these labels have lost their utility," Prescott said, trying once again to close the discussion.

"What about you, professor?" Elliot was not about to let it rest.

Cole realized he hadn't considered the question of how he would characterize his philosophy in a word, a label. "I would love to claim fidelity to the classical liberal model. But I fear that in the sweep of history it may be a failed model. It requires cultural homogeneity or radical decentralization with limited federal authority. We have neither at the moment."

Travis chimed in. "So what's that make you, big brother? I need a handle. You're losing me here."

"A reactionary, I'd say," Elliot snapped.

Cole tried to clarify his position. "If by that you mean someone who thinks we might be better off taking a step back, maybe. I would go back to a system that allows localities to live as they see fit. When you federalize every individual freedom, you limit the freedom of the community."

"Give me an example?" Marisa asked.

"We already heard one. Porn. The First Amendment provides that *Congress* shall make no law abridging freedom of speech. This has been interpreted to protect all manner of obscenity as 'speech,' a proposition that is—if you take a look at the stuff online—clearly absurd. But let's accept for the moment the First Amendment precludes federal prohibitions. Should that preclude a local community from drawing different lines? Abortion is another example. Should a community in South Carolina that believes it's murder be made to accommodate the practice because New Yorkers think it's fine? If they are required to provide something they find morally objectionable, are they more or less free?"

Travis had had enough. "So, Grandpa, we're getting off the subject. What about pot?"

"I think it's a terrible idea for Santa Ynez, regardless of what the state of California thinks." He turned to Elliot. "And I'm sure your father can figure out a way to right the ship while preserving the honor of the polis," Prescott smiled.

Prescott's comment was read by Elliot as a double-edged blade. He seethed with the anger building all evening.

"Well, thank you for the treatise on government. Exactly the sort of irrelevant bullshit I would expect from the professor and his mentor." He looked at his father. "Easy to pontificate when you spend all your time reading in the manor house of a ranch you lost," Elliot added pushing himself back from the table. "Well, I'm trying to save this one. Good night."

Elliot stormed off. Victoria followed, a little wobbly. The evening ended. The seal bled out.

The next morning Cole had retreated to the porch with his coffee. Elliot joined him.

"So why wasn't your old lady there? And don't give me the bullshit about her being under the weather,"

Elliot said as he sank into a chair next to Cole.

"Her name is Jessica."

"Trouble in paradise?" Elliot mused.

"No. Not really. Change the subject or, better, just drink your coffee."

Elliot complied. "Who's goin' to Vegas?"

Cole thought the question curious. "Top fifteen money winners."

"I know that, smart ass. Who? Is it settled?"

Cole relented. "All but the last couple slots."

Elliot sipped his coffee. "Olly Davis, I assume."

"What do you care?" Cole returned to his coffee hoping that would end it. But Elliot's stare told him otherwise.

"Odds are he will. But he hasn't qualified yet. Only reason he's here," Cole said.

"Who else has a shot?" Elliot asked.

"Travis for one."

Elliot gave his son a double take. "That'd be a miracle."

"What would you know? Don't remember you in Vegas."

"Nope. Never made it. Probably why you're so hell bent to get Travis there," Elliot added.

"Who says I am? That's Trav's deal. I'm just trying to patch some of the holes you've blown in this place."

"Ranching is tough these days. May have to sell if things don't turn around."

"Not yours to sell, Elliot," Cole retorted.

"Hell it ain't. Your mother made me manager."

"Yeah, and me and Travis owners. You have fiduciary responsibilities, not that you've noticed. I'm sure a court wouldn't look favorably at you selling shortly before you were to hand over the reins."

Elliot stood up and lit a cigarette. He shook his head. "You been talkin' to a lawyer? Your mother intended I make the decisions until you two grow up. I think we're shy a' that."

"You'd be the last to know what she intended."

Elliot stared at his oldest son, the anger flaring, then let it pass. "Your mother and I did have our challenges."

"That happens when you're banging every cowgirl dumb enough to lay down for your bullshit."

Elliot smiled. "I do not remember philandering on that scale."

"Probably too drunk."

"I did like to drink. Never bothered your mother."

"Till it killed her," replied Cole.

Elliot tossed his cigarette. His brooding anger flared. "That's a shit thing to say, but I'm going to forgive you, son. You've obviously screwed up your own marriage, else you wouldn't be here."

Elliot retrieved his coffee cup and stepped to the door exiting the porch then turned.

"What's eating you is knowing you didn't fall far from the tree."

Elliot left, his words hanging in the air. Cole could not dismiss them, as much as he tried. Inside the crevices of Cole's mind, he feared Elliot was right; that he hadn't fallen far from the tree; that, but for the consciously different path he had chosen, he could become his father. The thought haunted him as he got in his truck and drove.

Ten minutes later he pulled into the parking lot of his favorite local bar and grill. Parrilla de Manolo—Manny's to the locals—served coffee to locals in the morning, food and drink to everyone the rest of the day. It was a tradition to begin, and end, one's day at Manny's. It was owned by Manolo Pastore, patriarch of a local family with whom Cole had more than close ties. It felt more like home than his house in Santa Barbara when he walked through the front door.

Manny's was nearly empty: Three cowboys were playing pool with two girls who worked nights. Cole walked to the bar and sat to the side of two coeds fortifying themselves with coffee for a day of wine tasting.

The barkeep had his back turned. Cole wanted his attention: "Hey, big man."

Billy turned and smiled. He poured Cole a cup of coffee. "I'm assuming that's what you want."

"You put on some weight, Billy? Almost didn't recognize you," Cole said, sipping his coffee.

"I'm a large man. You can't stuff this much wisdom in a scrawny body like yours," Billy replied, wiping the bar top. "Thought you were in PALo Alto."

"Why does everyone say it that way?"

"To express our disdain."

"Had to finish my degree," Cole replied.

"You guys competin' in our dinky rodeo?" Billy asked.

"We're in the ranch sorting. Travis is in the bronc deal."

"Didn't you win one year?" Billy smiled, knowing the subject made Cole crazy.

"Ancient history." Cole shook his head and sipped his coffee.

Billy polished the brass handle of a beer keg dispenser. "Hey, this is a cow town precariously suspended between LA and Frisco. We live on our history, amigo."

"When'd you get so philosophical, Billy?" Cole quipped.

"I'm a bartender. We have to be deep. Sells beer." Billy turned and retrieved a slip of paper from the register. He placed it on the bar in front of Cole. "I hope the Clays win something. Your tab's as long as my dick."

The coeds smiled. Billy blushed and turned in their direction. "Forgive me, ladies."

Cole reached in this pocket and placed a nickel on the counter. "This should cover it."

Billy laughed. "Not a chance, but I'll take it up with management." He nodded behind Cole.

Cole turned. Samantha Pastore smiled and they embraced. Sam was Cole's age but looked ten years younger even with no makeup. Cole could not remember her ever wearing makeup. Maybe at the prom they had attended together a lifetime ago.

"I was going to send that to collection," she said.

"Hold off. I'll buy you a coffee as a gesture of good faith."

They walked to a two-top. A waitress poured Sam coffee. They didn't speak for a long moment.

"Haven't seen you around," Sam said.

"Had to finish my degree."

"So do I call you Dr. Clay now?"

"Yes," he smiled. "How's your father?"

"He's good. Retired. Turned the place over to me."

"That explains it."

"What?"

"The new policies, like making locals pay their tabs and such," Cole said.

"Exactly."

"You still seeing the lawyer?" Cole asked.

"No."

"Why?"

"None of your business."

"When'd that ever stop us?"

"About the time you married a *gringa* and became an Episcopalian."

Cole smiled. "Buy you breakfast?"

"On your tab?"

"Sure."

"I ate, but thanks."

The waitress arrived. "Sam, where do you want the pinot stored?" she asked.

"Leave two cases out for tonight and put the rest in the back," she directed.

"Pinot?" Cole asked. "I thought this was a cowboy bar."

"We sell a lot of wine now. Dad and I leased a small vineyard and do some private label stuff. It's all about wine now. Seen the Valley lately?"

"Yeah. You serving pot, too?"

"Not yet."

"From the look of things, you will."

"Substance abuse," Sam said abruptly.

"Not in the view of our enlightened leadership," Cole said, assuming they were still on the subject of pot.

"The lawyer. You asked what happened," she explained. "Oxy, cocaine...me, whatever."

Cole did not respond. He could have predicted it. An LA lawyer with a condo in Marina Del Rey. What was she thinking?

"How's it going for you?" she asked.

"Me? Oh, I've lightened up. A little Jack Daniel's once in a while, that's about it."

Sam smiled. "No, I assume you still abuse substances. I meant on the relationship side."

Cole paused. "Me and Jess? We're good."

Sam took his measure. She shook her head and smiled. "You could never do it."

"What?"

"Lie to me."

Cole looked away for a moment, then back. "That's a good thing, I guess."

Sam smiled, more resignation than joy. "It would have been. Might be better now if we could bullshit each other." She stood. "Pay your tab, cowboy."

"Ex-cowboy. Dr. Clay now, remember?"

"Can't shed your skin that fast, Cole, though God knows you've tried."

As she walked away, Cole called out. "Hey we're gathering tomorrow. Why don't you come? We could use the help."

Sam turned. "I have a date."

"Bring him." But she walked away with no answer. Just then Jace entered the bar with two buckle bunnies, one on each arm. They were ending an all-nighter or starting early. Cole couldn't tell. It made no difference. They were lit.

"Hey, amigo!" he greeted Cole. "Meet my friends…" There was a long pause. He hadn't a clue of their names.

Cole tried to save him. "Nice to meet you." He tipped his hat to the girls, barely eighteen by Cole's measure. One chirped: "Say, Jace says you went to Stanford and are real smart. We want to talk but first we gotta pee."

As they walked away, Jace leaned into Cole, his breath heavy with liquor. "Reminds you of that old line, eh? Cowgirl's saddle ain't the best thing—"

"Yeah, I know. But next to it. I have to go." Cole grabbed his hat and headed for the door.

"You're gettin' old, Cole."

That afternoon, the temperature hit ninety degrees, still and dry. Cole walked to the round pen and climbed up. A young bronc bucked his rider hard, oblivious to the heat. When he tired of the effort, the horse slammed against the boarded slats of the pen. If he couldn't eject the rider, he'd scrape him off. But the rider stuck, and the young stallion finally eased into a jiggy trot.

"Should have stuck it like that in Salinas," Cole said as Travis climbed the rails of the round pen. Cole handed him one of the two beers he carried.

"I woulda if that nag had fought back," Travis returned. They both drank their beer, comfortable in the silence.

"What's up?" Travis asked. "I read you like a book."

"I can honestly say I have never seen you read a book," Cole replied.

"It's a figure of speech."

Cole took a deep breath, reluctant, as if saying it would make it more real. "Me and Jess."

Travis killed his beer and threw the can in an open cooler near the pen. "Shit, that ain't new."

Cole did not respond. It wasn't new, but it seemed worse.

"Sometimes it's best to jam your fingers down your throat and puke. Get it done," Travis offered.

Cole stared, a little incredulous. "You always know just what to say, little brother."

A dented, dirty pickup truck approached the pen where Cole and Travis talked. The interior of the truck was cluttered with tools. Their ranch hand Carlos had somehow never grasped the idea that tools could have a place, a tool shed for instance. Every device he might conceivably need rested comfortably, if generally undisturbed, within three feet of the driver's seat. Wire cutters, gloves, hammers, a hot shot, the branding iron he used once a year. The rear of the truck carried two bales of alfalfa, barbed wire, a bucket, and some tack. That said, Carlos was a good hand and, more importantly, honest. The ranch would crater without him.

Carlos cranked the window down. "*Necesito ayuda, jefe.*"

"Okay," Cole said.

Carlos began to push crap off the passenger seat to make room.

"We'll walk, amigo."

As Carlos drove back toward the cattle pens, Travis and Cole climbed down from the rails of the round pen. Travis pulled the saddle off the bronc and turned him out. The horse threw his head and kicked out as he cleared the gate, as if to say he wasn't broke yet. Fifty feet out he stopped dead, sniffed and rolled, the sandy soil coating his sweat-laden flanks like a brown Pendleton blanket.

The brothers began their short walk to the cattle pens.

"Dustin'll be better off, you both happy," Travis offered.

"That's what people say to feel better about divorcing. It's bullshit. Dustin'll be worse off. Broken home, seeing me on weekends. Some asshole in Jessica's life trying to act like the father he'll never be."

"How ya know he'll be an asshole?" Travis asked.

"Look at her track record."

"Probably right," Travis smiled, then grew serious. "Wish to hell they'd divorced."

"Who?"

"Who do you think? Elliot and Mom. Everybody'd been better off," Travis explained.

"Especially her," added Cole.

As they reached the pens, Carlos was pulling hypodermic injectors and dark blue bottles of bovine meds from a cardboard box. He stood to the side of a large metal "squeeze," essentially a cage whose sides could be collapsed with a lever to hold a heifer still while the meds were injected. A narrow chute traveled from the squeeze to a tub that held the unwilling participants, all braying nervously. They would travel from the tub one at a time through the chute and into the squeeze. Carlos stood to the side of the chute with a long yellow rod, the "hot shot" delivered a sharp electric jolt to the flanks of beasts reluctant to make the trip.

The afternoon sun bounced off the sides of the black metal bars of the squeeze and alley. The paint on both was scratched and chipped and rusted in the places that held no paint. A breeze kicked up and cooled the sweat beading on Cole's back beneath his shirt. It carried the scent of dry grass and dust and loose dung, the herd's only means of protest.

Travis waved to Carlos at the tub and Carlos pulled a lever which opened a gate from the tub to the chute. Six eight-hundred-pound cows rumbled forward channeling to single file, resigned to their fate. As the first one entered the squeeze, Travis pulled another lever that collapsed its sides and slammed a gate behind the animal's butt end.

"Looks light," Cole said as he screwed a thick metal needle onto the injector.

"Drought's killing us," Travis explained.

Cole poked the needle into the bottle of antibiotic liquid and pulled a dose. He jabbed the bovine's right flank. He pulled a rope and the front gate of the squeeze opened. The unhappy animal lunged forward and out. Another entered and the process repeated.

The light and the smell and the sound, the very sameness of it all, began to restore Cole's mood. At least it made him forget, for a moment, a fear that had begun to gestate within him, a fear that, ultimately, things might not turn out as he had always expected. But for now, in this place and at this moment, things were as they had always been.

"There's folks looking for vineyard. Victoria knows them. There's the whole marijuana deal. Those guys pay four times what we can earn from cattle pasture," Cole observed. "Hate to say it. But we have to do something."

"Hate to say it, don't." Travis kept working the herd one at a time. "We could also turn this place into a guest ranch for spoiled brats from Santa Monica. But that's not who we are. It's not about money, big brother."

Cole pulled the lever on another thin cow. "Apparently not."

4

———⟡———

A t that moment, Prescott Clay sat in the library of his home in Los Alamos twelve miles north of Arroyo de Zaca. He gazed up at hundreds of books lining the shelves of the wood-paneled room that had become his frequent retreat. He loved how the sundry colors of their linen jackets speckled the white-washed room in color. But mostly he loved the ideas encased within their pages, like rare insects preserved for all time in a block of transparent plastic.

He pulled a title from the nearest shelf. He had read *The Last Lion* by William Manchester and Paul Reid during his first year in California. He recalled the story of Churchill's irrepressible determination to ensure that England would endure and, eventually, prevail. He began to reflect upon the jagged trajectory of his own life and the dark forces he had been called upon to battle.

Prescott had been born in Connecticut of what he called "good Scotch-Irish stock." He was proud to relate that his father's people had immigrated to "the colonies" from Ulster twelve years before the American Revolution. He was less proud to admit that they had changed their Scottish surname "Cay" to "Clay" upon arrival at Ellis Island the better to "fit in." But that they did. The newly Americanized Clay clan prioritized education and excelled in business. Prescott followed suit. He attended Andover and Princeton, married his high school sweetheart, and went to work. His facility with electronics and his Ivy League connections landed him a job at the CIA. He spent the next twenty years practicing the dark art of electronic espionage during the height of the Cold War. Their son Elliot was born in Sibley Hospital in Washington, DC, in 1962. They were unable to have more children and Elliot became the center of their universe.

In 1984, the Federal Communications Commission, with a push from the federal courts, deregulated American telecommunications. The venerable Ma Bell was "divested," broken into seven regional operating companies that were, importantly, no longer shielded from competition. The "C-lecs"—competitive local exchange companies—were birthed in a bloody battle to win consumers away from the staid incumbents and offer a panoply of ever-expanding electronic services made possible by the transition from analog to digital communications.

Almost simultaneously, fueled by faith in the proposition that the "public interest" was best served by competition, a second revolution began: wireless. The Federal Communications Commission was not convinced there was anything magic about the provision of cellular telephone service. As such, it determined to grant only one of the two cellular licenses in each local market to the local phone company. The other would be awarded to a new entrant who met minimal financial and technical requirements. The flood of "non-telco" entrants into the pool of would-be providers presented the Commission with a dilemma: It was nearly impossible to distinguish among scores of qualified applicants. So the Commission threw its hands in the air and held a lottery. If the ping-pong ball marked with the serial number of your application was drawn from the tub, you won and were on your way to owning a multimillion-dollar telecommunications franchise. Scores of centimillionaires and not a few billionaires were launched that day.

With a background in technology, Prescott Clay had seen the revolution coming. It wasn't difficult. The Commission's intent to foster competitive entry and to use lotteries in the process was entirely public. He left government service and entered the game. He leveraged his two lottery wins to finance the acquisition and consolidation of several more, assembling a northeastern regional "cell-co" network that would enjoy significant economies of scale in marketing and operations.

On paper, Prescott was worth millions. But he had tired of the long hours required to run his growing company. Worse, his beloved wife Franny was diagnosed with breast cancer. To spend more time attending to her needs and to enjoy the success he had earned, he made a decision that would radically alter the trajectory of the Clay family. He sold his company and moved his family West. He invested in technology stocks and land, specifically, a sprawling cattle ranch in Los Alamos in the center of California's idyllic Central Coast. At its apogee, Camino de las Olas covered some six thousand acres. The ranch residence, Casa de Barro, was an original adobe updated in a manner befitting the "tech" titan he had become.

Elliot took to the move west with abandon. He learned the cattle business, became an expert horseman and tried his luck in rodeo. His family's wealth, his good looks, and rakish charm combined to establish Elliot as one of the Valley's most eligible bachelors. He exploited the status fully. From Montecito to Santa Ynez, Elliot Clay was on everyone's A list, sure to show with a beautiful date and a boisterous story fueled by his growing affection for strong drink.

Prescott had been a legendary drinker in his day. Now sober, he watched helplessly as the family's congenital weakness consumed his son and delivered its predictable consequences in embarrassing gaffes, lost work, and worse. Elliot had been arrested for drunk driving once. As a juvenile, he escaped with a suspended license. But when a call from the sheriff's department announced Elliot's second arrest for drunk driving, this time as an adult, Prescott knew it carried a high probability of jail time.

Prescott wrestled with the nagging truth: Unless Elliot was made to suffer the consequence of his actions, he would never defeat the demon resting snuggly in the biochemical crevices of his brain. Prescott did not rush to secure Elliot's release. He let him spend the night in a dank holding cell of the county's "drunk tank" in Gaviota, a short drive from the ranch.

But upon Elliot's release the next morning, with a hearing date looming, Prescott succumbed to every father's instinct to protect his son. He called the deputy district attorney assigned to the case. It didn't hurt that Bob Murphy intended to challenge the more liberal district attorney when she stood for reelection in the fall. Murphy was counting on Prescott's support in a race that carried no campaign finance restrictions on donations. None of that was mentioned as a deal was brokered. Elliot would accept probation, a one-year suspension of his license, and the "suggestion" he give back to the community by serving in the California National Guard.

Elliot joined the reserves and trained as a "tanker." He met his obligation on weekends once a month. All in all, he thought, not a bad trade, until events eight thousand miles from Santa Ynez dramatically shifted the costs and benefits of the arrangement he had accepted.

Saddam Hussein had badly miscalculated American resolve when he invaded and "annexed" the neighboring nation-state of Kuwait.

On August 2, 1990, President H.W. Bush launched Operation Desert Shield. Inevitably, it morphed into Desert Storm. Within thirty days, Elliot Clay was called to active duty in Saudi Arabia with coalition forces amassing in response to Iraq's invasion of Kuwait. In January of 1991, he joined coalition forces in the invasion of Iraq. He was assigned to the 3rd Brigade of the 2nd Armored Division. He was a gunner on an M1-A1 tank.

In a war that concluded in one hundred hours and saw only twenty-six American losses to enemy fire, a number of American soldiers were killed by "friendly fire." Among them were six US servicemen killed when gunners of the 3rd Brigade mistook enemy rocket explosions bouncing off the skin of American tanks as enemy cannon fire. They opened up on what they erroneously believed were enemy tanks and killed six American soldiers in the process.

An investigation officially cleared members of the 3rd Brigade of wrongdoing, the mistake attributed to confused images presented by the tank's thermal sighting devices. But despite the official explanation released to the press, Elliot's last fitness report made reference to "subpar execution of accepted procedure." He was pressured to resign his reserve commission under a cloud.

Save once, Elliot did not speak of the incident again, but never shed the anger. He succumbed to bitterness born of the belief that the Pentagon had *unofficially* scapegoated soldiers asked to execute perfectly in a thirty-hour running gun battle, at night, with poor visibility and inadequate intel on the enemies' position.

Elliot changed. He had left for the Gulf War a scion of tech wealth, everybody's favorite dinner guest; he returned taciturn and bitter, unavailable to the many friends with whom he had cowboyed and drank and laughed before the war. Except one. Elliot had met Valentia Flores at the opening Gala of Santa Barbara's annual Fiesta Celebration in 1989. The landed *patrona* of Arroyo de Zaca, she had been, at the time, only one of many eligible young women with whom he had shared an evening of revelry and drink. But he had never forgotten her. She was, as he recalled, utterly unimpressed with his wealth; nor did she laugh easily at his many stories, as if, unlike other women, she would make him earn her favor. Unless his interest was real, and important, she didn't care and would not pretend otherwise. Stripped of the persona he had carefully crafted before the war, he now sought her honesty as if she might find in him something he had lost.

And so he called her and they talked. They talked in ways with which Elliot was unaccustomed. He told her things he had never told another. He confessed to her, and her alone, not only the anger, but the shame he carried from the Gulf War. He believed, more than any member of the crew trapped inside the claustrophobic confines of the metal death trap in which they had found themselves that night, that he was responsible for the mistake that incinerated six American soldiers. And Valentia made no attempt to dissuade him; she neither exonerated nor judged him. She spoke instead of the genuine sorrow that inhabits every life; she spoke of her own irretrievable mistakes and the sadness that attends them; she placed that sadness squarely in her understanding of her Catholic faith, the inevitable consequence of man's Fall from grace. But she also spoke of forgiveness, and the utter uselessness of guilt. Sorrow and regret, she explained, were appropriate and necessary preconditions to forgiveness. Guilt, on the other hand, was all about self, about the ego; ultimately, the retention of guilt was a rejection of redemption.

Elliot had never been particularly religious. His father's Episcopalian faith had seemed somehow appropriate for the circles in which they ran back in the East, but never an important part of his life. He found comfort, however, in Valentia's words and the certainty with which she seemed able to order both the sadness and the joy in the world around them. By abandoning the effort to rationalize his mistake, by accepting the sorrow around what followed, he was able to move past the anger and, to some extent, the guilt. He began to shed memories of the Gulf War and the darkness those memories had triggered.

Elliot and Valentia fell in love. Soon they married. Elliot moved from his father's Camino de las Olas to Arroyo de Zaca and became the *patron* of its sprawling cattle operations. While not the life he had expected, it was a good life and, for a time, his drinking in check,

Elliot Clay was happy. All the more so when Valentia delivered him two sons in the early years of their marriage. Elliot and Prescott combined their cattle operations and enjoyed a seemingly idyllic life, all the more enriched by the ever-present engagement of young Cole and Travis, anxious to learn the cowboy's ways.

At the time, neither Elliot nor Prescott fully recognized that the edifice of their ranching operations was built on a fragile foundation. Ranching on the Central Coast of California is generally unprofitable, the costs of operations, labor, and taxes overwhelming any profits squeezed from ranches unable to achieve significant economies of scale. The Clay family ranches were subsidized by Prescott's wealth. And that wealth soon proved vulnerable to forces beyond their control.

Believing he understood the tech industry, Prescott had invested heavily in the emerging dot-com sector with proceeds from the sale of his East Coast-based cellular operations. For several years, those investments seemed prescient. The Nasdaq had gained four hundred percent between 1995 and 2000. But on March 10 of 2000, the bubble burst. Day traders who had driven the Nasdaq to speculative new heights awakened to the reality of valuations that bore no relationship to expected earnings. The shiny bubble had grown to volumes its translucent skin could not sustain. By the end of 2002, tech stocks had lost five trillion dollars from peak values. The Nasdaq fell seventy-eight percent.

Prescott Clay lost his fortune. Not only did he sustain dramatic losses on the equity value of his portfolio, worse, he had levered his investments and thus owed debt on his trading account. Technically, he was bankrupt, but refused to engage the lawyers and process that would sanctify by court order the breach of what he considered a personal obligation. So he sold his assets, including his beloved ranch. He managed to save only "mud manor," his home on the smallest of what had been six parcels. The land and most of his liquid assets were lost.

Franny's cancer flared. Prescott would always believe it was triggered by the stress of their financial meltdown. She died in 2008. She was not the only casualty. Without the economies that had been derived from combining operations with Prescott, Arroyo de Zaca fell deeply into the red. Elliot began, once again, a slow descent into bitterness born of shattered expectations. All of his earlier assumptions about life's deck being stacked against him came to full and inglorious fruition. He retreated to the familiar solace of drink.

Prescott retreated as well. He now spent most of his time in the very library in which he now sat, cocooned among the books and ideas that mapped his understanding of life's journey.

It all came back with a photograph, a black-and-white snapshot of Elliot smiling broadly on his first horse shortly after they had moved to California. It had been pressed between the pages of *The Last Lion* and fell to the floor as Prescott opened its cover. He retrieved the photograph and, glancing briefly, carefully returned it to its hiding place in the folds of the book. Suddenly he was overcome with the thought that, unlike Churchill, he had failed. It was not the loss of his money, or his ranch, that disturbed him most. It was the abiding sense that he had failed his son, that he had somehow not forged in him the character to see things through. If, as Aeschylus said, the mark of an upright man was that he should not waste his life railing against the gods of misfortune, then Prescott had surely failed Elliot. And Prescott believed that if you fail your son, you have failed; that one's only true legacy is the legacy of blood and the hope one's progeny makes the mark that escaped oneself.

He closed the book and got in his car. He drove south on Highway 101 passing Arroyo de Zaca and pressing on to the ocean. It always made him feel better to see the ocean. The cold Pacific Ocean, dimpled by light wind, laid up against jagged coves from Gaviota to Santa Barbara. The one-hour drive into the city passed quickly. He parked on State Street and walked by its assortment of restaurants and shops. He paused to take in the majestic façade of The Granada Theater, home to the Santa Barbara Symphony. The tallest building in the city, it had survived the otherwise devastating earthquake of 1925 as if to underscore the community's determination to make Santa Barbara more than a weekend destination for foodies and surfers. Never profitable on ticket sales, it floated on the buoyant backs of Santa Barbara's uber-rich happy to signal their support "for the arts" and sustain the illusion they lived in a "real city." Attendance was optional.

Prescott took in the art deco façade and looked up at the billboard: "The Jupiter Symphony—Friday 7:00 p.m." It made no mention of Mozart. The patrons would know.

"Fuck! Watch where you're going, cocksucker!"

By the time the words registered, Prescott had stumbled to the sidewalk, his hand landing in a puddle of brackish yellow. Disoriented he looked up at a homeless man and realized he had tripped over his sleeping bag. He struggled to his feet.

"I'm sorry, I'm sorry I didn't see you…"

"Yeah, whatever," the man muttered as he kicked his sleeping bag closer to the curb. "Hey, can you spot me a buck or two?"

But Prescott moved quickly past, rubbing the wrist that had braced his fall. Slowly, he regained his composure. He reflected on the irony of homelessness in Santa Barbara. On any given night, up to a thousand souls sleep somewhere on the beaches or sidewalks of America's fourth most expensive city. Why choose here? Maybe, Prescott thought, Santa Barbara chose them. The city council had adopted a "compassionate" policy and lax enforcement of the vagrancy laws. But was the policy truly compassionate? He did not know anymore. Despite the encounter, he found his visceral hostility to this assortment of souls had softened. Even in his own life he had come to see fate as an indiscriminate shooter.

Mindlessly, he walked. Now at the east end of State Street near the wharf, he turned left and entered Santa Barbara's "funk zone," a collection of uber-hip shops and wine-tasting rooms that had risen almost overnight from the rusted ruins of the city's industrial zone. Cavernous warehouses of cement and steel now housed the city's most expensive boutiques, their metal bones and exposed ventilation systems only reinforcing the "too cool to shop at Neiman's" vibe.

He wandered past a clothing boutique stocked with the sort of casual but trendy clothing the locals prefer. Prescott hadn't seen a tie since he arrived on the West Coast. But the locals still spent plenty on fashion. Buying cool stuff that looks like you don't care is expensive. "One off" shops like this one simultaneously signaled a commitment to local business. Heaven forbid you shop a chain.

Prescott walked in. The walls of the shop were festooned in vintage rock posters. A sales girl approached sporting a purple tee shirt emblazoned with the psychedelic logo of The Jimi Hendrix Experience.

"Hi!" she chirped. "I'm Amy. Can I help you?"

He pointed at her shirt. "You ever see them live?"

"No, I wasn't alive when he was alive so never live."

"Of course. How silly of me. Well, I saw them. He was amazing."

"I bet. Can I help you with something?" Amy was on commission and didn't see him buying a lot, his nostalgia rush to the contrary notwithstanding.

"Well, I do need a pair of jeans. Seems all anybody wears out here."

"Sure. Let's start with these." She pointed at a dozen or so neatly folded jeans on the table to her left. "This is our vintage line." She picked up a pair of faded black jeans strategically torn and threadbare in all the right places; one knee was missing.

Prescott leaned down and eyed the price tag: $325. He hesitated as his brain shuffled an entire deck of possible responses. They ranged from the obvious "are you out of your fucking mind?" to something more playful. Finally...

"Impressively vintage. But I'm new to this. How *does* one distinguish between this type of artistry and the sort of tear you might see in a pair of jeans at, say, Nordstrom's?"

"Oh, you can tell. *Please.* You can tell," explained Amy.

"One of those 'you know it when you see it' deals?" Prescott mused.

"Exactly."

"Another question, Amy. Why, exactly, are these signs of wear—tears and such that will doubtless show up over time in the life of any pair of jeans if you wear them long enough—why are they so *expensive?*"

Amy scrunched her face as if the answer was obvious. "Real aging takes too long to happen! Why wait when you can have a cool vintage look *now!*"

"Good point. And without all that nettlesome life experience that gives rise to the worn and torn spots! Who needs the experience, give me the tear!"

Amy smiled. "You got it. And you have to pay for that shit."

Prescott paused to ponder the gargantuan gap between himself and Amy. He wanted to tell her about his favorite pair of jeans, the ones still stained by the blue paint he had chosen for Elliot's room when they found out they were pregnant with a boy; or the ones whose cuffs were frayed and tattered by the hours he spent trying to "sit a horse proper" during his first year in California. He wanted to tell her that "vintage" is not a look, it's the mirror of a life; that its meaning is not in the tracks that remain but in hard experience that left the mark. But he knew it would all be lost on her and that made him sad.

"Prescott?"

He turned and found himself face to face with Jessica, as surprised as she was. He hugged her and pushed back to give her a good look.

"What are you doing in here?" she asked, her smile wide and genuine.

"Stocking up on my John Varvatos gear. Can't have too many pairs of skinny black jeans."

She played along. "Cool. I didn't know you were into the hard rock look."

"Please. My generation *invented* rock. Your generation invented boy bands."

Jessica laughed. "Time for coffee?"

Prescott turned to Amy. "I'll have to think about it. Vintage is a big decision."

Prescott and Jessica walked to a nearby Peet's Coffee.

"Get me a small dark roast if you will. I need to wash my hands, or at least one," Prescott said, bolting for the unisex sign on their left.

He emerged and joined Jessica at a small table in the back. "What'd you get?"

"An oak-milk, skinny cappuccino with one shot of almond, no foam."

"Of course. The foam ruins everything."

"How so?" she asked.

"Lays on the upper lip like a mustache. Requires excessive wiping."

"Not worth it," she agreed.

They settled in. Prescott and Jessica had always had a certain simpatico born of similar upbringings on opposite coasts.

"How is the little prince? I refuse to say great-grandson," Prescott inquired.

"He is good. Great in fact."

"Not surprising. Strong stock."

"Yes, yours. That whole flinty Connecticut Yankee thing, right?"

"Yes, and more."

"Do you miss your ranch?" she asked.

"I do. I miss the land. Land is everything. It must

be the Celtic in me. We treasure land; because we have so little.

Jessica smiled, comfortable in their easy banter. "But you have the house, Casa de Barro?"

"Yes. But without the land it seems more like a ship rusting in port with nowhere to sail."

"You ever think about moving back? To the East?"

"I do." He warmed to the subject. "It's so different here."

"How so?"

"Many ways. People mostly. In the East, when someone asks you what you do, they mean 'what is your occupation?' In Washington, what they really want to know is, what is your proximity to power? In New York they mean 'what is your proximity to money?' Here, if someone asks you what you do, they generally mean do you play tennis or golf or ride or something."

Jessica laughed. "I'm not sure which is worse."

"Nor I. But it's different. The other day, I was stuck in traffic on 'the 101,' as you say out here. I looked around and everyone was laughing and talking on their cells, even rolling down their windows and talking to each other! On the East Coast, that traffic jam, that interruption to productivity, would have induced a stroke, road rage at least. But here? Everybody's fine with it. And I finally realized why. They really have nowhere to go. They are late for nothing. If they are, it means delaying a tee time."

"Well, selfishly, I'm glad you are here. I hope you stay," she said.

"This is where my family is now. That's most important. Speaking of which, how are things with Cole if you don't mind me asking? He seems to be in the Valley a lot."

Jessica paused. "Not great."

"I'm sorry to hear that," he responded.

"Maybe you could help. Cole, I mean. I think he's struggling with a lot right now."

"I was precious little help to his father."

Jessica smiled. "Some things can't be helped."

"I wish I could believe that." He thought about Elliot, then about Cole. "Cole is not Elliot."

"No, he's not. But he's caught in the same web."

Prescott finished his coffee. "It's not my place to comment."

He stood and leaned forward to hug her. "It's great seeing you. Please give my regards to your parents. I will see you at the branding next weekend?" he asked.

"I'm afraid not. I'm going to give Cole some space."

Prescott now took in the full measure of what she was saying. "Well, remember what Epicurus said: We do not develop courage by being happy in good relationships; we develop it by surviving adversity."

"Yes, and Socrates said, by all means get married; if you find a good spouse you'll be happy and, if not, you can become a philosopher."

"Very good. A bit of a non sequitur but nice. Not every granddaughter-in-law can quote Socrates."

"I took one philosophy class at Stanford. That's all I remember."

"It might be enough."

5

---◇---

Back in the Valley, Elliot was leaning over a pool table in the back of Manny's. Cole watched his father and waited his turn. He cracked the cue ball hard and spread the table. The bar was quiet, the evening revelers just filtering in.

Cole leaned in for his shot and missed. "Beef prices at an all-time high and we can't pay our taxes. Taxes are on *income*, last I checked."

Cole took a shot and missed.

"Not property taxes. And we have debt," Elliot responded sourly.

"For what?"

Elliot hesitated. "Started with a loan to drill that new well, bank debt." Elliot sunk a striped three ball. He lined out another shot.

"We have three wells."

Elliot sunk another. "Yeah, doing ten gallons a minute. We need ag water and a lot of it."

"For what?"

"State of California's going to restrict water access, sure as shit. The morons. We need to drill to protect our right to access that water. Then farm. Something. Lots of crops make more money than cattle. Cattle don't pencil anymore, Cole. Simple as that." Elliot missed his shot.

Cole stepped up. "Used to before you started drinking all the profits." Cole sunk a solid ball.

Elliot smiled, "That's what profits are for. Discretionary expenses."

Cole leaned in and struck the cue too hard. It flew off the table. Elliot picked it up and lined out his next shot.

"What about the stock contracting?" Cole asked.

"Makes some. Could be more if we had top-notch stock to breed out. Which is why that mare had to release. She's our only prospect at the moment."

Elliot sunk his shot and continued: "Even then, it's not enough. We need to adapt to the times, Cole." Elliot cleared the table and lined out the eight ball. "You'd know that if you'd pull your head out of your academic ass." He missed.

Cole sunk a solid, but missed the second.

Elliot sunk the eight ball. "You're a shit pool player," he said turning and walking toward the door.

"I don't have as much time to practice," Cole responded.

Elliot exited the door from Manny's as two men entered. Tommy Kyel was bearded and large; his companion skinny and young with shoulder-length hair hiding a neck laced with tatts. Cole walked to the bar where Billy, the barman, was prepping for the evening rush.

"Nice to see you two still get along," Billy said, wiping the bar top.

Cole ignored him. "Give me a Jack with a beer back." He pulled cash from his pocket and a prescription bottle spilled onto the bar.

"Not a healthy habit, amigo," Billy said, taking in the items on the bar.

"Neither's overeating," Cole retorted, shoving the bottle back in his pocket quickly.

Billy poured the shot and slapped the beer on the bar as a young guitar player connected his mic on the small stage with a loud crack.

"Test one, two, three. Test, test."

"What's this all about?" Cole downed his bourbon.

"Her passion. She wants music every weekend," Billy explained.

"Check, check."

"Then she ought to hire a musician." Cole looked at his watch as the guitarist continued to tune. "It works," he said to the guitarist. "Play something."

"Hey, bite me. I don't get paid till five."

"Bite me?" Cole said to no one in particular.

Tommy called out from the table he had commandeered. "Hey, Billy, what's it take to get a drink in this dump? Bring us a bottle of Stoli."

"No dice. I will serve you at the bar." Billy turned his attention to the young couple who had assumed seats at the bar near Cole. The male was about twenty-five, dressed in a vintage bowling shirt over skinny jeans. His companion wore shorts and a loose Rolling Stones tank top.

"Been wine tasting all day," Skinny Jeans explained.

"Really?" Billy replied trying to hide the sarcasm. "What can I get you?"

"I'd love a Viognier, on the fruity side," Tank Top said with a slight slur.

"I'm afraid we're plum out of Viogniers on the fruity side. But I'll get you something fruity."

Tommy moved to the bar and crowded between Cole and the tourist couple. "Shit, Billy, can I get that bottle?"

Billy set a bottle of Stoli on the bar with one glass. "Your friend there is underage. If he wants a soda, let me know."

Tommy laughed and turned back to his table. "Him? Hell. He's seventeen going on thirty. That's Hammer, my brother's kid. Complete shit bag. I wouldn't share horn toad piss with him."

"How is Frank? Haven't seen him around," Billy said.

"That's cause he's in rehab."

"Figures. Been hitting it hard since I've known him."

"It wasn't his drinkin'. He's doin' his rehab in Lompoc at the federal facility. They got him on some trumped-up tax deal. All bullshit," Tommy added before turning his attention to the tourists.

He leered at the girl. "I like your shirt. Especially from the side. You up from LA?"

"Yeah, how'd you know?" she squeaked.

"Wild guess," he smirked. "You gamble? I can spot you a stake at the casino just down the road."

"Oh, no, I don't gamble," she replied.

Tommy sized up her date, "Looks like you do." Her boyfriend stood up immediately, but quickly realized it was a mistake. He did his best to stare Tommy down but his bowling shirt diluted the intended menace. Tommy smiled, itching for the fight.

Cole hated moments like this. He had a good buzz on from the Jack and beer.

"Let it slide, Tommy," Cole offered without turning.

"Fuck yourself, Cole." Tommy stepped toward Cole and stood menacingly.

A standoff. The tourist couple used the diversion to bolt, leaving the fruity wine on the bar.

"Hey!" Billy called out, pointing to the check.

"I got it, Billy," Cole said. He turned to Tommy. "Impressive. Intimidating kids on a date. But then, I forgot, you're a professional. Isn't that what you do at the casino? Customer relations and such; or is it bouncer? Guess it depends on the customer, eh?"

"You always were a smart ass," Tommy replied, taking a step back from Cole.

"Humor runs in the family," Cole said, returning to what was left of his beer.

"Well, that's good. You may need it."

"Why's that Tommy?"

"Cause someone's about to take a chain saw to your family tree." Tommy stood, glass in hand. "Hang around, you're apt to lose a limb."

The guitar player leaned into a Jason Isbell cover as Billy returned and handed Cole two tabs. Cole put down cash.

"Seen Travis?" Cole asked.

"No. Might try the casino," Billy answered.

Cole drove the short distance from Manny's to the casino and parked. The soaring stucco building contrasted sharply with the modest farm and ranch architecture of Santa Ynez. It never failed to deflate his mood. He wondered how, in a county that could delay a septic application for months, the Native community was able to build an entire self-contained city almost overnight. But he knew the answer. They were not citizens of Santa Ynez. They were a sovereign nation. And nationhood has its privileges. Small consolation for what Native peoples had lost, Cole thought. Still, he hated the casino's architecture and, worse, the clientele it attracted, one of whom was the brother for whom he searched as he entered a smoky cavern of whirling chimes and flashing lights.

Cole walked past a sea of nonnative patrons slavishly pumping tokens into brightly colored machines whose rolling neon images promised great riches if only they'd settle in the right sequence. They rarely did. But the addiction held and many came back night after night hopelessly optimistic or too drunk to care.

Cole spotted Travis engaged in a heated exchange with a casino official just inside a door marked "Employees Only." Cole recognized him as a local who went by the name Yellow Sky. He was accompanied by a uniformed casino security guard. Just as Cole was about to reach them, the guard reached out to grab Travis by the arm.

Travis, obviously drunk, wasn't having it. He pushed the guard into Yellow Sky, who slipped on the smooth cement flooring. A pistol slipped from his belt and hit the floor with a loud metallic crack.

Cole stepped between them. "Whoa. Calm down. What's this all about?"

Yellow Sky calmly retrieved his pistol. "We were just suggesting to your brother that he needs to settle some accounts."

"What accounts?" Cole asked.

"Ask him."

Travis looked from Yellow Sky to Cole. "It's nothing. Little dispute among the homies. You remember Yellow Sky, don't you? I think his name was Tony Alavara in high school. Not sure when he discovered his Native roots."

Yellow Sky smiled and looked at Cole. "Lots of posers around town. I remember when your brother here was a Mexican. But that was before he married a white chick and moved to Hope Hills and all." He laughed out loud and holstered his gun. "Why don't you get your little brother out of here before we have him arrested."

Cole nodded. "Just what I had in mind."

Cole and Travis walked into the parking lot and sat in Travis's truck. Light from the casino's blinking neon sign bounced off the windshield as they spoke.

"What's that all about?" Cole asked.

Travis hesitated. "Nothing to worry about, big brother."

"Tell me, Trav," Cole pushed.

"What's it matter?" he deflected.

"It matters when we're up to our ass in debt and you're spending time in the casino piling up more. That's how a casino works, in case you don't know. You lose more than you win."

"Yeah, well I've noticed that. But you're talking to the wrong guy." Travis packed some Copenhagen, rolled down the window and spat.

"What's that mean?" Cole asked, confused by his brother's response.

Travis didn't answer and Cole decided not to press. "We'll talk later. I promised to stop by Prescott's. Get to bed early. We gather and brand tomorrow."

"Sure thing. No problem."

Cole slowly climbed out of Travis's truck, looking back at his brother with a questioning look. He got in his own truck and was soon driving north toward his grandfather's house. As he drove the short distance to Casa de Barro, he replayed what he had witnessed in the casino. He had long since resigned himself to the Clays' congenital weakness. Addiction of one kind or another had cursed the family for generations. While Prescott was sober, Elliot had become the worst kind of alcoholic, one fully bloomed but still in denial. Cole's relationship to alcohol was complicated by simultaneous attraction and repulsion in roughly equal measure. Dopamine and the mild sense of euphoria it brought were useful when you're predisposed to depression and anxiety, anyway. To make matters worse, Cole had been injured on a bronc during his senior year in high school and Elliot, anxious for Cole to compete in the National Finals, arranged for a doctor who had prescribed prescription pain killers. Cole had used them, off and on, ever since. They were helpful when his back flared. But the truth was, Cole loved the gauzy detachment they offered, simultaneously hating the weakness in himself.

As these thoughts flooded Cole's brain, he pulled into the driveway of his grandfather's home. Cole approached the front door of the once stately home, its paint now faded, the garden unkempt.

The door opened before he knocked. Prescott smiled and gestured Cole into the library, its wood-paneled walls stacked with hundreds of books.

"How about a perfect Manhattan?" Prescott offered.

"I thought you gave up drinking."

"I did, but I love to make them."

"We drink our bourbon straight out here, Prescott. That's a Connecticut Yankee drink."

"Indeed." Prescott handed Cole his drink and poured himself a Dr. Pepper.

They sat in heavy leather chairs as Cole gazed up at the books. "You add some shelves?"

"Yes. Believe it or not, I hadn't unpacked the books

in all these years. I wanted them out and organized," Prescott explained.

"You know there are these things called electronic readers, about the size of any one book here. They could store and organize this entire library on a single device," Cole said.

Prescott laughed. "Cole, I made my money in tech. I was an early investor in Amazon. I have a Kindle."

"Any thought of using it?"

"None whatsoever. I like to feel a book in my hands. It has weight, substance. Permanence. Its contents are static. My hard copy of *The Wealth of Nations* reads as Smith wrote it. Does Kindle's? Who knows if Amazon edits titles? They certainly ban books, something to which the left used to object. They probably consider Smith's promotion of the 'invisible hand' of competition to be hate speech. Markets are about efficiency, not social equity. They can be cruel." Prescott sipped his drink and went on: "Most of the so-called tech elite would have wet their pants in the 1770s had they read the popular press. It was very hateful at times."

Cole smiled, comfortable in Prescott's presence. He enjoyed his wit and the unbridled force of his will. Mostly he enjoyed his mind. Secretly he wished that Prescott was his father or, more precisely, that his father was more like Prescott. He had always felt guilty he did.

"You laugh but there's a serious issue there. It will come to full fruition long after I'm gone, but, as an intellectual historian, you should be concerned," added Prescott.

"About what, our media censors being pussies?"

"More than that. The whole idea of 'hate speech' and the disposition of some to purge it from public discourse.

It's absurd! You don't need a First Amendment to protect the conventional wisdom. You need it to protect the minority view, the one considered 'hostile' to existing convention. Take, for instance, the abolitionist position in the early nineteenth century. I can guarantee you decrying slavery in the South in 1850 was very hostile speech! What if we'd have banned it? Sorting through minority views, some crackpot and some not, is at the core of the democratic process. It is how we evolve and progress," Prescott said in disgust.

"The left would argue that it's how we *devolve,* hence the need to filter," Cole pushed.

"Poppycock. Who's to say? That's the whole point. Our system trusts the people to separate the wheat from the chaff. Any alternative model is one form of tyranny or another."

Prescott sipped his Dr. Pepper and shook his head. "It's actually worse than that. We are well beyond the idea of purging 'hostile' speech. The elites have decided they can and should ban more than that; they're on to speech considered 'disinformation,' whatever that means. Take the vaccine debate. Serious scientists were silenced; questions as to its safety and efficacy suppressed. I have no idea whether the vaccines were safe or not, good or bad. But we sure in hell deserved a free and open debate about it." He laughed out loud. "It's such an ironic joke. Posing a hypothesis, *and then questioning it,* is at the root of the scientific method. 'Science!'—the very altar at which the elites would have us kneel."

"Facebook and Google are private; they are free to censor as they please. That is *their* First Amendment right," Cole observed.

Prescott nodded agreement. "The core constitutional issue. I would argue that where the private sector is openly taking direction from the government, their polices are vested with an element of 'state action.' Where social media companies enjoy immunity by federal statute, they are state actors. But constitutional nuance misses the broader point—collectively, FANG hold more sway over our public discourse than the federal government. So is speech in America today free?"

"So what's the answer? More federal regulation? I thought you boomer conservatives hated regulation."

"We did. But civilizations are not static. Especially technology." Prescott was getting wound up. "The Constitution is not a sacred tome. It was a political compromise optimized for the eighteenth century. It may have to be adapted to the twenty-first. The framework of our governance may have to be dynamic to sustain a static measure of freedom, at least of the sort the founders envisioned. That's the argument, anyway." Prescott leaned back in his chair, suddenly deflated by the picture painted by his own arguments.

Cole sipped his drink and sat back, happily immersed, for the moment, in *ideas* and not the *things* that occupied most of his time lately.

Prescott eyed his grandson warily. "You're baiting me."

"Maybe a little," Cole confessed.

"I'm preaching to the choir here."

"You're the last true liberal, Prescott. I am beginning to believe it's a failed experiment."

"How so?"

Cole finished his drink and put his now-empty glass on the coffee table between them. "You know damn well 'how so.' It's what we were saying the other night. If you believe that man is fatally flawed, that we are fallen, lionizing freedom as the greatest good, the *raison d'être* of governance, guarantees we will spin toward the peripheries. By protecting any and all individual freedoms, no matter how divergent from some moral core, some normative consensus, we guarantee the evolution of a society most of us would not want to live in. That's exactly where we are headed so far as I can see."

Prescott hesitated. "You know the problem with the argument, no doubt? Who defines the moral core? Your argument works if we suppose a benevolent monarch, possessed of that moral core grounded in some preexisting consensus that is just and right."

Cole smiled and nodded his head. "I understand. Yet don't we have that very problem today? A not-so-benevolent monarch consisting of an unholy alliance among the financial, tech, and media elite who have decided what we should think and say? Willing to censor and cancel, to shame and penalize to conform public discourse and behavior according to their moral code?"

"Indeed. We do. I just hope that those who once championed the cause of liberalism will recognize it and arrest the contradiction before it consumes us," Prescott added.

"I see no evidence of that. You're the last liberal. The new left is perfectly comfortable with tyranny as long as it is doing 'good' according to them."

Cole was slipping into a rare melancholy. He looked back at the shelves of books and changed the subject.

"So who helped with the new shelves? You're not the handiest guy with a hammer."

"That nice Mexican man who works next door."

Cole bristled. "Does 'that nice Mexican' have a name?"

"I'm afraid I don't know it. I use the term "Mexican" to identify, not demean."

"I'm sure, but if he were Anglo, would you have said 'the white guy' next door?"

Prescott considered the question. "Possibly not. Although I could argue that saying the 'white guy' down the street would not have been terribly helpful as a means of identification."

"Around here, neither is 'Mexican.'"

Cole knew Prescott was not a racist in any meaningful sense. He also knew Prescott was perfectly comfortable discussing race in a way most people avoided.

"You know I'm as much Mexican as Scotch-Irish," Cole continued.

"You are. Most of us are a mix of ethnicities. We draw both strength and weakness from our cultures, our heritage; our upbringing. At the end of the day, we are what we choose to be."

"What does that mean?"

"Life is about choice. Willfulness."

Cole shook his head, "Sometimes we don't have a choice."

"We always have choices, even if they are not perfect ones. There are tradeoffs. In weighing those tradeoffs, there is a choice. That choice reflects our values," Prescott explained.

There was a long silence.

"I saw Jessica today," Prescott said.

Cole shook his head. "You could have told me that

earlier. At least now I know what we're talking about."
He stood up and poured himself another drink, this time
straight bourbon. "She hates the ranch, thinks it's a lost
cause. Nothing but trouble with very little return."

"And what do you think?" Prescott asked, looking
away from his grandson at shelves bent under the weight
of books.

"I'm beginning to think she's right."

Prescott pointed to a section of books over Cole's
head. "Most of those guys would beg to differ. They
wrote a lot about lost causes."

Cole stood and pulled a book off the shelf. *I'll Take
My Stand: The South and the Agrarian Tradition* was a
collection of essays by twelve poets and scholars whose
defense of Southern agrarian culture launched a school
of social and political critique.

"Yeah. They also ignored slavery and romanticized
the antebellum South," Cole responded.

"They did, but they made some pretty compelling
points about the existential utility of agrarianism in preserving values we hold dear."

"Which raises the 'means-ends' question," Cole added.

"Indeed. And the end of preserving the agrarian South
could never justify slavery as a means. But there are closer
calls, as when we are called upon to support imperfect policies in pursuit of consensus or an 'electable' candidate."

Cole sparked to the example and smiled. "That would
appear to be the perpetual state of American electoral
politics. And the answer?"

"I suppose it depends on the nature of those imper-
fections when weighed against the utility of consensus or
the strength of the candidate."

Cole finished his drink and pushed back. "That sounds like relativism. Wouldn't Plato have argued there exists a perfect form of governance, a perfect candidate."

Prescott smiled. "Yes, but the example he used was a chair. Human beings are a tad less perfectible."

"So I say you're a liberal, a dying breed. How do you identify politically these days, Prescott?" Cole pressed.

"As an Aristotelian."

Cole laughed. "I love you, Prescott. California hasn't affected you a bit. What do you do all day, anyway?"

"I read."

"Is that enough?"

"For what?" Prescott asked.

"To be happy."

"That's the wrong question."

"And the right question is?"

"About purpose. The modern view of 'happiness' is about self. Real happiness, at least as Aristotle conceived it, is about balance and purpose."

"Even if we're miserable?"

"Quite possibly."

Cole shook his head, smiling. "Virtue amidst the ruins."

Prescott smiled. "It may be all we have left if things continue on the present course. Winter is coming."

Cole gave him a double take, impressed with his grandfather's command of pop culture. "You finally watched *Game of Thrones*?"

Prescott looked confused.

"I thought you were channeling Jon Snow," explained Cole.

"I haven't read Jon Snow. I was referring to the phil-osophical school that contends every civilization has its seasons with winter being its last."

Cole rose. "I have to go. I enjoyed the talk. Not sure we resolved anything but good to engage."

"I'm sure you'll do the right thing." Prescott rose to walk Cole to the door.

"You coming to the barbecue?"

"Wouldn't miss it." Prescott smiled.

6

———————◇———————

The traditions surrounding a ranch branding date to the halcyon days of Old California when vast ranches covered tens of thousands of acres. Many *vaqueros* were required when the entire ranch was to be gathered and hundreds of head branded, a number more than any single ranch could pay on a year-round basis. And so there developed the tradition of *"rancheros visitadores"*—*vaqueros* from neighboring ranches visiting to help, expecting in due course the favor would be returned. In the earliest days, cowboys would gather at the Old Mission in Santa Barbara in the spring where a priest would bless the coming harvest of meat and tallow before the first of these rotating efforts began.

A second tradition evolved: the ranch barbecue. If your neighbors help, you feed them when the work is done. One of the abundant fatted calves would be slaughtered on the spot and the feast was on, nothing going to waste. Large sides of beef were served with "mountain oysters," the bull calf testicles removed earlier in the day. Grilled bread finished the meal along with strong drink. Green matter rarely found its way to the plate.

The confluence of liquor and a cowboy's natural swagger birthed another tradition: competition. *Vaqueros* from neighboring ranches, often miles apart, rarely saw one another. They happily came face to face at these gatherings. Naturally, after eating, they had to resolve the obvious question: Who was the best cowboy? And so, having ridden since dawn, they jumped back in the saddle and competed. Roping, bulldogging, and bust'n the rankest horse in the string. Rodeo was born of this friendly competition in which the prize was more precious than a million-dollar purse: bragging rights.

It was all part of history, the history of California, and, to Cole, keeping this tradition, keeping this history alive, was important. Arroyo de Zaca would be gathered on this day and Cole would do it as it had always been done. He was up early to start the small oak fire that would be used later in the day to turn the branding irons crimson red to sear the ranch's ZC mark on the left hip of every new calf. After he was sure the fire was lit, he walked past the pens that would be used to separate mother cows from their calves, anticipating the complaining bellows that would fill the air. It was all part of the smell, sound, and sight that created this important day. As he walked back into the house for a quick cup of coffee, he saw Marisa, who had been up even earlier, preparing the meal to be served when the work was done.

By 6:00 a.m., truck and trailer rigs started rumbling up the ranch road. To Cole's surprise, Sam was the first to arrive. She and Jace Wyatt exited the truck and backed their already-saddled horses out of the trailer.

"Hope this isn't your date," Cole said.

"Him? Hell, no. He closed the bar last night so I invited him. Figured you could use the help. My date may come later."

Sam pulled her ponytail through a "National Finals Rodeo" branded ball cap and tied her horse's lead rope to the side of the trailer. "Where the hell is everyone? Let's go, cowboy."

Cole had to smile. "Calm down. You sure you're okay with this whole deal?"

"Of course. Why wouldn't I be?"

Cole was saddling Slick. "Probably don't ride much anymore picking all those grapes."

Sam bridled her horse. "It's not the picking. More the stomping that bothers me. Could hardly get my boots on for the swelling."

Elliot joined them already on horseback.

"Elliot, you remember Samantha Pastore?" It was more a statement than a question. Cole knew Elliot never forgot attractive young women.

"Indeed, good to see you Miss Pastore. It has been too long. You are a vision this morning," Elliot smiled touching the brim of his hat. He looked, as usual, perfect for the occasion—a pressed western shirt, center-creased Wranglers under well-worn leather chaps topped by his perfectly shaped Stetson, a little dusty, lest anyone mistake him for a civilian. Generally abrasive around his family, Elliot Clay could be smooth as the silk scarf that circled his neck when he wanted to be. And that was generally around an attractive woman. But his attention to Sam irritated Cole.

Travis joined the group on horseback. Marisa stood to the side near a coffee station she had set up before dawn. Dustin stood by her side, his eyes wide with excitement. In his ever-present hat and boots, he had added a rope whose loop rested on the ground three feet behind him.

Cole imagined it wouldn't be long before he was throwing that loop, but not today.

Several more cowboys joined. They were ready. Cole mounted and turned his horse to face the group.

"We've got forty pair out, and twenty-four steers from last year's crop. That's one hundred and four head. We need to gather and sort, brand and vaccinate the calves, and cut the yearlings out to sell. Truck arrives at 1:00 p.m."

Elliot was mounted next to Travis. Dustin had climbed into the saddle with his uncle and listened intently, desperate to be part of the group.

Cole continued, "There's some holes in the fence line on the southeast. The neighbors run a Brahman-Angus crossbreed, so you see any cattle with an ear on 'em, they're probably not ours. Just run 'em back over if you can."

Elliot spit a long line of tobacco and turned to Travis, "Bullshit. They wouldn't push ours back. Don't worry about it."

Travis shook his head at Elliot and looked down at Dustin. Elliot dismissed the concern. "Ah, don't sweat it. He ain't trackin' this."

"Grandpa. Don't they all have ears?" Dustin asked.

Travis gave Elliot a look.

"Yes, son. They all have ears, but a Brahmer steer's got longer ears is all," Elliot explained, no longer sure Dustin wasn't tracking.

Cole continued: "Let's split up here. Jace, why don't you and Elliot take two more riders and sweep the southeast. Travis, you take the rest of these guys to the southwest where most of them are. Sam and I will pick up the stragglers in the north so I can get back and get the pens ready. Go easy. They haven't had a horse on 'em in a while."

Sam and Cole walked their horses out toward the north end of the ranch. The sun had fully crested Figueroa Mountain to the east. It was a beautiful spring day. A black-and-white border collie named Tucker trailed along with them, tongue out, head weaving anxiously side to side.

"You remember the first time we gathered here?" Cole asked scanning the pasture ahead.

Sam looked at Cole and didn't speak at first. "Of course I do. That's not a day one forgets. For better or worse."

Cole was more embarrassed by his gaffe than the memory itself. It had been the first time for both of them. "I'm sorry. I meant the gather of course."

The moment lingered awkwardly—a rush of memories and history, of roads taken and abandoned. They reached the top of a small rise and spotted the six steers Cole had expected would stay in the north end.

"Tucker, go round," Cole directed. With that, the border collie snapped into action, head down, moving swiftly, but not running, intense but focused. He circled to the right and pushed the group into a tighter circle. One baldie steer stood his ground. Tucker placed a sharp nip on his nose. Tucker was a "header," rarely biting at the heels, one reason he had lasted seven years without a disabling kick to the head or ribs.

"This is going to be easy. Tucker's on it," Sam laughed.

"Going to get a lot harder when they reach that draw on the left. They're going to break for it. And that baldie will lead the charge," Cole warned.

"How do you know?" Sam asked.

"And that's your side," Cole continued.

With that, the cattle broke hard to the left making a run for the draw. Sam gave her mount a quick kick and jumped into a lope. But the runaways upped the ante in a flat run to reach the steep incline down which they would be hard to follow. Sam followed suit, pushing her horse into a gallop.

Cole knew it was a shit show. If you have to gallop, you've already lost. Cowboys don't gallop on ungroomed terrain unless they absolutely have to. It's dangerous for horse and rider. One rabbit or ground squirrel hole and you're down.

He reluctantly pushed his mount into a fast lope but lost sight of Sam as she dropped over the crest of a hill. The next thing he saw was a plume of dust.

Sam was down when he reined up, the cattle nowhere to be seen, doubtless meandering down the rocky draw, their pursuers far behind. "You hurt?"

"Yes," Sam replied quietly.

"What?"

"My pride."

"You have no pride. You're a vintner," Cole parried.

"Okay, my foot. It hurts."

"Damn. And it was already swollen," he smiled.

"You're a jerk."

"Can you get up?"

Cole reached down to help her up, his arm around her back. She stood but grimaced when she put weight on her right leg. She reached for him with both arms to avoid falling and they were, for a brief moment, in each other's arms. Maybe in the same field where it began a lifetime ago.

Sam pulled back, balancing on her left leg. "I'm okay. Get my horse."

"I'll call Carlos with the truck. I'll pony yours back."

"No. I'm okay. Get my horse."

Cole left Sam standing gingerly, gathered her horse and returned to her. She took the reins balancing on her left leg and grabbed the saddle horn. In one easy motion she swung both legs over the saddle and mounted. She had not used the stirrup.

"Damn!" Cole said, impressed.

"What?" Sam was mounted and ready. "Get your horse. Let's go. I'm not going back without them. We'd look like pussies."

Sometime later, Sam and Cole trailed the six north-end renegades back to the pens. Jace and Elliot were already back, relaxing in their saddles looking over the fifty-one head circling nervously in the pens. Travis and the rest of the crew were still out.

As Sam and Cole added their quarry to the group, a white Prius pulled up to the conclave of diesel trucks and trailers already there. Tucker ran to the car and christened the right rear tire of the new arrival. Cole smiled. He shared Tucker's disdain for environmentally correct vehicles. It wasn't so much their beneficent contributions to the environment he resented as the virtue signaling of their drivers. He was never quite certain their owners were serious when they extolled the "quiet hum" of their engines or they just wanted you to know they were environmental warriors. He assumed Tucker shared the skepticism.

Sam hobbled over and back, now arm in arm with her date, the warrior. He was dressed like a hipster trying to dress like a cowboy. He wore jeans an inch too short to adequately cover the shaft of his boots, which should have been a priority given that they zippered on each side. Inevitably, the outfit was topped by a vaguely "western" fedora. Cole was convinced that the popularity of fedoras among Gen Xers would one day haunt them from the memory bank of their iPhones, much the way pictures of Elliot's high school mullet still haunted him.

That said, Michael was six feet, two inches and stupidly good looking. He looked like the guy in high school you wanted to hate but couldn't because he was impossibly nice. The jury was still out on Michael.

"Cole, I would like you to meet Michael. Michael, this is our host, Cole Clay."

They shook hands.

"Michael is an environmental engineer in Goleta," Sam noted.

"Actually, an environmental scientist. We have different core competencies. We are more about what to do, the engineers the 'how,'" Michael explained. "I'm surprised you guys heard me arrive, that thing's so quiet," gesturing toward the Prius, its right rear fender now dappled in yellow.

"Bingo," Cole thought, but said nothing.

"You have a beautiful place here, Cole. I love how underdeveloped it is."

Cole wasn't sure if that was a compliment or an insult. He gave him the benefit of the doubt.

"If it weren't for the methane problem, I'd bet you have a net negative footprint," added Michael. "I might be able to help with that."

Cole was confused. "I'm sorry, with?"

"Bovine gas. The methane problem."

Okay, thought Cole. Jury's in. "Great. We should talk."

Cole looked at this watch. "Listen we have a truck coming at one. We only have half of them in. I'd better see if I can help Travis. Enjoy yourself. Sam can show you around. She knows the ranch."

Cole walked toward his horse but turned back mid-stride and called out to Michael. "Maybe we can steal a few minutes this afternoon to talk about the farting. I could use your expertise there."

"Sure thing!" Michael replied, oblivious.

An hour later, Sam and Michael, leaning against the Prius, watched Cole and Travis emerge from the south end pushing a large group of cattle, two riders trailing behind. At the pens, Cole counted as they fed in. "We're three steers short. They'll show up in the morning looking for their buddies. Let's get started."

Jace and Elliot had started the sorting process. The entire herd was pushed into a center alley ten at a time. A rider with a good "inside" horse stood mid-alley, separating calves from mother cows and pushing the calves to a catch pen on the right. The mother cows were kicked loose to bray nervously as their offspring were processed. The steers were separated and pushed to a catch pen on the left to await the truck.

Michael had strategically placed himself at the corner of the center alley on top of the metal pipe fence rails. Cole approached on horseback from outside the pen.

"You might want to find a different spot to watch," he offered.

"Oh, no, I'm fine," Michael said.

"Well, actually, you're not. We have to push them to this end of the alley to separate them. They see you here, they're going to duck off."

Michael climbed down making clear he wasn't happy about it.

"Seems like a primitive process," he opined as he awkwardly climbed down the pipe rail fence.

"Well it's been done this way for two hundred years."

"Yeah, I guess that's my point," Michael answered.

"I see what you mean," Cole lied. "Well if you can think of a better way, I'd be open. Maybe one of those 'how' guys you work with, huh?"

Cole rode away and entered the small corral they were using to rope and brand the calves. He turned Slick toward the action, prepared his lasso, and waited his turn. Two riders worked as a team, the "header" moving in first to throw his loop over the calf's head. If successful, the "heeler" would follow to rope the calf's two hind legs. Once roped, the ground team would step in.

Cole and Jace teamed up. Jace's first throw hit the mark. Cole's first throw missed, but he quickly pulled his rope back and caught both hind legs on this second throw. Travis was working the ground. He moved to the roped calf and "bulldogged" the two-hundred-and-fifty-pound animal to his side. Cole and Slick, as if partners in a dance, backed up slowly until the rope was taut and the calf stretched out on the ground.

Sam had joined the ground crew administering injections, working alongside those who were branding and, when necessary, castrating. Michael was right about that piece. It was primitive. A special knife, mercifully sharp, sliced the scrotum, the cords were cut, and the testicles removed. One shot of spray antibiotic and the calf was up and out. The testicles were thrown in the "ball bucket" for the barbecue and the ground crew was off to the next calf, likely already down, roped by another team. The whole process took about four minutes per head.

As the branding wound down, Cole exited the arena. Sam had left the ground crew and now stood with Elliot next to Carlos's pickup, the back cluttered with a cooler of beer, various bovine meds, and an open box of donuts. Cole approached on horseback. Elliot was in a full charm offensive with Sam. "I'd love to come by and sample some of your wines. I had no idea—"

"Hey, can you hand me a beer?" Cole interrupted. "Where's your boyfriend, Sam?"

"I don't know. He said the smell of burning cow hair made him nauseous."

Cole finished the beer, threw the empty in the truck bed. "He's a jackass." Cole gathered up Slick and rode off.

"Your son has a way with words," Sam offered.

Elliot nodded in agreement. "Got that from his mother. She was a plain-spoken woman. I was grateful most of it was Spanish. Didn't understand a word of it." Elliot finished his own beer and extended his arm. "I wonder if you would accompany me to the *hacienda*. We have a barbecue to organize."

Sam threaded his arm. "I'd be happy to help."

"Along the way we can look for your jackass boyfriend."

"Jackass date," Sam corrected him.

On the grassy knoll near the main house, sweaty cowboys soiled from the branding, mingled with fiesta-attired neighbors and guests from nearby Santa Barbara, drinks in hand. More cars and trucks arrived by the moment.

Cole's view was you invite the neighbors whether they helped or not. The branding was an annual event whose symbolism Cole would not let pass. It was, he thought, a sort of hybrid of Thanksgiving and Easter. It celebrated bounty, good fortune, and new life. It was very much part of Old California.

Billy was the chef, a sideline business and a break from bartending at Manny's. He wore a large, flat-brim hat and an apron emblazoned with his catering logo. He had even waxed his mustache for the occasion. Stiff and glistening in the afternoon sun, it extended an easy three inches on either side of his prominent nose. He was as proud of his "stash" as his signature tri-tip and beans, which he now served with charred sourdough and the "mountain oysters" for those disposed to sample. Always ready with a well-timed compliment for the señoritas, he served the cowboys their food and insult in roughly equal measure.

Jace reached the front of the line and took the offensive. "Hell's bells, Billy, I had no idea you could still get that thing up. May have to get me some of that wax."

Billy pushed some rare beef onto Jace's plate. "Sorry to hear that, pard. When I was your age I didn't need a stiffener."

Travis reached Billy in the line and held out his plate for the tri-tip. "I took you for a vegetarian, Trav, you sure? Maybe a tad rough for that pinot 'nowaar' you fancy."

Cole and Sam stood to the side and watched. It was, he thought, exactly as it should be. Neighbors and friends, cowboys from the Valley and centimillionaires from Santa Barbara, Mexicans and Anglos, without class or pretense, joined in common cause—celebrating the land and a shared history.

Jace, Cole, and Sam joined Prescott who had found a shady spot at one of the tables just as Victoria's twins, Leaf and Summer, arrived at the party. They strolled through the crowd sharing a bong, oblivious. Their attire was gender-neutral, postmodern cowboy.

"Holy shit. Who's that?" Jace asked as if he'd seen an apparition.

"That's Leaf and Summer. They're Victoria's kids from her former marriage. Be nice. They're coming over," Cole responded calmly.

Leaf and Summer approached in a thick haze of smoke.

"Hey," Cole opened. "Sam, Jace, this is Leaf and Summer." He gestured to Sam and Jace, "These are my friends Samantha Pastore and Jace Wyatt. You know Prescott, of course."

Jace jumped in, extending his hand. "Great to meet ya. You sisters?"

Cole held his breath. Leaf answered, "We prefer gender-neutral nouns and pronouns."

Jace looked at Cole, then back at the two standing in front of him, "Well, I'll be fucked."

It was an honest response.

Leaf continued undisturbed, "You can use 'ver' instead of him or her, 'verster' instead of brother or sister."

Jace took a deep breath and then a big hit of his Crown and Coke. He had had several.

"Well, versters, I guess I'll damn well call you what I please."

Summer rolled ver eyes. "Then you're a primitive bigot, as I might have guessed."

"That's kinda harsh," Jace said. "I'm just tryin' to understand."

Leaf leaned in. "What don't you understand? Gender classification reflects deeply ingrained cultural misogyny. You need to evolve."

Jace's tone turned serious, almost apologetic. "You know, you're right. I need to evolve." He gestured across the lawn full of cowboys. "We all do. Can't blame us. We're a product of this environment."

Leaf and Summer both nodded their heads. Jace stepped closer, placing his hand on Leaf's shoulder. "To evolve, I need to understand."

Summer was still skeptical. "I'm not sure where to begin."

Jace looked at his boots as if considering. "Well, let's start with an easy one: Which one of you has a penis?"

"Oh, my g-a-w-d!" growled Summer. "I think we'll leave you to finish your animal flesh."

Jace laughed heartily as they left.

Sam looked at Cole. "That went well."

"About what I expected," said Cole. Jace just smiled, proud of his work.

Cole surveyed the crowd as more guests arrived. In one corner, Indigo had had his minions set a table that morning with an assortment of his wines. They were serving when Indigo arrived. He checked on his table and began working the crowd talking endlessly, as usual, about his wine. Victoria joined him, leaving Elliot alone at the campfire with Travis.

To Cole's surprise, Tommy Kyel blew through the gate, Hammer in tow. They both took a glass of wine from the Indigo table and strode over to join Elliot and Travis. Cole had no idea who invited Tommy or why he would come. But his attention was diverted by Marisa who approached with a plate of empanadas, Dustin tracking closely behind.

"Hey, cowboy!" Cole greeted his son. "You having fun?" Dustin nodded enthusiastically. "Marisa," Cole added, "you don't have to serve. Let someone else do that."

"I don't mind."

Jace reached out and took one, downing the delicacy in two bites. "Damn, those are good."

Just then, Dustin bolted down a rocky embankment behind them. He had spotted a California horned toad lizard, there could be no higher priority than its capture.

Cole, Sam, and Marisa watched the hunt with obvious delight. Cole recalled his earliest days on the ranch and seeing his first horny toad. Flat, spiked, and sporting a crown of horns, the black-eyed reptile was surprisingly calm when captured and made a manageable pet as long as you provided the requisite number of insect snacks. They were said to be good luck, their presence on your property a positive omen.

But not today. Dustin soon scampered back in tears wiping at his eye. Marisa put the empanadas down and pulled Dustin into her arms.

"It's okay, buddy. Let me see." Cole held his son's face and wiped blood from beneath his eye. "It's just his way of defending himself. Horned toads excrete their own blood to ward off predators. He just thought you were going to eat him." Cole patted Dustin's back as he settled down.

Cole did not settle. Horned toad lizards could expel blood, but rarely did. This was not a good omen. Maybe superstition, maybe a tale from his *abuela*, but the moment stuck in Cole's chest.

Cole was brought back as his attention was drawn to the fire pit and loud voices. Elliot's voice.

"Get your damn ass outta—"

Cole and Jace ran to the commotion just as Elliot took a drunken swing at Tommy. Tommy ducked it easily and caught Elliot square in the nose with his left fist. Elliot was on the ground when Cole reached the fight. He never slowed his gait, running into and over Tommy who hit the gravel hard, nearly busting his head on the river rock surrounding the fire pit.

Hammer scrambled to pull his uncle to his feet. Travis helped Elliot up. Cole stood his ground inches away from Tommy, ready for his next move. But none came. Tommy brushed himself off.

"Not very gracious hosts."

Cole stood down. "What are you doing here, Tommy?"

He smiled and picked up his hat. "Hey, it's a branding. Ain't everyone invited?" He looked squarely at Travis. "Wanted to see what you got out here."

"Get out," Cole said.

Tommy just stared, then turned to Hammer. "Let's go, boy. I guess they don't understand the tradition."

Cole's guests soon returned to their food and drink, retreating beneath oak canopies and away from the summer sun. But the warm and easy atmosphere Cole had worked so hard to provide had been altered irretrievably. His guests soon began to take their leave and Cole found himself wishing just one would say what they were all thinking: What in the hell was that all about?

The barbecue came to an end. Elliot decided to drive to Santa Barbara ostensibly to see a doctor about his nose. For all Cole knew he had a girlfriend in town and why not? Victoria had left with Indigo to "inventory the wine" they had sold at the barbecue. Elliot had offered to drive Dustin home to Jessica in Santa Barbara, an offer Cole declined. Elliot was in no condition to drive himself, let alone his son. Prescott was on his way to Los Angeles for a reunion of his "agency" colleagues. He had agreed to see Dustin safely home.

The guests departed, Cole walked back to the grassy knoll and took a seat next to Sam, the last guest. The summer heat was cooling. They watched the cattle, recently released from the pens, their heads down, stealing a last meal before their silent standing sleep.

"Well, that was pretty western," Sam said.

"Yeah, that sort of thing doesn't happen when you serve pinot," Cole replied.

A sliver of moon appeared, the sky still light. Most found that beautiful or, at a minimum, curious. It made Cole anxious, as if a reminder that the light and the dark exist simultaneously. He knew that. He didn't need billboards in the sky.

"What was Tommy doing here, anyway?" Sam asked.

"I don't know."

"Probably just being an asshole."

"Maybe. But I think we have trouble at the casino."

Sam turned her attention back to the view, the sky now darkening.

Cole read her reticence, sensing she knew more than she was saying. "Spill it," he demanded.

Sam took a deep breath. "Word is Tommy takes bets under the table. On sports, I guess," Sam hesitated. "Elliot was spending a lot of time at the casino for a while. He met Tommy sometimes at our place. It never looked pleasant."

Cole thought about it, then stood. "I guess you need a ride. You could stay in the guest room. But Mr. Clean Energy wouldn't like that. You could tell him we were saving the fossil fuel needed to get home, I guess."

"He's not the jealous type," Sam replied.

"Figures."

"What's that mean?"

"He's a jackass. He should be."

Sam smiled and they walked toward the main house.

"I'll show you to the guest room," Cole offered.

"No need. I've pretended to stay there many times," she smiled.

About 4:00 a.m., Cole tired of staring at the ceiling of the room he had occupied as a child. For Cole, coming home was always bittersweet. He loved the ranch and the *hacienda* that sat dead center in its rolling hills. It smelled as it always had, of wooden beams and leather chairs, vague remnants of cigarette smoke indelibly etched into the crevices of its wood-and-plaster bones. A thousand memories lived there, waiting while he was away, stirring to life when he entered. But never quite gone. Coming home was inevitably regressive. It required a conscious effort to be the person you had become, and not the person you were when the role you played as a child became part of the DNA of "home."

Cole had been the "good son." His father's constant companion, confessor, and counselor. It was an unnatural role and exacted on Cole a heavy toll of unspoken resentment. He yearned for Elliot to be his father and not his friend, ever in need of advice and encouragement, all the more so as Elliot's marriage began to unravel and his dreams escape. But it was a role Cole could not seem to escape, as if some innate need to "make things right" compelled him to be the gravitational center in a constellation of stars being pulled out of common orbit.

Travis occupied a different role in the family and had from the start. He was the cowboy, the pure play, oblivious to the rest. It was his capacity to put the family's problems on a shelf, to emotionally remove himself from the fray, that most distinguished him from his older brother. In truth, for most of his life, Cole had been jealous of his little brother's capacity for emotional isolation.

He rolled over in bed. Why could he not be more like Travis, boxing the snakes in his mind and placing them on a shelf, to be opened once a year, briefly, then put back? Like visiting the zoo.

Cole gave up pretending that he was going to go back to sleep. He got up, pulled on his sweats and walked to the living room.

Sam sat curled up in a leather chair, bundled in a robe, cigarette in hand.

"I didn't know you smoke," Cole said.

"I don't. Sometimes I like the way they smell. Who knew they taste like shit?"

Cole sat across from Sam in his father's favorite chair. "Couldn't sleep?"

"The room was too crowded," she said.

Cole smiled. Their high school ghosts occupied the house as much as the faint echoes of his mother and father fighting.

Sam crushed the cigarette. "Let's eat."

The first hint of dawn pushed grey light behind the black contours of mountains to the south. Cole moved to the kitchen and Sam sat at the counter on a bar stool. Cole began to unload the refrigerator. Tortillas, orange and red peppers, chili sauce, meat from the barbecue.

"Can I get a latte?" Sam asked.

"No. This isn't a wine bar. I'll make some coffee."

"Spare me the usual brew. I think I had adrenal failure in high school from your coffee."

"Cowboy coffee is strong. Not like the watery stuff you serve at Manny's. Been meaning to mention that."

"I'll have you know that is a new Ethiopian-Honduran blend. We have our own roaster now, not that you'd know the difference."

"Probably not."

Sam soaked it in. The light, the smell of coffee brewing and tortillas beginning to soften and sizzle in butter. It felt like everything she loved about the morning in Santa Ynez, the soft delusion of safety.

"I'm making *migas*," Cole volunteered.

"Good. For a minute, I thought you were cleaning the refrigerator."

Cole smiled. "Your boyfriend would be happy. *Migas* are environmentally appropriate: Nothing goes to waste."

"He's not my boyfriend. We are friends."

"That is such a female thing to say. There is no such thing as 'just friends' between a man and an attractive woman. At least in the beginning. You're either a girlfriend, a potential girlfriend or you're toast."

"Leaf and Summer were right. Visiting Zaca is like a trip to Jurassic Park. You should issue 3D glasses at the gate," she replied.

Cole began to crack fresh ranch eggs in an iron skillet over the diced vegetables and meat.

"It's like nothing has changed," Sam said, as if to herself.

"But everything has," Cole answered. He poured her a cup of coffee and handed her a small pitcher of cream.

"Not everything," Sam quietly added.

Cole looked his first lover in the eyes, then let it pass. There was no upside in going there. He heaped the *migas* on their plates and tossed two warm tortillas on top.

"Let's eat."

They ate in silence for long moments as bright light vanquished the grey pastel of early morning.

"When we were kids, I thought life was like a ride at Disneyland or something," Sam said finally.

"We back to amusement parks?" Cole quipped, hoping to deflect.

Sam watched through the window as Carlos walked a young gelding from the barn. "I'm serious. Like our lives were on a track or something. Scary twists and turns, but it all works out. Guaranteed, as if life's wheels are bolted to a track that will always take you back to a safe place."

She turned to Cole and smiled, but her eyes carried a hint of sadness, as if to apologize for what she was about to say.

"There is no track is there?"

Cole put his fork down and watched as Carlos turned the gelding out in an adjacent pasture. He had no idea how much Sam knew, or sensed, about his own growing fears. But he wasn't ready to tell her.

"No, I guess not. Who knew?" he said dismissively.

Sam reached for a second tortilla. "Well you should

have. Supposed to be so damn smart. Historian for heaven's sake."

"You're right. History confirms the futility of our struggle. After the Fall, man, separated from God, was doomed to eternal struggle."

"That's bullshit. That is why we have the church. There's a path. Makes the struggle less onerous. At least there's a road map," Sam retorted giving Cole a look of mild disapproval.

Cole smiled. He envied her blind faith. Her serenity in surrender. "I think I lost the map."

"That's not the problem. You know what your problem is, Cole?"

"Tell me."

"You *want* to be a martyr, to trade everything for that one moment of existential glory."

"It's not like that," Cole asserted, feeling less sure than he sounded.

7

---◇---

"L *adies and Gentlemen, welcome to the opening after-*
noon of our own Fiesta Rodeo and Stockman's Show."
The PA boomed over a packed house in the
Earl Warren Equestrian Showground Arena. Cole,
Elliot, and Travis were saddled and ready, waiting in the
covered staging arena adjacent to the small arena.

"Today we kick things off with our ranch competition
where local teams from area ranches compete in various com-
petitions meant to showcase the skills a vaquero *uses every*
day in cattle ranching."

Cole was nervous. He had long since retired from
competition and he knew this meant a lot to Elliot.
Cole's legs communicated the anxiety to his horse as if
by telegraph. Slick jigged left and right.

"Our first competition is team penning. For all you city
folk, that's where our cowboys cut three steers marked with a
given number out of a herd of thirty and put 'em in a pen at
the other side of the arena. The trick is, if any animal of the
wrong number crosses the center line, you're done. It's a timed
event, low time wins, ninety seconds max."

Elliot approached. "Okay, Travis, how do you want
to do this?"

Travis laid out the strategy. "Dad, you take the first
cut. Cole, you turn back and I'll work the pen. Then we

rotate. That means I put the last one in for the money."

"Okay, don't fuck it up," Elliot instructed as he moved to the starting line.

The first team rode. The buzzer blew at the maximum ninety seconds. They had penned one steer.

"Our next team is from Arroyo de Zaca and includes at least one pro cowboy. This should be fun."

Cole, Travis, and Elliot walked their horses out to the starting position and waited for the number that would identify their targets.

"Number five. There are three steers marked five in that mess. Go get 'em, cowboys!"

In a deliberate but unhurried manner, Elliot rode into the herd and easily cut out the first number five. He pushed it toward the pen at the other end of the arena as Cole held the rest of the herd back. At the other end, Travis made a good cut and nudged the first steer marked with a number five into the pen at twenty-three seconds.

Cole rode into the churning herd, missed his first cut but made the second, pushing the second number five to Elliot, who penned it. They had used another thirty seconds of the clock.

With thirty-seven seconds remaining, Travis was up. He rode into the scrum too hot. The herd scattered. Elliot kicked his horse into overdrive to simultaneously turn them back and push the last number five toward Travis. A second chance.

With twenty-four seconds remaining, Travis blocked his target's retreat to the anonymity of the herd and drove it hard toward the pen at a full gallop as the clock ticked down…

Nine…eight…seven seconds…

Travis realized he did not have time to hand off to Cole. He stayed on his prey...six...five...pushing hard for the pen...four...three...

But the ninety-second buzzer sounded with the last steer just shy of the pen's threshold.

The crowd groaned, then applauded the effort. "*Tough break for the Zaca boys. Two in at ninety seconds.*"

Cole, Elliot, and Travis reined up together as they exited the arena. Elliot was livid. "Pro cowboy? What kinda dip shit amateur rides in that hard?!"

Cole had seen his father angry many times but he had never seen his face flush the way it did in that moment. Years of drinking had thinned the skin of his face so that the translucent tissue of his cheeks revealed cobwebs of hard time. At that moment, his face looked like a road-map of Los Angeles and Cole knew, somehow, this was not about team penning.

The next night, the parking lot outside Manny's was packed with pickups. Cole and Jace parked three blocks away and walked back. A neon sign flashed "Welcome PRCA Cowboys." A bouncer named Tiny checked IDs at the door. Tiny's stature belied his name. He weighed two hundred and fifty pounds stark naked, not that anyone would want to see it. Cole had known him in high school. A Hawaiian, he often bragged his relatives had eaten Captain Cook. Cole didn't doubt it. Tiny honored his Polynesian heritage with tatts covering both beefy arms; they ran up his shoulders and onto his thick neck. Letters inked on the five fingers of his left hand spelled out "A-L-O-H-A," which Cole assumed was intended to be ironic, but never asked. Tiny never smiled, but nodded when he saw Cole. He waved Cole to the head of the line. Cole blew through the door, Jace tagging behind.

They stood shoulder to shoulder in the packed barroom, their ears adjusting to the volume of the band.

"You think I got a chance?" Jace yelled as if in a wind tunnel.

"Of course. Elmer Fudd could score in here. Half these girls are pros."

Jace stared back blankly, then shook his head. "No, I mean in the bronc deal, beating Olly?"

Cole spotted his father and brother at a table inside. "I don't know. Maybe, yeah." They moved through the crowd to join Elliot. Travis sat to his left. Jace tipped his hat at Elliot as the waitress descended.

"What'll it be, gentlemen?"

"Bring us a bottle of Jack, four glasses with ice," snapped Elliot. "Oh, and some beer back. Firestone DBA, unfiltered, if you got it."

"Well, thank you, Elliot. Kind of you to order for us," Cole said.

"Prelims tomorrow. I'll have a beer," Travis said.

Elliot waved his arm dismissively. "Shit, in my day a good hand couldn't ride sober." He turned to Jace, changing the subject. "How'd you do up north?"

"Shitty. Drew a dink," Jace offered.

Elliot turned to Travis. "What's your excuse?"

Travis was irritated by the question. "I rode her to the buzzer."

"Yeah, but what'd y'a mark?"

Cole jumped in. He hated Elliot's constant needling. "What was the name of that horse. I forget."

"T-bone. A complete burn out," Travis offered.

"Well, sure she was, son," Elliot explained.

"How would you know?" Travis asked.

"Getting your draw these days is like computer dating. They match profiles."

There was an awkward silence. And then Jace burst into laughter. They all followed, even Cole. But their moment of comradery was interrupted by a commotion near the entrance. Cole looked back but couldn't make out the cause. Elliot turned to Jace. "So who'd you draw in this deal?"

"Ragged Edge," Jace answered.

Travis exchanged a nervous look with Cole.

"Feel terrible about Wade but that's a money horse for sure," Jace said.

"Be happy when we can turn her out for breed stock, the bitch," Elliot snapped.

"I'd think you'd be happy to have her in your string," Jace said.

Elliot shook his head. The waitress returned carrying the bottle and balancing the four beers on a tray. Elliot watched until she had deposited the drinks then went on: "That's because you think this is about the glory of going to the bell on a great horse and all that happy horseshit."

Noise at the entrance broke their attention again. Olly Davis and his entourage emerged from the scrum. Olly led the way for his two cowboy keepers, followed by three young "cowgirls" in a bouncy blur of bosom and blonde.

Cole turned back to Elliot, anxious to move the conversation away from Ragged Edge. "Give it a rest, Elliot," he suggested.

But Elliot had downed his first Jack 'n ice and damaged the second. He gestured toward Olly. "You think guys like that asshole give a shit about pitting himself against a great horse? He just wants to get to the show where the money is." He killed his second drink. "Same for the stockman. Our mare makes it to the show, she's worth some money. That's all I care about. This is a business. A shitty one, but a business."

Travis stood abruptly, "I'm going to the head."

Olly and his group had taken a table. More laughter.

"Olly's gonna be hard to beat," Elliot slurred.

Cole shook his head, "He's overrated."

"I wouldn't bet against him, son."

Cole considered the comment, but dismissed it as drunken ramble.

Travis returned. Cole stood. "Good, you can babysit awhile."

Cole walked toward the head and ran into Sam. They stepped to the side where they could talk.

"Sorry about today. I heard," Sam said quietly.

"No big deal. It was team penning."

"When does saddle bronc start for Travis?" Sam asked.

"Tomorrow, short round next day if he makes it."

The band began a waltz. One of Olly's crew approached Sam.

"Was wondering if I might have this dance, miss?" he slurred.

"No, thank you. I'm working."

"Well, it don't look like you're workin'," the cowboy came back.

Sam didn't blink, "It will. When I have Tiny come over here and throw your sorry ass on the street."

The cowboy returned to Olly's table and they laughed, loud enough to make sure everyone heard.

Cole turned back to Sam. "So you coming to the bronc deal?"

"Maybe, if Travis makes the short round," she smiled. One of her staff approached. "I gotta go."

Cole used the head and set a course back to his table. He had to pass Olly's table on the way. He could hear their drunken chatter as he approached.

"He ain't hittin' that."

"Oh, I don't know. Heard his ol' lady threw him out."

As Cole neared, Olly chimed in. "Can't blame her. Guy can't stay in the saddle to the bell. Bet I could ring it."

Their heads bobbed about in waves of silent laughter as Cole stopped just behind Olly. The entourage saw him first. It was a moment that freeze frames in the brain, where everything else fades, where choices are crystalized even if, as Prescott had reminded, there are no good choices among them.

Cole tapped Olly on the shoulder, the laughter faded quickly as Olly stood. "You have a problem?" he said.

Cole shook his head. "No, but you will."

Olly smiled and looked back at his crew as if to say "watch this."

He turned to Cole. "When's that?"

"Tomorrow morning." With that, Cole punched Olly in the face as hard as he could. He felt the cartilage in his nose snap as Olly fell backward, only to jump back to his feet and start swinging, his nose awash in thick red blood. Cole experienced the fight as if floating above it, observing film in slow motion.

Unlike the movies, what he saw was not an elegant, choreographed dance, opponents trading perfect punches to the face and body without apparent effect, heroically coming back for more. What he saw were gangly punches rarely connecting, grown men tripping and falling in their own blood and spit, then connecting with a lucky punch that did real, bone-crushing damage. It was chaotic, violent, and ugly.

Travis and Elliot were on them in seconds. Travis pulled Olly off his brother and punched his already broken nose while Elliot cleared the deck with wild swings of an overturned chair. Jace kicked the legs out from underneath the last of Olly's crew and stepped on his neck to keep him immobilized.

Then Tiny was on them and it was over.

Jace and Travis were at Cole's side when he was cuffed and removed by a Santa Ynez sheriff's deputy. Elliot returned to their table and finished his drink, a slight smile drawn through weathered cheeks.

The next day marked the opening of the Santa Barbara Fiesta Rodeo. The showground's bleachers were packed with a disparate assortment of cowboys, families, and teenagers wandering the aisles in a last-ditch effort to score any seat other than the one their parents were holding. Most were unsuccessful. The event had sold out weeks before. The quarter walls that lined the arena itself were papered in logos that defined both a sport and a culture: Cactus Rope, Skoal, Carhartt, and John Deere. Junior Rodeo participants loped their ponies around the outer edge of the arena sporting colorful flags of their choosing. Behind the bucking chutes, riders and their handlers readied.

The small indoor arena made the whole affair somehow more intimate and, for the fans, more exciting. Some came to see their favorite cowboy compete; most came to see the inevitable wreck. The air crackled with nervous energy.

Behind chute number two, Travis prodded Ragged Edge into position. Elliot joined him.

"How's she doin'?" he asked.

"Like always. Being a bitch. How's she supposed to be doin'?" Travis replied.

"She's supposed to stand the chute proper and kick his ass when the gate swings," Elliot said.

"Well, we'll sure do our best, Dad."

Jace approached. "Where's Cole? He's supposed to flank for me."

They all watched as Olly and his entourage readied in chute number one. Olly glanced their way. His nose bandaged, his right eye purple and blue. He climbed the chute and mounted his draw as the rodeo announcer called the event to order.

"Ladies and Gentlemen. Welcome to our rodeo and the opening round of our saddle bronc competition. First up is PRCA's reigning saddle bronc champ, Mr. Oliver Davis. Let's give him a nice round of applause."

As the applause faded, the crowd grew silent. Olly nodded his head and the gate released.

From their position on the ground behind chute two, Elliot, Travis, and Jace could see only Olly's raised right arm and head intermittently punch into their field of vision with each successive buck of the bronc.

As the seconds ticked down, the crowd cheered. The buzzer sounded. Jace climbed the panels and mounted.

"A good opening ride for the champ. That'll put Olly Davis in the short round tomorrow, I'm gonna guess. But we'll see. Next up in chute number two is Jace Wyatt. He'll have his hands full with this mare."

Ragged Edge reared and tensed, trying to buck. But

a horse can't buck unless she can get her head down. Frustrated, she thrashed side to side.

Jace sat the chaos and waited. "He should be here."

"I guess the sheriff had a different idea. Doubt he'll make it," Elliot said without emotion.

At that moment, Cole was lying on a cot in a county jail sweating profusely. He was bruised, sore, and pissed. Whether his anger centered on Olly or his own bad judgement was unclear to him. It didn't matter. What mattered was the time. They had taken his watch and phone. He assumed he had already missed the bronc competition at the arena a few blocks south of the jail. He wanted to be there for his brother.

The afternoon sun peered through the Plexiglas and wire window that rested high on the one exterior wall of the cell. It cast a filtered yellow light on the concrete floor and a naked toilet bolted to the wall. Cole had never seen a more depressing tableau. He wondered why he had always been so sensitive to the color of light.

He heard keys push into the metal door to his cell. It swung open.

"Get up, shit head. Your lady friend made your bail," came a low voice. The sheriff's deputy smiled oddly, as if he'd been rooting for release.

Cole was escorted to a small office outside the cell block where he was given his wallet, phone, and watch. A clerk pushed paper at him.

"Says you'll show up for your arraignment. Date's on it. Sign there and take your copy," he said without looking up. Cole signed and waited.

The clerk looked up, "Well? Get. Glad we could be

of service."

Cole took his possessions. "And that was?"

"Twelve hours of detox. You'd pay big bucks for that one of those places in M-A-L-I-B-U," the clerk laughed, convinced he was clever.

Cole turned and exited to brighter light. Sam was waiting, the engine running. She gestured him in.

"Thought you weren't coming till the short round," Cole said as he opened the passenger door and got in.

"At this rate, doubt the Clays will make it. Too busted up and all."

They drove quickly to the arena. Sam slid her car to a stop on the gravel just outside the arena. Cole bolted through the contestant's entrance. A clutch of cowboys stood to his left, Jace at center court.

"Thought you were in the can," Jace said.

"Sorry I wasn't here to flank you."

"No problemo. Did okay, anyway. Hope to hell that shit ass brother of yours crashes," he smiled. "He's gettin' set. You better go."

Cole turned to go, but ran straight into Olly Davis and his posse.

"Shoulda stayed in jail, professor. Your little brother'd have to score an eighty-one to make the short round. Odds are he's just gonna embarrass himself."

Cole moved past him without speaking.

As Cole reached Travis's chute, there was no sign of Elliot. A rodeo staffer whom Cole did not recognize attended his draw, already saddled in the chute. Travis stretched and chalked his hands. He smiled broadly as Cole approached.

"Hey! Didn't think you'd make it, big brother," he

said. "Glad you did. Give that flank a yank. Need this fucker to buck!"

The buzzer signaled the end of the last ride. Travis climbed the panels and settled on the back of a black gelding. Cole reached into the chute ready to pull the flank strap as the gate released.

"Bad break for Johnny Solet. Our last rider is Travis Clay."

The chute released. Cole had delivered a clean, tight pull on the flank strap and climbed up the catwalk to watch his younger brother.

Travis marked out well, immediately assuming an even rhythm, spurring the horse high on the shoulders and hard in the flanks with each successive buck. The bronc responded in kind, bucking harder and higher with each successive application of the spur.

The buzzer sounded and Travis slipped off and onto the rump of the pickup man's pony, then onto the ground to wait. He stared at the score clock....

Finally, it flashed...eighty-three. He lifted his hat to the crowd to a cacophony of cheers from the hometown crowd.

Travis took his time exiting the arena shaking the hands of strangers and friends with an equal measure of innocent joy. He walked to the catch pen to collect his bronc saddle, then left for the parking lot looking for any sign of Cole. He needed a ride home.

Cole was sitting in his truck, his expression dour. Travis threw his gear in the back and got in the passenger side.

"Where were you?" Cole said as Travis slammed the door.

"Hell, big brother, had to accept my congratulations. Olly was first in line," he said with a shit-eating grin.

Cole did not reply. He stared at a text on his cell.

"What's wrong?" Travis asked, knowing something was. His brother would be the first to celebrate his success.

"He died," Cole replied flatly.

"Who?" Travis said, still confused.

"Wade Roy. Never regained consciousness. Had a bleeder deep in the brain. Too deep to fix."

Travis slammed his hands on the dash. "Fuck!" He hesitated, then turned to his brother without speaking.

"What?" Cole demanded.

"There's video."

"What video? We saw the video."

"We saw the PRCA video. It was a bad angle. Or maybe I should say it was a good angle," Travis said.

"Spill it, Trav!"

"Some fan shot video on an iPhone. You see the whole deal. From the front. It doesn't look right."

"Travis, what was in the syringe?" Cole asked his brother without looking at him. Cole waited for it, knowing a significant chapter of his life would be divided by the moments before and after learning whatever Travis was about to say.

"A little Acepromazine. That's what Elliot said. He loaded it," Travis replied quietly, trying to take in what his brother had just revealed.

Cole was calm now. Back in slow motion. Seeing it all, watching it unfold the way you watched a mare birth a breech colt, knowing one or the other or both would die. His breathing settled into a rhythm, his eyes closed for a moment and he was back in a hospital room with a young wife and a cowboy who would never regain consciousness, never know the sequence of the events that led to his death; details Cole knew he would inevitably unearth, for good or ill.

Cole opened his eyes, looked at his brother who was slumped next to him, and started the truck's engine. It rattled the way diesel trucks do, the last comforting sound either would hear for a long time.

They rode in silence over the San Marcos Pass, the spacious starry night not calming to either of them. Even the smell of sage and dust on the ranch road leading to home added no comfort.

Cole exited the truck and went to the desk in his room. It was cluttered with mail. One piece caught his attention but he set it aside to turn on his computer. He wanted to see the video on a larger screen. He brought his desktop screen to life and searched the Internet. It didn't take long. He googled "accident Salinas Rodeo" and it appeared under six different headers.

He clicked on the video. It had been shot by a fan directly opposite the chute from which Wade released. It showed the first moments of the ride in a way that could not be seen on the "official" footage shot from behind.

Cole sat back and watched the grainy footage unspool. The gate opened, Ragged Edge hesitated, then clearly stumbled coming out, her legs unsteady and loose. Broncs sometimes stumble on release if they catch a hoof on the lower panel frame, but this was different. She touched nothing coming out. The last seconds of the ride were not unlike what they had seen before: She bucked off all fours, twisted in the air, and collapsed as she hit the ground. But now, from this perspective, it was clear her legs, unable to support her weight, just collapsed as she came down.

The flickering film stopped and began to replay. Cole turned it off and sat back in his chair. He heard loud voices. When he walked into the darkened room, Elliot's back was to Cole, Travis cowering before him.

"Keep your damn mouth shut and do as I tell you that's what," Elliot bellowed.

Travis saw Cole over Elliot's shoulder. Elliot turned.

"This isn't about him," Cole said quietly. He stepped up face to face with his father.

Elliot turned and calmly walked to the makeshift bar. He poured himself a drink.

"Accidents happen. Best way to deal with this is to keep our heads low and mouths shut," Elliot said evenly.

"Well, that might prove challenging given the PRCA suits want to talk," Cole said. He held up the now-opened piece of mail he had found in his room. He didn't wait for the response. He was somewhere else, putting it all together.

"That horse wasn't right," Cole said.

Elliot scoffed. "Well, I guess we all know that. Especially you, seeing as you gave her the injection."

It wasn't so much what he said; Cole had already figured it out. It was the dismissive arrogance with which he said it.

Cole charged Elliot. "You son of a bitch. That's right. I gave her the injection you prepared. A little Ace, a mild tranquilizer, so she'd quit fighting the chute."

Cole spun around and looked down at Travis still trying to disappear into the folds of the overstuffed leather chair in which he sat, then spun back toward

Elliot. "Make sure she releases so Elliot gets what he wants, right?"

Elliot replied in an even tone. "What this family needs. You're damn right."

"No matter what the cost. To Wade, to me, Travis..." Cole turned to the portrait of their mother which hung over the river rock fireplace in the center of the room. "To her."

Elliot's calm under pressure had its limits, like an egg you can squeeze from both ends, he usually held; but tap the fragile sides of his twisted psyche and he cracked.

"You arrogant bastard! That was an accident!" he bellowed.

It was Cole's turn to seek the refuge of calm, knowing as he did, that what he was about to say needed to be said clearly and directly. Words that had been gestating in his gut for years.

"Of course it was, Elliot. No one said you intentionally threw her head through the windshield. But that sort of thing happens when you're driving blind-ass drunk."

"Fuck you, Cole. They investigated," Elliot seethed.

"Yeah. Your old rodeo buddy on the sheriff's department. The one you called after you sobered up."

Elliot slumped into his chair, his yolk on the floor. But Cole gave no quarter. "Sure it was an accident. Just like this one. The predictable consequence of stupid decisions."

"What was in that injection, Elliot?" Travis asked.

Elliot looked to Travis then back at Cole. "It wasn't Ace. It was stronger."

Travis was on his feet. "That's not what you said, you son of a bitch!"

Cole turned to Elliot. "Why?" he calmly asked.

"Because he couldn't score. Wade had to lose."

Cole turned back to Elliot, "What was in that syringe, Elliot?"

Elliot was now somewhere else. He answered as if talking to empty space. "What's it matter? You were happy to inject the Ace. That ain't exactly kosher."

"It's not a narcotic or stimulant. That's what the rules prohibit," returned Cole.

Elliot scoffed, the old crust coming back. "Sure, son. Tell yourself that. A little Ace. It's grey. Where you like to hide. Well, this ain't grey."

Cole turned to Travis. "I'm going to ask you this just once, Trav. Did you know?"

Elliot answered for him. "He didn't know a damn thing. I gave him the syringe and told him to Ace her. An ignorant tool in this deal. Just like you. Keep you two out of it. Carry the weight myself."

"Don't you dare play the martyr. You screwed us all, Elliot. Again."

Elliot slumped into his chair and took another long pull on his drink. "We were going to lose the ranch, everything."

"Why?"

"We had debt. Bank debt. And taxes. I paid some but they still had us by the balls. We were going to lose the ranch. Everything."

Elliot took another pull on his drink and almost smiled. "I used to be a fair poker player. I was up for a while. Then those assholes got me in the high roller deal. Lost my ass."

"So you start betting under the table with Tommy. You rig the finals and tip him off, everybody wins. How stupid can you be?" Cole said, putting it all together.

"IT'S RODEO! Something we know!" Elliot was losing his calm.

"Apparently not!" Cole screamed.

Elliot went dark, almost inaudible, "It doesn't matter. Bottom line, we got money on Davis. He qualifies for Vegas, we're good. That's all we promised."

Cole thought about it. "But you didn't count on it being close, so you screwed with Wade's ride, made it harder to score."

"Exactly. Couldn't have the kid challenging." Elliot stood and looked directly at Travis. "Or you. You need to stonewall those assholes from headquarters...and lose tomorrow. You don't, it's gone. Everything."

Cole retreated to his room but did not sleep. He arose at about 4:30 a.m. He wandered in a daze to the dark kitchen illuminated only by tiny blue flames on the stove top, flames warming tortillas piled high in an iron skillet. He poured himself coffee and pushed through the door that opened to the porch.

Marisa sat there alone, her coffee in the delicate china cup she preferred, its flowered pattern matching the embroidered black vest she wore to ward off the morning chill. She was staring at the black horizon, waiting for dawn to slip over the edge of the distant peaks. She was clutching her rosary as if she knew all that had transpired last night. Cole had no idea if she did.

"You're up early," he said, kissing the top of her head near the ivory comb that pulled tight her black-and-grey hair. Marisa had never succumbed to the slovenly style of dress that the Valley's near-perfect weather brought forth in others. She looked as if she might be entertaining the provincial governor of Alta California at any moment, the one who had rewarded her great-grandfather's loyal service with the ranch.

She smiled without turning. "Your grandfather demanded it. Fresh tortillas and coffee each morning at dawn."

Cole sat. "And you still do it, for them?"

"And why not?" Marisa smiled at her grandson.

"Because their stupidity may cost us a ranch that has been in your family for generations? Because it already cost us your only daughter?"

"And if I hate them for this, will Valentia come back to us? Will we have the ranch for many more generations?" Marisa replied looking out over the scene that had marked the start of her day since she could remember.

Cole shook his head, jealous of her facility with the quality that grounded the faith they shared: forgiveness. If Cole went to hell, he was sure it would be a result of his inability to forgive.

"The past is…" Marisa searched for the words in English but they failed her. "*Un agujero negro.* If you look into the darkness long enough it will swallow you."

Marisa stood and touched her grandson's face. "We cannot hide in the past or control what others do. We are free only to choose our own path." Cole's eyes took in the horizon and the first hint of day. When he turned back, she was gone.

He walked to the paddocks knowing he needed to clear his head of all that he had learned in the preceding twelve hours, to reorder his thoughts and tamp down the anger. To do so, he would surrender to mindless and familiar routine.

Slick had his head down in alfalfa, unhappy for the early morning interruption. But he, too, succumbed to the routine, lowering his head as Cole slipped on the halter. Cole tied the lead to the corral's pipe fencing and began to brush him out. Each stroke left tiny parallel lines in his chestnut coat and sent dust dancing in the morning air. It was the smell of that dust and the leather that provided the comfort. That and the smell of fresh horse manure. It was the smell of a ranch, of land, safety, and home.

He blanketed and swung his saddle over Slick's back in an easy motion, gently bringing the rig to rest just behind the withers.

He tightened the cinch, buckled the stampede, and untied the lead. He pulled the halter off and the bridle on in a single motion, then lifted lightly into the saddle.

He moved Slick out in a walk, then a slow lope into early morning air. Tucker joined the ritual. Cows and calves looked up as horse, rider, and dog slipped into their company. With imperceptible signals from his legs, Cole keyed Slick on a bull calf and easily separated him from his mother. First one, then the next. Tucker held the separated calves back as Cole sorted the small herd.

Cole reined up. He signaled Tucker to release the calves, which he did reluctantly. Steam rose from Slick's sweaty neck. The sun, now fully blossomed, bounced yellow off worn spots on Cole's saddle and he thought about what Marisa had said, about the "black hole" into which he had descended. And how he might find the light. He knew where he was supposed to look.

Cole had been baptized a Catholic and taken his first communion at the Old Mission Santa Ines. He hadn't been back in years. His study of history had challenged his faith. In all of history he thought, there existed a profound and abiding conflict between matters of secular reason and matters of faith. The history of western man progressed from attempts to order and understand the world with philosophy, to efforts to master that world with science, and finally to bring the world to heel. This effort to understand and, later, to master the natural order of things found its apogee in the scientific advances of the late industrial age. It found its philosophic expression in the Renaissance. Humanism and secularism eroded older beliefs rooted in the universal truths of Aristotelian philosophy and provided, Cole thought, the seedbed of modern relativism. The secular humanists believed that matters of this life, the here and now, should take precedence over the imponderables of an afterlife. Humans, they argued, were capable of ethical and moral judgements without religion or even God.

Cole was no longer so sure. As an adolescent, Cole had chaffed under the rough nap of the Catholic cloak. The inviolability of the church was a difficult sell, and that conclusion was reinforced by his study of early European history. Even a casual reading exposed the greed and avarice of powerful political institutions. The Catholic Church was no exception.

But was the church these *men*, these very human and flawed men of history? Or was it the teachings of a moral order that had remained, largely unchanged, for two thousand years? Doctrinally, the church had largely held the line against the incoming tide of modernity. And what, he thought, had man's journey away from matters of faith, away from blind acceptance of doctrine inviolate,

rendered? The modern world was a mess, spinning inexorably away from the foundations of moral order: family,
selflessness, community, truth. Higher purpose. Pretty
basic, but increasingly challenged. Even in his own life.

He unsaddled his horse and turned him out and got
in his truck. Within minutes he was sitting on a cool
wooden bench in an otherwise empty chapel at the Old
Mission Santa Ynez. He began to pray. He prayed for a
way to save the ranch, for Travis and Elliot, for the soul
of young Wade Roy. He prayed for forgiveness.

Mostly he prayed to see his path.

PART TWO

"We do not act rightly because we have virtue or exellence, but we rather have those because we have acted rightly."

—ARISTOTLE

8

―◇―

Travis delayed his departure for the rodeo as long as he safely could. He even considered not showing up at all. It would accomplish the same result with less humiliation. But he couldn't. Ducking the event entirely, after the buildup all week, would be suspicious. Besides, it's easy enough to blow a bronc ride—a lackluster job of spurring will do it. He was confident the mission could be accomplished with no one the wiser.

He pulled into general parking at the Earl Warren Equestrian Showgrounds, too late to park in the contestants' area. The lot was packed. Excited fans seeped through parked cars collecting in a scrum before the single ticketing booth for general admission. A sign overhead announced the evening's business: "PRCA Rodeo Finals Tonight."

Travis sat and watched the crowd. He loved the energy and the unabashed enthusiasm for the tradition of rodeo. Cowboys and their fans mingled together, the former in their everyday work attire, the latter in the hat they bought an hour ago, their feet pinched by boots worn once a year. No matter, everyone was there to celebrate tradition.

A few minutes later, Cole pulled into the arena parking lot. He would, as usual, be Travis's flank man. He opened the glove box in his truck to retrieve his gloves and picked up a bottle of prescription pills with them. He exited the truck and walked through the throngs of fans. He blew past the entry gate with a nod to the attendant. He could hear the announcer's opening remarks inside the small arena as he walked to the paddocks behind the chutes.

"Welcome to the finals of our Santa Barbara Fiesta Days Rodeo! Let's get started!"

He passed a trash can full of empty beer cans. He dropped the pills in the trash and entered the contestants' ready area. Cole knew the bareback finalists would compete first and he had time to find Travis. He could feel the rhythmic pounding of hooves beneath his feet as he climbed the steps that would allow him to see the arena floor.

This year's rodeo queen, a local high school senior, pushed her palomino mare around the perimeter of the arena. She carried the American flag on a wooden standard to her side. The crowd stood and removed hats as she passed each section, first in a lope, then a gallop, before pulling her mount to the center of the arena and reining up hard.

"Ladies and Gentlemen: Please join us in singing our national anthem lead by the Guest of Honor, Marine Corps Captain and Veteran, Marjorie Darby."

The crowd mostly mouthed the words, letting the captain carry the weight. But they tried, and Cole wondered where else could one find a collection of disparate citizens so willing to engage in this unabashedly patriotic display?

He watched the rodeo queen. Her mount jigged nervously side to side, but she sat ram-rod straight in a silver-laden saddle, eyes forward, the flagstaff now tipped slightly forward, colors unfurled. She was overweight. A thin line of sweat ran from her hatband into her left eye, her abundant mascara trailing down one rosy cheek. But she wouldn't wipe it away. Not during the anthem. Not now. She held her smile. The Vaseline on her teeth helped.

Cole's attention was drawn to a section of the grandstands just to his right. Fans still standing at attention rustled as a late arrival pushed past them. Elliot was oblivious, careful not to spill his beer, driving to an open seat in the center of the row. He came to rest as the anthem ended. Sam was seated to his left. Cole watched as they stiffly embraced. He considered how different they were: Elliot privileged, but bitter; Sam proudly working class, grateful for the possibilities. Sam always said we "cannot change the past" as if that were a revelation. And yet the manner in which she embodied the idea, the degree to which her sense of the future seemed unshackled by the past, *was* a revelation to Cole. Cole scanned the audience for Jessica and Dustin. He knew Dustin would not miss his favorite uncle's big night. He thought of the disappointment he would soon feel.

"This is it, folks! Our 'short round' of finalists. At stake, a whole lot of prize money and, just maybe, for a couple of these cowboys, a trip to the National Finals Rodeo in Las Vegas. So let's get started with the bareback bronc competition. Leading off, Blaine Fross on Bruiser..."

The gate swung open and the bronc charged, its hapless rider snapping forward and back until the eight-second buzzer visited mercy on them both.

Cole descended the stairs and joined a group of contestants waiting their turn, Jace and Olly among them.

Jace reached out to shake Cole's hand, uncharacteristically sober. "Hey, Cole, haven't seen Trav. Wish him good luck. Heard he got a nasty draw."

Olly passed Cole to leave. "Won't make much difference, professor."

"Rick Mattack in the chute. Pete Cliff on deck."

Cole retreated to the side of the staging area to wait. The buzzer sounded on another ride and Cole knew it would only be moments now. He spotted Travis checking the rigging on his draw. He averted his eyes from Cole's gaze.

"Tough break for Pete Cliff. Saddle bronc contestants should be in the staging area."

Cole approached Travis at the chute as the buzzer announced the last bareback contestant's effort.

"We'll take a short break to ready for our saddle bronc finals."

"I hear this one's pretty rank. He'll swap ends on you if you let him," offered Cole.

"Well, that should help," Travis replied. "I'm sorry, Cole."

"For what?"

"The whole mess. I shoulda told you earlier how deep we were."

"You're not the architect, little brother."

"Okay, let's get started. Ladies and Gentlemen, we've got an exciting saddle bronc contest about to begin. Cowboys qualify for the National Finals Rodeo based on cumulative winnings over the course of the season. The top fifteen money winners go to Vegas.

"We have three contestants with a shot at qualifying. Reigning World champ Olly Davis will earn that last ticket with a first or second place finish. But if Davis were to place

third or lower, either Jace Wyatt or Travis Clay could take that last slot with a win. Right now in the chute and ready to rock is Nevada Cowboy, Jace Wyatt."

Travis and Cole heard the gate swing, then the crowd erupted in applause as the buzzer sounded.

"*A great ride for openers...eighty-one! That sets a high bar for the competition tonight.*"

Another rider released. Elliot had wandered into the staging area and approached his sons. He ignored Cole, turning to Travis.

"Heard about your draw. Tough horse. No one could blame you, I guess," Elliot remarked evenly.

Travis held his father's eyes. "No, sir."

With that, Elliot turned and left. Cole climbed the chute panels to watch the next rider, Olly Davis. Olly nodded the release and marked out well, but, after three strong bucks, his horse spun hard to the left and Olly lost his center for a moment and that moment cost him. The buzzer sounded and Cole held his breath...seventy-nine flashed on the scoreboard.

"*That'll put Olly in second place with a ticket to Vegas. But we've got two riders to go.*"

As the penultimate rider settled, Travis climbed his chute. Cole adjusted the flank strap. The buzzer sounded. It was Travis's turn. Cole stood on the catwalk eye to eye with his brother.

"*Tough break for Mark Colly. Our last rider is Travis Clay. This is it, folks!*"

"How should I do this, Cole?" Travis asked.

In the time that would follow, Cole would not remember consciously making a decision, nor experiencing a moment when the answer formed. Was the script written, or did he exercise free will? Had God answered his prayers at the Mission or had he known his path all along? And what if, as Marisa had offered, God had granted free will knowing all along how it would be exercised?

Cole didn't know. But in that moment and for the time that would follow, his course was clear.

"Like you always do, little brother. I'll give you a clean flank. Ride this cocksucker."

Travis was stunned, but couldn't suppress a smile. "You sure, big brother?"

"Sure as I've ever been."

"Okay, then."

Travis settled, then nodded the release. The gate opened and his draw exploded into the arena, spinning to the right then bucking hard, high and steady. Travis spurred viciously until, at four seconds, the horse bucked off all four and spun almost one hundred and eighty degrees before touching down. But Travis had seen it coming. He sat the landing and kept spurring.

The crowd erupted in applause even before the buzzer sounded. When it did, Travis dismounted and stood center arena waiting for the score.

Finally, it flashed: eighty-six.

Travis threw his hat high into the air as Olly, in the paddocks, threw his to the ground. In the grandstands Sam was on her feet, waving her arms wildly. Somewhere, Cole knew, his son was jubilant.

Elliot remained seated, his head down.

That night, Manny's was packed. Pro cowboys and locals, shoulder to shoulder, there to celebrate the end of Fiesta and Travis's victory. He pushed into the room to a cacophony of cheers and whistles.

The lead singer of the Bakersfield Brothers stepped up to the microphone. Cole and Travis knew him well. He had been born and raised in Anaheim, California, six blocks from Disneyland. Why he talked like a Texas farmer had always been a mystery. Maybe too much time in Frontierland as a kid.

"Listen ya'll, this here goes out to our own Travis Clay! Damn if he ain't goin' to the NFR!"

There was another round of cheers, back slaps, and high fives all around. Neighbors and friends shouted their support.

The band opened with Robert Earl Keen's "The Road Goes on Forever and the Party Never Ends." The crowd settled in to make good on its promise.

An hour in, Cole searched the room for Travis. He spotted him on the patio. Alone at a table, two empties in with a fresh can on the table. Cole took a seat.

"Hey. Congratulations, little brother," Cole said.

"Thank you. Wouldn't have stuck it without you telling me about him swapping ends." He finished his beer. "Cole, we're going to have hell to pay. They probably bet heavy on Olly, like we told 'em. We're in deeper now."

"We'll deal with it," Cole offered, not sure how.

Just then the band fired up the opening licks of "Night Rider's Lament." Jace called through the open patio doors, "Travis! Get your ass over here!"

Travis left his brother on the patio and joined the now-drunken crew in a tight cluster in front of the stage. Together, they bellowed the lyrics of the song most knew by heart.

Cole watched from the patio, happy to see Travis enjoying his victory. He wasn't sure how long it would last. He picked up his hat and left. Forty-five minutes later, Cole knocked on the front door and waited.

When Jessica opened it she did not smile or register surprise. "I thought you'd be celebrating."

"It's Trav's night."

"Do you ever carry a key?" Jessica asked.

"Sure, but I didn't call. Figured if I just blew through the door this late I'd scare the hell out of you."

"And why didn't you call?"

"I wanted to think."

"About what?"

"Everything. Can we sit?"

They walked toward the den and passed Dustin's room on the way. Cole opened the door and looked in. He was fast asleep, the room dimly lit by a night light shaped like a cowboy boot, a fading reminder of his childhood.

Cole watched his son sleep. "He's the best thing we'll ever do."

Jessica ushered them out and closed the door before answering.

"No question."

They fell into two chairs in the den facing each other. The room was dimly lit and laced in melancholia. It was more how the room felt than how it looked. It looked the same. The same framed photographs and memorabilia. The same books lining its shelves. But they felt like reminders of what had been, like a room cluttered with debris from last night's party.

Cole began slowly. He had to try to make her understand. "When you study history...of cultures, ideas, our so-called progress, the industrial revolution and the rest, you come away with the impression, this assumption really, that the most advanced time in a people's history is the most advanced stage in their development.

"I'm not sure it's true. I mean, look at us now, Jess. We have cars that drive themselves, private space shuttles, more computing power in your iPhone than NASA used to reach the moon. We are the wealthiest civilization in history by orders of magnitude. And where are we? We're fucked, that's where we are. We are alienated and juxtaposed by race and class, individually isolated, technology obsessed. We are drowning in a hot cauldron of materialism and self-obsession; every institution that grounds values we cherish—family, religion, local civic organizations—the institutions that bind us together in common cause, all collapsing in a sea of relativism. We subscribe to no truths, no absolutes. And what we have lost is replaced by what? By things of no inherent value—money, power...status symbols. We are obsessed with virtue *signaling* because we possess, inside, precious little virtue. Is that the world we want to leave Dustin?"

Jessica had grown impatient. "Of course not. But that's the world we live in and you and I aren't going to change it."

"You're right. But shouldn't we try? Isn't there value in the very act of resisting? And who says we can't live a different life?"

"Where? How?" Jessica asked.

"Here."

"I knew that's where you were going. Damn it to hell, Cole, we're back to this?"

"I'm not going to LA, Jess. I'll take a job teaching

high school history here if I have to. I want to live and raise Dustin in a small community, where people know each other. Where neighbors show up to help a neighbor. Where people aren't embarrassed to go to church on Sunday and work in jobs with their hands making things that are real."

He watched her face and knew she was waiting, waiting for him to talk about the real issue.

"Listen, babe, I know the ranch has been a huge source of trouble. Money, conflict in the family. All of it. But that ranch, what it represents, is important."

"And what exactly does it represent besides financial ruin and social isolation?"

"Something permanent. Something we can hang onto, something Dustin and Dustin's children can hang onto."

"To what end?"

"To its own end. To the end of sustaining things that are real and enduring..." He trailed off. "An honest life...I don't know exactly, but that's how I feel."

Cole took a deep breath. "There's more, Jess. Things I haven't told you yet. Elliot's got things up there in a bad way. Travis is involved. I can't walk away."

Jessica stood. "Oh, but you are. You are walking away from your own family."

"No, I'm not, Jess. Don't make this a zero-sum game. It's not. We're all family. Blood. All of us. If you want to take that job in LA, okay, I understand. We can work something out. We've done it before."

"And where does that leave Dustin?"

"Here. There is not a damn thing he can learn in LA he can't learn here. At least, nothing we'd want him to learn. Come on, Jess. LA's pretty much the epicenter of forces pulling us away from every value we want Dustin to have."

"And those values would be rodeo and a good bar fight on Friday night? A high school education?"

"Jess. It doesn't have to be that way. You know that."

"Good night, Cole."

Cole would have stopped her if he could. He knew he couldn't. He had said what he needed to say. They would sleep on it.

The next morning, Cole awakened and made coffee. It was early, still dark, but he had heard her up. He walked into their suite with two cups in hand. He could not see Jessica, but he heard her. She was dry-heaving in the bathroom. She was ashen when she returned to sit tentatively on the edge of the bed and Cole knew.

"Holy shit. You're pregnant."

"I'm sorry I did not tell you last night. I would have but it wasn't the time, obviously. You had things you needed to say and I'm glad you did."

"That's okay, babe. Hey, it's great. I mean—" Jessica held her fingers gently to his mouth.

"Stop. Let me talk." She gathered her strength. "I'm leaving, Cole. I sat up most of the night thinking about what you said. I understand your thinking but I do not agree. I won't live the life you see for us. I will rent a house in LA near Mom and Dad and a good school. Mom and Dad are going to forgive the debt on this place, the mortgage, so we own it free and clear. It's a lot of money, half yours."

"Are you kidding me? What's that? A bribe? Take some money and go away? Screw the money!"

"If you don't want it, put it in a trust for Dustin. But it's yours."

Cole tried to collect himself. "Wait! What are we talking about, Jess? Things are screwed up, but we're married. We will work this out."

"Some things you can't work through, Cole. I love you. But I'm not in love with you. That's not something you talk through."

"You're talking like this is a high school crush. Well, I'm sorry you're not in love with me but *we're married*, Jess. We have a son. You work through it. And I love *you*, by the way."

"Do you? You love the *idea* of me. This pretty rich girl from LA marrying the cowboy who isn't really a cowboy but, well, now you are, I guess..."

"Jess, listen," Cole pleaded.

"No. God knows you do most of the talking. Now you're going to listen. You are one of kindest men I know. I love your passion, even when I don't share it; your willingness to martyr yourself for principal. I know you love Dustin. You'd lay down your life for him in a second. And that won't change. I know that. But the *idea* of love is not enough. It has to be real. In the DNA of the relationship. It's not something you have to declare, or martyr yourself for. It just is. Or isn't."

She started to cry and caught herself. "You're a good man, and the smartest man I have ever known. But at the same time, without a doubt, the dumbest. You don't know shit. You certainly don't know much about me. If you did, you wouldn't have said what you did last night. I'm glad you were honest. It wasn't really a surprise. You're never going to leave the ranch and that's not the life we planned."

Cole had finally absorbed what she was saying, that she was serious. For a moment, he could not speak.

Jessica took his hand. He pulled back. "Wait. Wait. You're pregnant. How does that work?"

Jessica took a deep breath. "It doesn't. I'm not having it."

With that, any semblance of control in Cole was lost. A noise began in his head. A shrill whistling sound. It seemed to get louder and louder until it drowned out his thoughts. What he thought, what he *believed* and what he *felt*, anger and revulsion, panic and pain, all merged into white noise so that he could not tell one from the other.

"Don't tell me that, Jess. No matter what else happens, don't tell me that. You're not going to kill our child."

"Don't emotionalize this. It's not a child. It's an embryo. And I won't bring another child into a broken marriage."

"Oh, my God." He took a deep breath and with that breath tried to focus his thoughts. The stakes were too high. "Do you know what an embryo is?"

"Yes."

"No, you don't. It's what people call a baby they don't want. It's much easier if you depersonalize it. It's why we called Native Americans 'savages.' They were easier to kill."

"Cole, you're being hyperbolic."

"And accurate."

"Cole, it's my body. Not yours."

"Of course it is. But don't hide behind the sophistry that it's *just* your body. It's not just your body now. It's a human life, our child. That's just the inconvenient truth."

"You are so out of touch."

"With what? Prevailing culture? So were Southern abolitionists before the Civil War, but they were right!"

Cole walked to Jessica and tried to take her in his arms. She pulled away.

"Jess, I know this is shitty timing. It's hard. It's inconvenient as hell. More than that. And I know it's easy to believe something is okay when you desperately want to, and when everyone tells you it's okay. But you know in your gut it's wrong."

She replied flatly and without emotion. "This is an issue you don't understand and can never understand. So I won't try. But the law is clear. It is my decision alone until viability. We are way short of that."

Cole looked away. He knew he had lost. "Another piece of crap. Viability. His liver won't function on its own right now. So what? You think the morality of taking human life turns on how fast you do it?"

"Cole, we are talking about a speck. Some cells. You don't know shit about the science."

"You want to be scientific? Then tell me when life begins if not at conception? Trust me, it's begun. All we have to do is let it happen."

Jessica's face flushed with anger. "'All we have to do is let it happen!?' You don't know what you're talking about! First, I'm only a few weeks pregnant. Fifty percent of embryos at this stage *fail*. This is far from a done deal. It's a process and it's just barely begun."

"Yes, but it's begun. And it's our job to give our child every chance."

"Really? What about the pill you were so happy to have me use?"

Cole, confused. The pill?

"You know how they work? Did you ever ask? Of course not. One of the ways they work is by preventing an impregnated egg from embedding in the uterus. By your definition that's a chemical abortion!"

Cole hesitated. He had never thought about it. "Maybe that's why the church opposes it, I don't know. But we know you're pregnant now. You're not on the pill. It's a choice, a decision to end a life."

"You're right. My choice! And there are good reasons for that!"

Cole raised both hands. "Listen, please. I know you bear the costs and risks in a way I never can. I can't change that. But the fact it's in your belly doesn't mean it isn't a life! And it carries half of my DNA."

Jessica turned. "You're right, but *I carry it!* That's why it's called a *women's health* issue, not an issue on which you have a vote!"

"Except it's not."

"What?"

"A health issue! If it were, this would be a different conversation. You have no health issues, like the vast majority of abortions. This is about the fact you don't want another baby right now, with me. At least be honest with yourself. You're doing this for *you.* You're talking about taking a life because it's inconvenient."

"Screw you, Cole, you and your judgement. This is an issue you can never understand."

Cole stood. "I understand, Jess. And you do, too. But you will wrap yourself in consensus and try the rest of your life not to think about it."

Jessica held his gaze. "I didn't want it this way. We

can talk. There's a therapist. I'm not saying we can save our marriage, but we can save our relationship."

Cole put on his hat. "Jess, if you want to end the life of our unborn child, there is nothing to save. I think you just confirmed everything I was saying last night. You think this is okay, we're lost. I won't be part of that world, and neither will Dustin if I can help it."

Cole left the room, his marriage, and the life he had expected to live.

Cole reached the ranch just as the sun cleared the mountains to the east. He poured himself coffee and stepped onto the porch. The glint of morning sun sparked gold on the tips of wild oat grass. He watched cattle graze thirty yards from the house. A newborn calf stood wobbly, its umbilical cord still wet and stringy. The mother cow licked him furiously, as if it were her first. But it had been her sixth in as many years. His fight with Jessica flooded his mind. The seeming incongruity of it all. It was only the human animal, he thought, that could use political consensus and "reason" to deny the natural order of things.

Cole felt sick and retched over the porch banister. Elliot stepped onto the porch as Cole wiped his mouth and sat down, as unhappy to see Elliot in that moment as he had ever been.

"Tie one on last night, son? Can't say that I blame you seeing as you pretty much flushed us all down the toilet yesterday."

Cole looked at his father with profound sadness, then tossed the remainder of his coffee and left. He had an appointment.

The meeting had been arranged at a makeshift office

in Los Olivos just minutes from the ranch. Cole was ten minutes late when he pushed through the door. Two men in western-cut suits sat behind a folding table cluttered with documents, a laptop and several Styrofoam coffee cups. They both stood as Cole entered. One was Clive Westgate. Cole did not recognize the one who spoke first.

"Mr. Clay, my name is Lanny Briggs. Don't think we've had the pleasure." He extended his hand. Cole tipped his hat, shook his hand and sat in front of their table.

Briggs continued with that false air of familiarity that characterizes the chatter of men when they don't know each other, as if they were meeting at a church social, as if their purpose was insignificant. But all three understood, without acknowledgment, that the matter at hand was deadly serious.

"I guess you know Clive here. He's headquarters. Can't rodeo anymore so they kicked him upstairs." They both chuckled, but the façade was thin as wet tissue. Cole wanted to get on with it.

Westgate spoke next, "I'm sorry we didn't get to finish our conversation at the hospital."

"Yes, sir," Cole said. He offered no explanation because none existed. He had intentionally avoided the earlier exchange and he knew Clive knew it. These words didn't matter. They would soon. Cole waited, impatient for the kill shot coming.

Westgate teed it up. "We have some questions about the accident in Salinas that resulted in the death of Wade Roy."

Westgate stopped to take a swallow of his coffee. "PRCA has received a letter from his widow and her lawyer. They are raising some questions about the horse. We understand that mare was in the Clay Ranch string and you and your brother were there at the chute. Now—"

Cole interrupted, "I drugged her. Between the first and second go. That mare needed one more release in a qualified event to be eligible for the finals. She was fightin' the chute so I gave her an injection of what I believed was a small amount of Ace. I was trying to take some of the fresh off and, instead, I helped get Wade killed."

There was stunned silence in the room. Westgate and Briggs exchanged glances. Briggs spoke first, "In light of your statement, Mr. Clay, I think it best to suspend our discussion at this point. There will be follow up, but I think it best for all concerned if we involve counsel at this point. You might want to retain someone yourself."

Cole stood and put on his hat. "I appreciate the suggestion but that won't be necessary. I know what happened. The only issue is what happens now and that's up to the PRCA and Ms. Roy."

Cole returned to the ranch and backed his truck between the jacks that hoisted his camper trailer. He had decided to park it in some remote spot on the ranch, to find some cover from the storm. Mostly, he wanted to avoid hearing Elliot make more statements against interest in an effort to coordinate their testimony in the investigation. Cole would have no part of it and would not tempt Elliot to further damage his position by being around to hear it. Cole had told Briggs and Westgate the truth—that he had injected what he believed to be Ace. The next shoe was doubtless soon to drop—what Elliot had actually loaded in the syringe.

Cole lowered his camper into the truck bed and bolted it down, but not before Elliot charged from the *hacienda* like an angry boar. "What in the fuck did you do now? You haven't done enough?"

"What?" Cole turned to face his father.

"You know what! I just got a call from those assholes at headquarters. They want depositions under oath!" Elliot was seething.

"I told them the truth. I didn't volunteer anything I did not know. I did not mention you or Travis but it's obviously coming. I suggest you tell them the truth, but I'm sure you'll do as you please."

Cole got into his truck and slipped it into four-wheel drive. He began to edge forward. He spoke to Elliot through the open window. "You keep digging this hole, Elliot, it's going to get deeper and you're not the only one gonna get buried."

The truck lumbered forward as Elliot was still screaming: "None this woulda happened had you just held the line, damn it!"

Cole stopped the truck and thought about it. It was true, and that reality was something Cole would have to live with.

"You're right, Elliot. But we screwed up and someone got killed. Lying about it is not a line I'm going to cross. I'm sorry you feel otherwise."

Elliot turned cold and calm. "I wish I lived in your world, son; all books and theory; but most of us don't— not me, not Trav, Marisa, or Carlos. You drive off and go read some more theory, Cole. We'll eat the shit and lose. And you know what? Wade'll still be dead!"

Cole managed to bounce and drag his rig to the most obscure spot he knew at the south end of the ranch. He set up a dry camp and opened a beer. He lit a lantern and picked up his copy of *The Republic* and started to read where he had left off the night of Wade's accident. As Prescott had said, in his most famous work, Plato postulates a perfect "form" of all that we know; by implication, a perfect construct for organization of the polis, a perfect conception of justice, a perfect civic virtue. Cole wondered if the damage we do in pursuit of these perfections was not, in the end, the most imperfect of paths; as if man's separation from God rendered the quest for God-like perfection a dangerous, even sinful arrogance. But in the end, he thought, he could not give up the idea that there existed perfect forms of being. And he knew that if he gave up the struggle to achieve those ends, he would have nothing.

He camped out in the same spot for four days, periodically recharging his cell from the truck's engine battery. He had heard from no one and had made no calls. He knew the calls would come in time and was happy for the break. But on the afternoon of the fifth day, he resolved to break camp and restock on food. As he exited the ranch gate and turned left on Highway 101, his phone signaled a message.

It was Sam and the message was short. "Travis is here, with Tommy. You better come now." Cole panicked at the possibility it was an old message, just loading now. But it wasn't. It had been left two minutes before. She had probably called as he traversed the dead spot on the ranch road just east of the gate.

Cole turned right out the ranch gate and headed for Manny's, ten minutes away. He dialed Elliot but got no answer. He left Elliot the same message and sped up.

When Cole pushed through the door at Manny's,

it was mid-afternoon and the bar was empty. Billy and Sam stood behind the bar. Travis was seated at a small table with Tommy and Yellow Sky. Cole stepped in front of the bar.

"Let's go, Trav."

Travis tried to stand. Tommy slammed him back in his chair.

"This doesn't concern you, Cole," Tommy said.

Cole responded in an even tone, trying to keep the lid on. "If this is about the ranch and my brother, I guess it does."

"Got nothing to do with you. The Clays got some debt. We tried to help out and your brother here cocked it all up. We're just discussing how to make it all right," Tommy offered.

"Looks like a one-way sort of discussion."

Tommy laughed. "Whatever."

"Tommy, if we owe any money, we'll pay it. But from now on, you talk to me."

"Or what?"

"Or I'm going to come over there and put your smug face through the window behind you."

Tommy's face flushed. He and Yellow Sky stood and moved just behind Travis. Tommy pulled a pistol from his belt. "You just try, asshole. I'd love that."

"Tommy, get a grip. You really going to shoot me in a public bar over this?"

"It's a shitload of money. And I don't think I'm goin' have to shoot anyone, professor."

Cole looked from Tommy to Travis.

Tommy smiled, feeling the energy shift.

Without turning, Cole tapped the counter behind

him and Billy handed him the shotgun he kept behind the bar. Yellow Sky immediately pulled his gun.

Tommy smiled. "So, what now, amigo? You think the spread on that thing will cover us both before I drop your ass?"

The room fell silent.

"It won't have to."

They all heard it at the same time and turned.

Elliot had entered through the back door and stood in the shadows to the right of Cole. He held the Colt 45 as he always did, with two hands, arms extended. He was aiming directly at Tommy.

"Tommy, you're a lyin' sack of shit. So is your lawyer and those blood-sucking bankers. You have about three seconds to stand up and walk out of here. And I don't wanna hear another thing about the money."

Tommy's smug smile was gone.

Elliot spoke in a low and even tone: "Cole, you remember how this works."

What Cole remembered was that it rarely did. They had little success hunting the ranch side by side, Elliot with his vintage pistol. But it didn't matter. For all the posturing, Cole didn't believe Tommy was dumb enough to pull the trigger and he knew he wouldn't. The shotgun Cole held was all posture, no purpose.

Then Travis lit the fuse. Without warning, he stood and swung his left fist backward as hard he could into Tommy's throat. Tommy's gun discharged and Travis fell...

In the next instant, the room exploded in a cacophony of gunfire as, simultaneously, Elliot emptied his pistol at Tommy, Yellow Sky fired at Elliot, and Cole leveled Yellow Sky with both barrels of the .12 gauge.

It was loud, violent, and over within three seconds of the first report of Tommy's pistol.

In the quiet that followed, before the cursing of the wounded registered, Cole heard only the hum of beer logo lights. He saw their flashing neon reflection in the grey-blue smoke of gunpowder and thought to himself... what a stupid waste.

9

---◆---

Cottage Hospital in Santa Barbara had been remodeled in a multi-year effort launched in 2009. The elegant entrance was now lined in bronze plaques naming donors who had financed the project. Names at the top had contributed more than ten million, the next group five, and so on. Cole wondered how so many people had so much money and why, if they did, they needed everyone to know it. He admired the last name on the list: "Anonymous."

After checking in with the candy striper at the front desk, Cole and Travis wandered the long gleaming halls unescorted. They finally found the intensive care unit and spoke to a duty nurse who took them to Elliot's room. For a moment, Cole thought he might have passed but the heart monitor said otherwise. His face was pale and drawn, his cheeks sallow. He had aged ten years. Cole and Travis pulled two chairs to his bedside and waited.

They had spoken to his doctor on the phone and knew that he was in critical condition. Bullets from Yellow Sky's Sig Sauer P320 had blown through his lung, liver, and large intestine. They had operated to repair the damage but his prognosis was compromised, less by the wounds than the general state of his health. Years of heavy drinking had taken a predictable toll—weakened immunities, fibrosis of the liver, a severe vitamin B deficiency, and evidence of colorectal cancer, something they would explore after he recovered.

A nurse entered and pushed a needle into the IV tube taped to Elliot's wrist. "If he awakens at all, he'll be groggy. He's on heavy pain meds. He may not make any sense."

Travis smiled. "Thank you, ma'am. We're used to it."

After about five minutes, Elliot opened his eyes with a start. "What?"

Cole took his hand. "It's me, Cole. Travis is here, too."

"I know who in hell you are. What happened?"

"We shot up Manolo's," Cole said.

"What was the score?" Elliot's voice was scratchy.

"You finally hit something," Travis chimed in.

"Tommy?"

"Yeah."

"Where? He dead?" Elliot asked.

"No. You hit him in the ass," Travis said.

Elliot grumbled. "What about the other little prick?"

"He didn't fare as well. I hit him with the shotgun. Pretty much blew his right knee off," Cole answered.

"What are the cops say'n?"

"Let it rest for now."

"Tell me, damn it!"

Cole looked to Travis, not sure it was the time to get into it. The investigation was being overseen by detective Alberto Plano. He was Native. He had joined the sheriff's office after six years with the tribal police. Travis and Cole had been interviewed twice, the investigative results still pending.

"We don't know anything yet. Tommy and Yellow Sky both had concealed carry permits because of their work at the casino. They're saying Tommy's gun discharged accidentally when Travis hit him, which I think is true. Yellow Sky is saying he fired in self-defense. Your pistol was not licensed so far as they know."

"Of course not. Bought it at a gun show," Elliot hissed.

"If they conclude Tommy's gun went off by accident, then you fired first. Although you can plead confusion in the moment. But you may get charged. I don't know."

"With what?"

"Let's just wait."

"With what!?" Elliot demanded.

"Attempted murder."

"They were holding Travis hostage and pulled guns first!" Elliot calmed himself, the pain in his abdomen obvious. "What about you?"

"I fired after Yellow Sky opened up on you. I don't know."

Elliot took a deep breath, his eyes closed. "It doesn't matter. I'll never stand for it."

Cole looked at his father and he knew. He knew he was right. Elliot had surrendered. Cole had seen death come, to a friend in college, then to his own mother. He believed there is a moment when the will to live passes and the body follows as sure as night follows day. Cole took some comfort in the idea that that was evidence of a soul, that we are not merely flesh and blood but spirit and essence, which, when surrendered, marks more a release than any physical end.

"Don't talk like that. Of course, it matters. Get some rest. Can we get you anything?"

"Yeah. Some bourbon, slip it in the IV. Got me on sugar water or some such shit. Kill me for sure."

Cole smiled and stood. Travis wiped his eyes, ashamed of the tears. "I'm sorry," he said.

"Don't get all teary on me, Travis. Glad you smacked him. Gave me an excuse to shoot the fucker."

Cole stood and leaned over Elliot's bed. "What'd you mean, what you said, at the bar?"

"I don't remember. What'd I say?"

"That he was a lyin' sack of shit. Tommy. Sack of shit for sure but what'd he lie about? And you said something about a lawyer, a bank."

Elliot looked out the window at the garden some planner had envisioned when the new hospital wing had been conceived. No doubt it was intended to reassure patients and families experiencing the worst day of their lives. For Elliot, it had the opposite effect, serving only to remind him of beauty he had never seen, of peace he had never accepted.

"She got me all doped up, that nurse…"

He dozed off, then awakened a few seconds later and continued…

"It's damn ironic."

"What?" Cole asked.

"How long the ride feels when you're on it; how short it feels now, looking back. Like a damn blink of the eye."

He looked back at his sons. Then his eyes closed. He continued, only half-conscious.

"You two are the only part of me that will last, only thing I didn't fuck up, despite best efforts." He looked out the window. "It ain't that hard. Gotta look at things the way they are and accept them. Some shitty deal happens, move on. Guess I never could."

There was a long silence as Elliot surrendered to the meds.

Cole stood and put on his hat. They walked to the door, then turned. Cole said it, almost a whisper: "I love you Elliot."

Elliot surprised them in a clear voice without hesitation, "I love you, too. Both of you."

Cole and Travis took the long route back to the ranch through the Santa Ynez mountains. They passed the casino as they entered the Valley on the other side of the mountains separating Santa Barbara from Santa Ynez. Neither had spoken.

Travis broke the silence. "What in hell was that all that about with Elliot? Accepting things? Moving on?"

"The war. What happened to him," Cole said.

The brothers rode in silence through the winding hills until, finally, Travis spoke: "They pulled my ticket."

"What?" Cole said. "Who?"

"The Rodeo Association. Suspended my eligibility pending the investigation into Wade's accident. I'm out for the finals," Travis explained.

"Travis, I never mentioned you when I spoke to them," Cole protested.

"Didn't need to, big brother. They've interviewed five guys there that night. They know I was there and carried the satchel with the meds to the chutes. I'm in this deal."

Cole shook his head, crushed by the news. "I don't know what to say. I am so sorry, Travis."

"Don't worry about it, big brother. Nothing to be done. Besides, I'd probably just get my ass kicked in Vegas. This way, I can just lie about how I woulda won and all. Hell, you should be happy! This way that high

school deal you won still gonna be the only championship buckle in the family."

Cole shook his head but had to smile. "You're an asshole. And you're never going to let me forget this."

"Nope."

The traffic slowed behind a black-and-gold casino
tour bus.

"Fucking Indians. This whole deal started with those
bastards and now Plano is the investigating officer. We're
fucked," Travis said.

"Race has got nothing to do with it. Tommy's white.
Yellow Sky's Mexican. Or half-breed. Like us. Plano's
an honest cop. You think the white guys running Vegas
wouldn't jam you up just as quick? Anyway, Elliot's the
one that let 'em," Cole said.

Travis packed some dip and rolled down the window.
"Issue is, what are we going to do now? We owe money,
blood money now. Elliot's hospital bill is going look like
the national debt. He cancelled our health insurance last
year."

"That I didn't know. I thought you had to carry insurance under Obamacare."

"Yeah. Elliot said that made it all the sweeter."

"Sounds like Elliot."

"Well, we gonna have to do something. They want to
do pot, lease the ranch for next to nothing."

"How do you know?" Cole asked.

"That's what Manny's was all about."

"What'd you tell them?"

"Fuck off."

"Good. We're not doing pot and we sure as hell aren't
going into business with those dirt bags."

"So what are we going to do?" Travis asked.

"You're going to clean up the rough stock business; we're going to sell the herd. Let the pasture rest a bit, restock with higher-end cattle. And wine, I guess. If Indigo's still interested."

"Thought you hated him, not to mention the death and destruction brought on by the vineyards around here," Travis observed.

"I do."

"Well, that's a plan, I guess." Travis packed more dip.

"Best I can think of."

"What about the debt?"

"Like I told Tommy, we'll pay any legit debt. We just need some time."

"Where's that leave Tommy?"

"Unhappy."

"You know he's coming back at us, don't you? Just a matter of when and where," Travis said flatly.

"Yeah, I do."

10

---◊---

B ut for shotgun pellets still wedged in the wall, Manny's bar looked no worse for wear. Billy, on the other hand, looked exhausted as Cole leaned into the bar. It was 5:00 p.m. the next evening, and the bar was nearly full.

"You're not goin' to shoot the place up again, are you? Took me two hours to clean up," Billy said. He pushed a beer in front of Cole.

"Hey, you handed me the scattergun."

"Good thing I did. You'd be dead."

"Might be preferable. Where's Sam?"

"Office."

Cole took his beer and walked to the backroom through the door where Elliot had entered. Where it had all started, where the Clays' journey had taken a dark turn. He knocked on the door to Sam's office then pushed in. She looked up but did not speak. She gestured to the chair and Cole sat.

"How are you?" he asked sheepishly.

"How am I supposed to be?"

Cole saw in her eyes something he rarely did, something he hated and understood in equal measure. Resignation; a sort of acceptance that things might keep getting worse at every turn.

"The police just left. They wanted my statement, again. Some things they needed to clarify. They're going to nail you, Cole, if they can. You know they've already decided to charge Elliot." Sam caught herself. "How is he, anyway?"

"Not good."

"Well, I'm sorry for that. Sorry about the whole thing."

"Obviously the apologies run the other way. Travis shouldn't have met them here and we...we might have handled it better, I guess."

"Oh, do you think?" Sam tried to stay calm. "Maybe not have Wyatt Earp blow through the back door with his gun out? And who are you? Frickin' Doc Holiday? You really think it's cool to blow a guy's leg off in a wine bar?"

Cole had no reply, but when he looked back at Sam she smiled, ever so slightly, and shook her head. "Come on, Cole."

"Hey, look at it this way. Manny's is going to be famous. I'll get Elliot's pistol, we can frame and hang it on the wall with the date of the Clay's Last Stand. We could even stage the fight every anniversary."

"Spare me."

Cole made a pivot.

"Sam, we may do some wine. We have to do something. I'm going to lease some pasture for vineyard, convert that old barn into a winery. I'm going to talk to Indigo. He seems to have more money than sense. Just the type of partner I'm looking for. I don't have a lot of choices."

"What does that have to do with me?" Sam said, returning to her paperwork.

"You and your dad, you know the business. I'll need some advice, and help."

"We do about forty cases a year, it's a vanity project. I won't be much help. Besides, I don't want to get in the cross fire."

"I would never let anything happen to you," Cole replied.

Sam looked up from her work and stared at Cole. "Really? What's changed?"

Cole gazed at his feet and absorbed the blow. No clever response occurred. He paused to reflect on how and when their paths had diverged.

When Cole had left for Stanford as an undergraduate, he and Sam had already discussed marriage. It had long been assumed because it was so obvious and right that they should be together. It wasn't something they had to think about. But the centrality of that relationship soon had to fight the opposing pull of everything Cole experienced at Stanford.

For Cole, leaving the tiny ranching community of Santa Ynez to join some of the nation's most elite students at Stanford was like being teleported to another planet. It seemed a world of endless possibilities and it fueled his ambition. Suddenly, living out his days in a tiny cow town seemed a life too small. He wanted to study the great thinkers of history, to have his own ideas recognized, to make his own mark.

All of his assumptions—about religion, natural law, and political philosophy—were challenged. Encouraged by his professors, he came to question everything, and so began to forget what he already knew. He told himself that was the very objective of a liberal arts education and willingly submitted.

And then he met Jessica. Jessica was Sam's mirror

image: a wasp from a "blue blood" family, she traced her ancestry in the United States to prerevolutionary settlements. Unlike the "best" families in Santa Ynez who were "land rich and cash poor," Jessica's people were just rich. Her Episcopal religion, at least her understanding of it, had seemingly released her from any discernible constraints, save being "a good person" who did not "judge." Cole had been taught to judge everything. Cole's Catholicism carried abundant constraint and an equalizing measure of guilt for constraints not well observed. It was *all about* judgement. At nineteen, that was a burden he was happy to lay down.

Cole's attraction to Jessica was immediate. She was beautiful and fun and, in her, Cole found an opportunity for abandon he had never allowed himself. But their love was also more aspirational than fully realized. They were, together, what Cole *wanted to be*. There were lines they could not and did not cross. Their relationship worked because they drove within the lanes. In the heady days of their courtship, Cole was happy to stay within the lanes because he wanted to. He willed it to work. He convinced himself that relationships were necessarily so.

Sam had learned of Cole's engagement from mutual friends. It was a wound that had not healed. He had, in fact, let "something happen to her."

And now she wanted to know what had changed.

He finally answered, "Everything. Or nothing, if you go back far enough."

Sam looked up from her work and stared. "I have no idea what that means, Cole, but I know what happened to us hurt. Hurt me at least. It's buried pretty deep, but it's still there."

She pulled an invoice from her desk and began to shuffle other papers. "I have to work. I hope Elliot's okay."

Cole left for an appointment he dreaded but needed to put behind him. He and Indigo had agreed to meet at the Grand Avenue Café, the restaurant made famous by Paul Giamatti's rant about merlot in the film *Sideways*. It was, Cole thought, the perfect backdrop for his sell out. Established originally as a local butchery supporting the ranchers, it was now owned by a local vintner. The owner paired his excellent food with his own wine. Business was all about leverage, and Cole was about to lever.

Indigo brought a bottle of his own wine, preferring a corkage fee to consumption of inferior wine, by which he meant pretty much anyone else's. Cole ordered an oatmeal stout. The fact that he was about to agree to make wine didn't mean he had to drink it. He watched Indigo sniff his own cork and feigned interest in the verdict. It was all quite painful but necessary. This was business.

"You still want to plant a vineyard on Zaca?" Cole opened.

Indigo turned cagey. "Depends."

"On?"

"The terms, of course."

"What do you suggest?" Cole said, sipping his beer.

Indigo made a show of sending back the olive oil which he found too heavy with garlic. "Planting a vineyard takes a long time and a lot of money. It would be three or four years from planting vines to bottling our first decent vintage. I want an option on that, but what I need now is a winery in Santa Ynez. I can buy grapes until our vineyard matures, maybe use some of my excess inventory up north. Main thing is, I want to establish my presence on the south-Central Coast. With a winery and a tasting room I can get some buzz going down here. Meanwhile we'll plant a few acres, see what you have."

"How much acreage do you want?" Cole asked.

"A couple of hundred acres; more if it works. Hell, the wine may taste like asparagus juice. Your sandy soil will stress the grapes. That can be good if you know what you're doing but it's tricky."

Cole smiled. But only because he so disdained the dance. While he considered farming an admirable endeavor, he detested haggling about money. There was something mildly parasitic about those who profit from the exchange of money, the deal, as distinguished from those who profit from the production of goods and services. Something real. Cole had no doubt this discussion was about money, the deal. But Cole needed a deal. He needed cash to drive the ranch to break even one way or another. So he would endure the dance with Indigo.

"I thought you liked our *terroir*," Cole said, trying to seem engaged.

"I said it's critical. Whether you have decent *terroir* is another matter."

Cole looked directly at Indigo and realized he had to make his move. "I'll option you two hundred acres. You buy the option to lease at the market price when you exercise."

"It's unproven vineyard land. There's risk here we have to account for." Indigo was not going to be outdone.

"So we'll structure the option to allow for you to exercise in twenty-five-acre increments. Only plant a few acres at first. That's up to you. And your risk."

"What about the winery? The vineyard will take a

while. I need production and storage capacity now. And a presence here in the Valley," Indigo barked as if Cole already worked for him.

"I understand. We have a barn we can use, easy access from Highway 101. But I'll need a loan to convert to a winery and tasting room, plus cash to buy the equipment."

"Terms?" Indigo asked as he slopped more olive oil on this bread.

"Cost of money, which is low these days. Interest only for three years. And I want to borrow twice the capital costs of the build out. Profits on the wine you bottle here is all yours. You pay rent on the facility, of course."

"Wait, twice the build-out costs? Why in hell would I do that deal?" Indigo said, some non-garlicky oil skating across his dimpled chin.

"Because I have other offers," Cole said having heard there were "plenty of wineries looking to expand" though he could not, at the moment, name one. "And I won't do it otherwise. I'm not going to bullshit you. This is not about wine for me. It's about money."

"It's always about money," Indigo laughed knowingly. "What's my security on the loan?"

"The winery. Not ownership, rent-free use if I default until you recoup. We'll have to specify a market rental rate."

"I don't know. The equipment I want in there, could be a big loan."

"You'll cover your cost of money and put it to good use securing something you want. More production. I suspect you've got some cash sitting on the sidelines," Cole said trying to use Indigo's ego against him.

"I have some," Indigo smiled. He swirled his wine in the glass. "Okay, but you build the winery to my specs."

"Within reason. Costs of production are on you; you recoup from sales. I also want to sell some local wine out of the winery. It'll help with the buzz and draw folks in. There is a lot of traffic up from LA every weekend. Sam has a boutique vineyard and resells some local stuff. I'm sure it won't compare or compete with your vintages."

"Well, shit, you sound like you've thought about this, cowboy," quipped Indigo. "Let me think on it."

"One more thing," Cole interjected. "I want a 'call' on the deal. The marriage doesn't work, I can call the deal and pay off all the debt."

"Why would I put up all this money to build a business just to see it shut down?" Indigo asked, not unreasonably Cole thought.

"Couple reasons. You want a footprint in the area, you'd get it. The call, if made, wouldn't kick in for a year, if it happens at all. I would give you time to unwind, find another place. Besides, you know I don't have the money to exercise the call so the risk is minimal. Even if I exercise, I can't see how you'd be out of pocket."

"You get a call, I get a put. Same terms. I may not like the marriage any better than you." Indigo was back on the dance floor.

"Fair enough." Both thought they had prevailed. Cole asked for the check.

11

⬦

A week after reaching his deal with Indigo, Cole was looking for his lawyer, Jack Callson, outside the building that housed the Santa Barbara Superior Court. His arraignment on charges stemming from his bar fight with Olly Davis was scheduled for 2:00 p.m. As he waited, he marveled at the oxymoronic façade of the courthouse. The business of the criminal division of the Santa Barbara Superior Court was disguised by palm trees and elegant Spanish Colonial Revival architecture. It looked more like a classy margarita bar than the last thing you see before a wall of vertical bars. But that's Santa Barbara, ever pleasant, he thought.

He spotted Jack nervously pacing back and forth in front of the hearing room's heavy oak doors.

"Glad you could make it," Jack said sarcastically.

"Had some business. Where do we stand with the deputy DA? I knew Jimmy Vega in high school. He should be a defendant."

"Well, he's not. But he caved. He couldn't get a hold of Olly so he's got a weak hand. His victim is out of town, I guess."

"Yeah, Las Vegas for the finals."

"I thought your buddy Jace qualified when they pulled Travis's ticket," observed Jack.

"He did, but Olly is back there protesting. Says some of Jace's winnings were in non-sanctioned events so he shouldn't get the slot."

"He's a prick," Jack said as they pushed through the heavy oak doors into the courtroom.

"Exactly. Is that a defense?"

"We'll see…"

The deputy DA was seated at counsel's table, the clerk to his left. No judge. Cole and Jack stepped to the counsel's table to the right of the DA and sat down.

The bailiff entered from a side door and addressed the courtroom. "All rise. Division Three of the Santa Barbara Superior Court in session, Judge Mary Tapinato presiding."

They all stood as the judge entered and sat, rather regally to Cole's mind.

Cole's thoughts drifted to the symbolism of the state and to the idea of impartial justice; to the idea, more specifically, that we vest in a judge the right to decide. He had seen Tapinato at Larry's a week before. Larry's was a favorite of locals mostly because its drinks were too strong by half and cheap. She was well lit by the time Cole had arrived, presiding loudly over a red leather booth of campaign operatives. She had already announced her intention to leave the bench and run for district attorney. That was a bad omen for Cole. He expected her to demonstrate she was tough on crime and he was a convenient vehicle. She knew his politics, and he knew hers. But, of course, in theory that didn't matter. This was about the scales of justice, scales held in balance by a blindfolded "Lady Justice." To Cole's eye, Lady Justice looked nothing like Mary Tapinato but there was nothing to be done. This was the social contract we had struck, leaving the state of nature in a grand experiment, trading our ostensible "state of nature" freedom for law as a bulwark against chaos. Or so thought Thomas Hobbes.

Cole looked up and was immediately struck by her apparent authority. Judges sit on a platform well above counsel and the defendant, whose fate they hold in their hands. One looks *up* at judges, their vestiges framed by the symbols of state power—a flag and the scales of justice. But it was the black robe that stood out. Judges wear robes so that we will see them as impartial arbiters of the state's authority. As if to hide their personage, to help them embody the state. But when he had seen her at Larry's, she looked like everyone else in Santa Barbara, as if she had dressed to wash her car and decided to go to dinner instead.

"The matter of the people versus Cole Clay will come to order. Counsel, announce your appearances."

Vega stood, followed by Jack.

"James Vega for the People, Your Honor," Vega announced.

"Jack Callson for the defendant," Jack followed and then continued, "May it please the court, Mr. Vega and I have reached an agreement that may expedite matters. I know the court's docket is quite crowded."

"Please," urged the judge.

"My client is willing to plead to a misdemeanor infraction of disturbing the peace in consideration of the People's decision to dismiss the assault and battery charges," explained Jack.

The judge looked disappointed. Maybe her docket

wasn't so crowded, or maybe the prospect of slamming Cole Clay had a certain countervailing appeal.

"Mr. Vega?" the judge asked.

Mr. Vega jumped back to his feet, too perky. "Your Honor, the incident that gave rise to these proceedings was most serious and the State is reluctant to compromise our efforts, which we know the court supports, to curb this type of lawless behavior. That said, the victim of Mr. Cole's conduct is out of town and was unavailable to lend support to the state's prosecution."

"I see. Mr. Clay, would you like to address the court before the court considers the plea?" She looked at Clay, her disappointment with the news obvious.

Cole noted the judge's reference to herself in the third person, "the court." He had an overwhelming desire to say, "Well, Mary, as I may have mentioned at Larry's the other night between your first and second margarita..." But he reconsidered: No upside there. She held all the cards. So he stood and assumed the position—feet back, spread wide. "Thank you, Your Honor. I would be happy to address the court. I regret the incident, of course. I am not prone to resort to physicality. I would accept the plea of disturbing the peace for the reason that, under any interpretation of the events, I certainly disturbed the peace, especially Olly's."

He knew immediately he had not bent over far enough. He should have dropped the reference to Olly. Too late.

"Mr. Clay," the judge opened, "I find your attitude curious. You engaged in an unprovoked physical and violent attack on a patron in a public bar while, it seems from the evidence, intoxicated. You could do time for assault and, I should remind you, this is the People's business. Whether this Mr. Davis wants to participate or not, my job is to do justice by the standards of this community."

Cole considered his response, "I understand the court's responsibility. But I also understand mine, as a husband and a father and, yes, as a member of the community you mention. It is a community of persons who must maintain, at least in my view, a certain decorum, a set of standards and unspoken rules of civility. On the evening in question, it was my view, as impaired as it was, that those standards of engagement, those unspoken rules of civility, could not sustain my ignoring the very crude and disrespectful comments made by Mr. Davis about my wife. You might say it's a matter of personal honor and that still counts in my book."

The judge was not pleased. She shuffled papers to stall for time. Finally, she spoke: "Mr. Cole, it's the court's belief that yahoos like you who believe they can get drunk and punch people in the nose as a means of redressing grievances, are the very persons who are the greatest threat to our standards of civility. As the People have withdrawn their assault and battery charges, the court has no choice but to render sentence on the remaining disturbance charge on which I impose the maximum sentence allowed by the guidelines: two years of supervised probation and a one-thousand-dollar charge. Good day, Counsel."

As they exited the palatial hall of justice, Jack pulled out his cigarettes and seized some shade under a palm. "Well, that went well. Why didn't you just threaten to punch her?"

"Sorry, Jack. But I wasn't going to leave my balls on her mahogany floor. Olly got exactly what he deserved.

Maybe we'd all be better off if we stopped pretending otherwise," answered Cole. He continued in a more serious tone: "Where do we stand on the deal at Manny's?"

Jack puffed away. Cole had not seen a real cigarette on State Street in months. Bongs and vapes, but a cigarette? He knew Jack was upset now.

"Your father has been charged with attempted murder and an assortment of firearms-related charges. I think we can clear you. You did not bring a weapon to the fight and fired only in self-defense, or so I'm saying. I don't think they could get a conviction and they know it. At least not in Santa Ynez."

"What's the strategy from here?" Cole asked.

"To keep you out of the courtroom for fear you'll screw up my good work again." Jack stubbed out the cigarette and started to walk to the nearby trashcan to deposit the offensive butt.

"Works for me," Cole said.

12

---◇---

The deal with Indigo had been signed. The Clays needed to convert the old barn into the winery. To do so, it would have to be expanded. That would require the county's approval. A land use permit cleared the right to build; a building permit would follow, if you were lucky. Their application to begin construction had been returned stamped "incomplete" and accompanied by a six-page, single-spaced letter explaining in detail the precise manner in which their application was "incomplete." Travis's last drunken rant at a county inspector made him an unlucky emissary to the county building department, so Cole reluctantly volunteered.

Cole walked into a nondescript building through a glass door that read "County of Santa Barbara Planning and Development." He immediately felt a deep and discomforting anxiety. That anxiety was grounded in history.

Arroyo de Zaca was created by a land grant concession made by the Mexican government to his mother's people in 1840. The Mexican government had looked to reward the loyal service of officers in the Mexican Army and, simultaneously, to colonize "Alta California" with Mexican citizens. These grants also served to reduce the land holdings, and influence, of the Franciscan missionaries whose loyalty to the Mexican government was suspect. The original concession had been granted to Cole's maternal great-grandfather. It covered almost thirty square miles stretching from Santa Ynez north to what is now the city of Santa Maria. But these grants were provisional and had to be surveyed and marked. Lacking the resources and means to do so formally, vast *ranchos* were informally marked by reference to the topography—a stand of oaks, a creek or, as in one famous case, a cow skull. Still, claims to land were generally honored and the vast *ranchos* were ignored by the Mexican administrators for many years. The *ranchos'* trade in tallow and hide was not a source of tax revenue, as was the robust import and export trade in Monterey farther north. For a brief period, these vast holdings and their *ranchero* families enjoyed halcyon days of idyllic self-sufficient isolation.

But those days were numbered. The Mexican-American War began in the spring of 1846 and ended shortly thereafter after an American rout. Ulysses Grant, then a young officer in the American army, would one day describe the engagement as "the most unjust" war in American history. It ended in 1848 with the Treaty of Guadalupe Hidalgo. Alta California became the thirty-first state of the United States in 1850 and with statehood came bureaucracy. The new government required all owners of land grant concessions to present their titles for confirmation to the California Board of Land Commissioners. It placed the burden on landholders to verify their titles and the boundaries of their land. The process took an average of seventeen years, and it was expensive. Lawyers and surveyors were necessary combatants in a war of administrative attrition. Many *rancheros*, including that of Cole's forbearers, lost vast portions of their estates by adverse rulings or foreclosures born of debt incurred to pay the lawyers.

And then it got worse. The gold rush of 1849 had brought three hundred thousand white settlers with an appetite for land, land largely held by Mexicans whose claim on this new American state was viewed with suspicion. The Preemption Act of 1841 came into full effect. Under certain circumstances, squatters could lay claim to one hundred and sixty acres by occupying and working the land. Land was lost to "adverse possession" and outright fraud. The great drought of 1863 to 1864 was a final bullet. Cattle that could not be fed or watered died by the thousands, their once valuable beef and hide left to rot or sold for pennies on the dollar. More land was sold to survive.

The net of this history was clear. Millions of acres of land were lost by their rightful Mexican owners, and the seeds of enmity between the white and Mexican occupants of this vast western land were left to germinate beneath a shallow topsoil of comity. Cole could not help but believe that those seeds were ever threatening to come to full and inglorious fruition. And yet he resisted the thought. Everything he had learned from history, and everything he had absorbed from philosophy, compelled him to resist viewing events in racial terms. He had met worthy and worthless men in every shade.

This was not to suggest Cole denied differences among the races, a reality which to him was obvious. Cole himself was born of a Mexican mother and a Scotch-Irish father. To suggest that there were no differences in the world view of those two peoples, forged from a thousand years of dramatically different history and culture, was to him absurd. The trick was to distinguish between the broad realities of cultural history and *the behavior of an individual* as that history unfolds. To acknowledge the differences among people was compelled by a clear-eyed view of history; to prejudge a person, in the midst of evolving history, was wrong and served only to reinforce a sort of corrosive social animus.

That said, the history of Arroyo de Zaca had had a profound effect on Cole. Once spanning over twenty thousand acres, Zaca was now just under two thousand acres. Cole gleaned from that fact and the history that drove it, two principles he would not easily compromise: He would not willingly concede another inch of the ranch; and he would never trust lawyers or the governmental bureaucracies within which they thrive.

These thoughts flooded his head as he entered the offices of the county's land use bureaucracy for an appointment with a government bureaucrat. More specifically, a county land use lawyer.

He approached the counter and the woman who stood behind it. She was on her computer and did not acknowledge him. Cole waited. Finally, she looked up and pushed her feline-shaped, aquamarine glasses down her nose and assessed her prey.

"Yes?"

"My name is Cole Clay. We own the Arroyo de Zaca off the 101 in Buellton," Cole opened.

"Do you have an appointment?" she asked.

"Yes ma'am. With a Ms. Hotchkiss," he replied.

"That's me. But I don't have an appointment on my calendar," she snapped.

"I'm sorry. I was sure it was set. I just have a question."

"Case number?"

Cole paged through the sixteen-page, single-spaced letter he had received from the county. "I'm not sure."

"It's on the second page." Exasperated, she pulled the document from Cole's hand. "There it is. 18LUP-00000-0088. What is your question? I can answer a few if they aren't too detailed. We are very busy."

Cole started to look back at the empty room but caught himself. When the enemy owns the battlefield, best to keep your head low.

"I guess my question is, did I get the correct letter? It's a form and, well, I was hoping there may have been a mistake."

"We don't make mistakes. I don't, anyway, and I see here I'm your planner. No, the letter is correct. You're doing new construction in a sensitive area."

"How so?"

"It's all there. According to county records, your ranch is within the tiger salamander range. That requires that a biologic survey be prepared by a qualified biologist as to potentially sensitive habitats that may be located within one thousand feet of a proposed disturbance. And the oaks—in addition to set-back requirements, we'll need a written plan to ensure protection of mature trees and their saplings. There can be no disturbance of critical root zones from grading, paving, or construction. You need a qualified arborist to do that study and craft the protection plan. All onsite mature oaks within twenty-five feet of disturbed areas will need to be fenced, the drip line plus six feet."

"Okay, then," Cole offered in surrender. "Is that it?"

"No. Your ranch is next door to the McBreen place, right?"

"Yes, it is."

"I thought so. They found some Native American pottery there last year. You will probably need a qualified archaeologist and a Native American representative to clear the area. Just as a precaution, of course."

"Of course. Hate to break any china on this deal," Cole said, his first mistake.

"It's not 'china,' Mr. Clay, it's heritage. *Ours*," she corrected. "Anything else?"

"No, I guess you have answered my questions. I appreciate it." Cole gathered his documents and tipped his hat to leave.

"What are you building up there, anyway? You already have a house, I see," she asked.

"We're just expanding an existing barn."

"Why?"

"We're converting it to a winery."

"Great. Just what we need in the Valley." She adjusted her glasses and returned to her work, then looked up for a final shot. "That reminds me, have you cleared the Agricultural Preserve Committee? I'm sure you know you may not remove more than two acres from your agricultural application, in this case grazing, not grapes."

"Well, I would think wine is also an agricultural application."

"Not necessarily on a cattle ranch. Different deal. You'll have to take that up with the committee. They're backlogged. It will take a while to get on the calendar," she added.

"Well, thank you again. You've been very thorough," Cole said.

"That's our job," she smiled.

Cole started to leave but couldn't resist. "Say, I'm a bit of an environmentalist myself. Have tiger salamanders ever been found near our place?"

"No. But you never know," she said, turning away from the counter.

"That's for sure, never know."

On the ride back to Zaca, Cole's thoughts bounced from salamanders to cat-eye spectacles to the government bureaucracies that spread in California like mold on soggy bread. More broadly, the history of Zaca flickered through his mind like frames of a silent movie. Finally, his thoughts settled on John Locke's *Two Treatises of Government* and his contention that man organized government for the purpose of *protecting* private property rights. What a dope he thought.

13

———◇———

Cole had a choice. Community service was a condition of his probation. As it turned out, there were several ways to serve, among them planting oak trees, removing graffiti from buildings along State Street, or mentoring "at risk" youth. Cole opted for the latter and was surprised when his probation officer agreed. There was some irony, Cole thought, in serving out a sentence for fighting in a bar by mentoring punk kids disposed to do the same. But it was better than the alternatives.

Cole sat in another bank of nondescript county offices with Luis Perez, his probation officer. Luis was engaging and articulate but looked, to Cole's eye, like a graduate of the mentoring program. Bearded and unkempt, his thinning hair revealed a tattoo Cole understood to be the symbol of a white nationalist gang. But Luis was obviously Hispanic. Cole was confused so he jumped in. What could Luis do? Assign him to tree duty?

"So your tatt. That's a gang symbol."

Luis smiled, "Yeah, how'd a Santa Ynez hick like you know that?"

"Learned some about gangs at Stanford."

"I'll bet you did. Those frat boys can be some mean-ass mo-fos. And the LAX bros? Wouldn't want to cross them. They carry metal sticks and shit."

"It was in a sociology course. Several chapters on dysfunctional social strata."

Luis laughed. "You didn't learn shit, homie."

"Well, I thought I learned that gang was a white nationalist deal? You look Hispanic, if you don't mind me saying."

Luis looked up and glared. "You a racist? What, you don't like Mexicans?"

Cole marveled at his own capacity to make bad situations worse. "No, actually, I am half-Mexican myself. I meant no offense, I just…"

Luis laughed out loud. "Don't go peeing down your leg, bro. I'm giving you shit. Lighten up. But, like I say, you didn't learn a thing. You're thinking of some other shit bags." He touched the tatt on his neck. "We were all about power and money. Kinda like the frat boys at Stanford, come to think of it."

Luis closed one file and opened another. "Head of our chapter was a Jew. Bunch of Mexicans join around here, Santa Maria and Lompoc mostly. There's some racist assholes but it's mostly just assholes."

"That clarifies it," Cole said.

"So here's the list." Luis tossed three pages of "candidates" for mentoring to Cole. Cole flipped through the pages. One name jumped out: Harold Allen Kyel.

"Hammer."

"What?"

"I know this kid. Harold Kyel. What's he in for?"

"He's not 'in' for anything. He got busted with some smack. First offense. Probation, just like you. You'd be a perfect pair. How well do you know him? Might be disqualifying if you guys are tight or anything."

"No, I just see him around."

"And what you think of him?"

"I think he's a flake, but he comes by it naturally. I think he's two clicks from serious trouble."

"Well maybe you can redeem yourself by saving his ass from the life," Luis said. He filled out the paperwork that would obligate Cole to see his candidate twice a week and file monthly reports outlining their progress on a range of "mentee" objectives which, in Hammer's case, included tutoring toward a GED and securing a job.

"I need you to stay in touch. And file those reports," added Luis, closing the file. "We can always convert your probation, or his, to time in the tank if you blow this off."

Cole stood and put on his hat. "No, sir. We'll both be on the path to redemption shortly."

As Cole left the county offices, he received a text from Travis. "Come to hospital" was all it said, but Cole knew what it meant. He drove the short distance to Cottage Hospital and made his way to Elliot's room. He knew the path well. He and Travis had visited several times since their first visit after the shooting and each time Elliot had slipped further from their reach and, for that matter, from that of the doctors. As Cole approached the room, he saw Travis standing outside. From his expression, Cole knew his father had passed.

A week later, Elliot was to be buried according to his written instructions. There would be no church service, no minister at the gravesite. He was to be buried on the ranch and, if it was ever sold, they were to remove the gravestone and "be done with it." He didn't want "strangers wondering who in the hell he was." The marker was to reflect his name and the dates of his birth and death and so it did, with nothing more. "No clever inscriptions," he had directed. He wanted to be buried on the "high point" of the ranch on the east-facing slope, the one with a view of the entire Santa Ynez Valley.

Cole had invited family and a few close friends. Victoria and Travis had arrived early, soon joined by Billy, Sam, and Jack Callson. Indigo's invitation to attend had been declined. Jessica had also declined but agreed to drop Dustin off at the ranch that morning. Marisa held her great-grandson's hand as they all waited for the service to begin.

Cole arrived last. He had driven out to retrieve Prescott. Prescott had taken the passing of his only son hard and did not speak when he exited the truck on the slope where the others had gathered. Cole walked to Dustin first and leaned down to hug him before stepping to the side of the flag-draped casket.

Cole knew the obligation to say something would fall to him but had no idea what he was going to say. As he prepared to speak, an older gentleman Cole did not recognize joined. He spoke to no one and stood at the back of the small gathering. He took off his cap as Cole began to speak.

"Elliot Everett Clay was a son and a father and husband. He was a marine and a rancher. He was a cowboy. He could be a son of a bitch at times, a hard man. I would like to tell you that he lived a long and happy life, that his dreams were fulfilled and that he died happy, content with the course he had followed. But I can't, and I won't. Because Elliot Clay hated phonies and phoniness above all else and so I will not stand at his grave and lie. Elliot had disappointments, chief among them some of the mistakes he had made himself. Unforced errors.

"The life he had expected to live, as a son of Eastern privilege, never came to pass. And so he seized another life and worked hard to make it real. For all of us. Whether that effort succeeded is a story yet to be told.

"For all of his faults, for all of his rough edges, I believe that Elliot Clay was a good man. He never gave up the struggle as he saw it. He never stopped trying to save this way of life, a life that history and progress and modern culture have conspired to extinguish. He believed this life and all it represents has value. He sought to preserve that value for his sons in the hope that they would preserve it for theirs. He was a good man because he never gave up on that, or us.

"The last time Travis and I saw him, at least the last time he knew we were there and could talk, he came closer to an apology than I had ever heard him come. He acknowledged his mistakes and, for that, I hope the good Lord looks the other way as he makes his run at the pearly gates.

"But he said something else that last day, that last opportunity he had to push us, me and Trav. He reminded us that this race we are all running feels long but it is, at the end of the day, profoundly short. And so, he urged us to make the most of it. To take the blinders off, to see and accept things as they are. To move past the setbacks. Now, you can take those words as the last gasp of a life-long cynic; that what he was saying was, 'yeah, the world is fatally flawed. Accept it and get your share as best you can.' That would be, knowing Elliot as we all did, a fair interpretation. But that is not how I read his words. Quite the opposite. I believe that Elliot, staring at the end, meant to express regret, and to glean from that regret the great lesson of his life; that what is good and true and right is clear; that we don't have to struggle to see it, save moving the debris of this world from our field of vision; that we don't have to seize it so much as accept it. And, as Elliot might put it, when bad things happen, accept them and move on. That is what I intend to do. And for that, I thank Elliot one last time."

Cole glanced toward the casket and closed: "May God bless and accept his soul into eternal salvation."

As the group began to disperse, Cole gently placed his hand over Dustin's shoulder for the walk back to the *hacienda*. Cole had debated whether Dustin was too young to attend, whether he would understand, whether attending might do him more harm than good. Jessica had strongly opposed Dustin attending but Cole had insisted. He knew that Dustin had idolized his grandfather and might benefit from the closure. As they walked, he prayed he had been right.

"You okay?" Cole asked.

"I guess," Dustin replied tentatively. "I hate it. It's sad. Grandpa in the ground like that."

"Grandpa's not in the ground. His body's in the ground. His soul is still around, just as cranky as ever, I'd guess," Cole ventured.

"Where?"

"We believe that when a good person dies his soul goes to heaven."

Dustin thought about it as they approached the *hacienda*. "Was grandpa a good person?"

Cole looked at his son and smiled. His father's son, he thought; right to the heart of the matter.

"Yes. He was far from perfect. He made mistakes. But I believe he was good man doing his best. What you should remember is that he loved you very much."

Dustin slipped from his father's reach and skipped up the steps to the *hacienda* calling back as he did, "Did Marisa make those cookies?"

The funeral party gathered in the *hacienda*. Marisa had prepared a meal of chicken enchiladas, rice, and sweet tea. She laid the cookies out for dessert once the meal had been served. The gathering didn't last long. It was early for lunch and the conversation was awkward. There were the obligatory condolences and the occasional story about Elliot, the attempts at humor. Billy tried his best to spin his recollections of Elliot as the antics of an "old school cowboy," a cantankerous but well-meaning "classic" from another era. They all laughed politely and knew, simultaneously, it was a lie. For the last twenty years of his life, Elliot had been disillusioned and bitter at best, plain mean at worst. They all knew it, and no entertaining anecdotes could change it. Cole had done his best to extract what good he could from the lesson of Elliot's life and his last words. But it had not been enough to crack the grey lens through which Elliot's life was being processed, quietly, in the filtered morning light of the *hacienda*'s great room.

One by one they made their leave with quiet words of sympathy and support; words that meant nothing, save smoothing the hasty exit of the speaker as, one by one, they escaped to their cars. Cole couldn't blame them. He wished he too could just drive away.

Jessica arrived to retrieve Dustin and waited in the car as Cole walked his son down. As he opened the passenger-side door, she spoke. "I'm sorry, Cole. Elliot and I had our differences but…well, I'm just sorry it ended this way."

"Thanks," was all he could think to say. He turned to Dustin and saw, for the first time, tears beginning to well in his son's eyes. "Hey, bud…what'd your grandpa always say when you start to cry? Cowboy up, eh?"

As Jessica drove away, she cast a final glance at Cole. Its message was clear: "I was right. He should never have come." It was not unlike a thousand other nonverbal reprimands he had suffered over the course of their troubled marriage, but this one stung. He wasn't sure. Maybe she was right.

The issue, unresolved, pressed like a cold hand on his chest as he turned to find himself face to face with the last guest. It was the older gentleman who had arrived late. He extended his hand and Cole recognized the logo of the 3rd Brigade Armored Division on his tattered ball cap. "You served with Elliot in the Gulf?" Cole asked.

"Yeah."

"I didn't catch your name."

"Name's Mike. Don't matter. I just wanted to pay my respects." He zipped up his leather jacket and took in the view, not quite ready to leave.

"Well, thank you for coming. It would have meant a lot to Elliot," Cole said.

Mike's eyes stayed focused on the view. "Not so sure about that."

Cole had no idea how to respond.

"Sometimes best not to be reminded. Not as easy as what you said, just move on and all that," said Mike. He reached into his pocket and pulled out his keys. "You think he ever did?"

Cole considered the question and regretted the truth before he spoke it. "No, sir, I don't. Not entirely."

Mike just nodded and walked across the gravel to his car. As Cole watched, he thought about all the injuries that never heal and the loss we never understand. And he thought once again of Dustin's tears and wished that he could shield him from those injuries and explain away all the losses that lie before him. But he knew he could not, and that fact filled him with a sudden, overwhelming sadness. He began to cry and he knew that, for the first time, he was crying for the loss of his father and for all of the nobility, and stupidity, of his life.

Cole turned and stepped back into the great room of the *hacienda*. Maybe it was the light, broken by curtains Marisa had inexplicably half-drawn, or the shimmer of dust in the air where the light found its way in, cracked and broken throughout the room; maybe it was the plates of half-eaten food randomly left on tables and countertops throughout the room, testimony to the hurried flight of friends and family. Whatever the reason, the empty room fueled a gestating anxiety; a sense that there were things he did not know or understand; things that might explain why Elliot had so recklessly courted death, then seemingly surrendered his life in a sterile hospital bed between aluminum guardrails. Neither seemed like the Elliot Cole knew. It was as if Elliot had written a plot for which there was no resolution; like he didn't want to see the third act.

Cole stepped onto the porch and was surprised to see Sam. She was sitting quietly to one side under the porch's single umbrella, her glass of wine near empty.

"I thought you left. I'm sorry we didn't get a chance to speak."

"You had a lot to do."

"Can I get you another glass of wine?"

"I can think of a hundred reasons to say no."

"Is that an answer?"

"No. I'll have one more. Then I have to go."

Cole returned with two glasses of red.

"I thought you were a beer guy," Sam said, accepting her glass.

Cole sat next to her. "I have to make the transition, hard as it may be."

"So what did all that mean—your remarks at the grave?" Sam asked.

Cole shrugged. "I don't really know what Elliot meant to say, that last time we spoke. That's what I think he was saying or, maybe I was just attributing to him what I needed to hear. It doesn't really matter. It's what I believe."

"And what is that exactly, Cole?" Sam asked. "What's the good and the true? And what's the...what'd you call it? The debris. That was it. Help those of us who didn't go off to a fancy college figure it out."

Cole sighed, the sarcasm registering. "Well, maybe you're lucky. That's where I waded through most of the debris. Phony philosophies, false equivalencies, moral relativism. Questioning everything to the end that nothing is truer than anything else. Self-obsession. Relationships that mean nothing."

"That's where you met Jessica," Sam observed quietly.

"Fair enough. And she was not debris. And Dustin sure isn't. He's the most important thing in my life.

But…" Cole trailed off, somewhere else. He had never said it out loud. He had never admitted it all to himself.

"The other day Jessica said I never really loved her, that I didn't even know her. That what I loved was more the idea of her. And I hate that thought. But there's some truth. I loved the idea of her and me together, from different backgrounds and cultures; her beauty, her family, the old money they represented. It was a world I thought I wanted. But the truth is, she and I never fit. It was always work. It was what I wanted but it wasn't who I was. So, no, she was not debris. But my desire for her was cluttered with aspirations and those aspirations had some debris, the stuff that makes you forget who you are."

Sam sipped her wine and looked away, back at the view.

"I'm sorry. That probably makes no sense," Cole said.

"As much as anything else right now. The problem is, who we are changes."

"Does it?"

Sam put her wine glass down. "Yes, or maybe who we were just gets buried in all the scar tissue."

She stood. "I have to go."

"May I see you?"

"I see you almost every day."

"That's not what I meant."

Sam hesitated. "Let's just see, Cole."

14

◇

In the end, a process that was supposed to take "a few weeks," took nine months. But after thousands of dollars in fees and hundreds of pages in filings, the biologists had found no rare salamanders; local tribal representatives had found no evidence of Native settlements; and the Agricultural Preserve Committee had agreed that processing wine grapes was still "agriculture" and therefore acceptable within the terms of the Williamson Act Agricultural Preserve program. With the regulatory green light, Cole and Travis had begun the process of converting their old barn to a winery and tasting room. With any luck, it would be finished for the following fall harvest.

Cole had imagined that actually building the winery would be simple once the regulatory hurdles were cleared. He was wrong. Converting the barn space to accommodate winemaking and visitors had been no small matter. But the scale and expense of the equipment required to turn grapes into wine had been a surprise.

Weeks into the process, Cole arrived at the new winery early, anxious to see the final pieces of equipment as they were unpacked. They had already received and installed a six-foot horizontal receiving hopper. Indigo had insisted on a particular model, one that would allow for a "constant metered feed" of fruit into the de-stemmer. "We need a consistent internal rotation," he'd said. Cole was assured that the hopper they'd purchased would be as gentle as a "gloved hand" for which Cole had expressed appreciation. "Wouldn't want to bruise those grapes before we crush the crap out of them," Cole had remarked.

An incline belt elevator would carry the grapes to the hopper, after which they'd be pushed into the de-stemmer. But not any de-stemmer. The one arriving this morning was fully adjustable to accommodate anything from one-half ton to two tons of grapes, a specification Cole found curious since they had not yet planted a single vine. Surely, he thought, when acquiring inventory, one could control volume but, as Indigo had said, "best to be flexible." Yeah, especially when Cole's end of the deal included setting up the winery.

Cole was regretting the deal already, less on account of cost than Indigo's constant fitful presence. Indigo arrived that morning in a foul mood and met Cole as the new equipment was unpacked. "That's a cheap ass de-stemmer. I wanted automated speed control. This thing has a damn knob with a pulley and belt."

"Wow, I had no idea," Cole deadpanned. "Will that affect the nose on your Viognier?"

"Screw you, Cole." Indigo stormed off just as Sam arrived. Cole was happy to see her.

"Just in time," Cole said.

"Wow. This is first-class stuff," she said.

"Not in my partner's opinion. Thinks we're cheaping out."

"Where are you going to put the waste from the de-stemmer?" she asked. "You're going to need some half-ton macro bins."

"We have them. They're called cows."

"That's not a bad idea. The lees are very nutritious for cattle," she observed.

"Yeah, and it pre-marinates your beef."

Travis directed another delivery truck to the backside of the barn. Huge pieces of polished aluminum emerged, each as mysterious as the next. "And these would be?"

"The must sump and pump," explained Sam as Indigo reappeared, now pleased. "Finally, a nice piece. I specially ordered this pump. The only pump in the industry that won't degrade overall oxygen; it self-primes. No dry operations. Beautiful."

He whirled away to direct his crew down from Napa to piece the equipment together. He did so with a harsh tone and heavy hand. As Cole and Sam turned, a tattered pickup arrived just outside the barn.

Hammer emerged from the truck.

"You're late," Cole opened.

"Whatever," Hammer mumbled.

"Hey, you want this job or not?"

"Not really."

"Okay, I'll let your PO know. Thanks for coming out." Cole turned back to Sam.

Hammer hesitated. "Okay. I'm here, ain't I?"

"Yeah. But it's not enough. You need this job and for me to say nice things about the great progress you're making in rehabilitating your ass. So drop the attitude."

Hammer looked at his feet.

"Grab that broom and sweep the floor in the back room where this new equipment is going."

Hammer picked up the broom and disappeared.

"Marriage made in heaven," smiled Sam.

"It's a marriage of mutual inconvenience," offered Cole. "So what's that?" Cole pointed at the latest pieces of equipment being unloaded.

"The pumps and filtration system. Those are your bottlers," explained Sam. "And that's your press," as she pointed to a huge aluminum box being hoisted off a large flatbed.

Cole shook his head in the direction of what he now understood would press the grapes into the juice that would ferment and age into their winery's first vintages.

"What's the problem?" Sam asked.

"I had envisioned you and me stripping down and stomping around in a huge wooden barrel."

"Not a chance," she said.

As Sam drove away, Hammer reappeared. "So what now?"

"Go find Carlos and help him unload the plants in the back of the truck."

"Plants? Why?"

"That's not a question you get to ask."

Hammer turned and dragged himself toward the *hacienda*, his unhappiness manifest.

Cole called out. "If you must know, we are going to plant the perimeter of the tasting room patio. You need a pleasant environment to fully appreciate a wine's subtle bouquet."

Hammer replied without turning. "That's why I prefer pot. All you need is a ratty couch and a game console."

The fermentation tanks and refrigeration systems arrived next, followed by the stainless-steel barrels in which their product would age. A day later they were assembled and Arroyo de Zaca had a winery.

Now all they needed were grapes.

They had pushed hard to complete the winery for the harvest and soon they arrived: several tons of Grenache Blanc from local Santa Ynez vineyards with excess capacity. Indigo's first vintage in Santa Ynez, he said, had to score "ninety-two or above." He was damn sure it would.

The team worked obsessively over the next few days until, finally, sorted, stemmed, crushed and pressed, the juice entered the fermentation process under the obsessive oversight of Indigo and his winemaker down from Napa.

The rapidity of the fermentation process was carefully monitored. Yeast would transform the natural sugars to ethanol and carbon dioxide but, Cole learned, the alchemy of great winemaking requires some intervention. The naturally occurring "bloom" yeast was preferred reflecting, according to Indigo, a vineyard's natural *terroir*. That said, it needed some help—to optimize the fermentation process, the yeast would have to be supplemented with cultured yeasts and have constant access to the correct levels of carbon, nitrogen, sulfur, phosphates, vitamins, and minerals. The temperature was carefully controlled in the refrigerated tanks that had cost Cole so dearly.

Cole concluded the natural *terroir* of the vineyards Indigo had chosen must be less than advertised. By the time Indigo let the brew rest, he had taken its temperature more often than the new mother of a sick child. He had added everything but the tail of the fabled tiger salamander. God's "natural elixir" my ass, Cole thought.

When the fermentation was judged complete, the wine entered aluminum tanks to age. That night, the team enjoyed a rare moment of comradery. Cole, Travis, and Hammer had transformed the old hay barn into a passable winery. The tasting room was nearly complete and the wine was in the "barrels." Sam had been a constant advisor, helping to soften Indigo's demands where prudence and money dictated a course south of Indigo's often unrealistic expectations. In the end, they were all pleased with the effort. Cole, Travis, Sam, and Indigo were joined by Marisa, Victoria, and Hammer. They had gathered to lift a glass to their efforts and to good fortune which, in this case, meant a good review from arbiters of good taste, the ones whose noses could decipher those hints of tangerine and lemon grass.

Cole raised a glass: "I never intended to be a vintner. And of course, even now, I'm not. Indigo and Alejandro are vintners. I guess I'm the landlord. But I'm proud of the job you did. Special thanks to Sam, without whose counsel I would have had to accept at face value all the bullshit Indigo was slinging. And to Hammer, who has actually worked pretty hard the last few weeks, something most thought as unlikely as me owning a winery. So to life's mysteries!"

After a series of short toasts, they settled into a liberal sampling of Indigo's Napa products. He had insisted the team become more familiar with the "infinite subtleties of God's special gift." They tried, but, after an hour, the subtleties were lost on most of them. The gathering disbanded. Sam stayed behind to arrange a display of her wines in the tasting room, making good on the one concession Indigo had granted in their negotiation. Cole watched, waiting to lock up.

Sam placed the last bottle of wine from her family's

boutique vineyard in a display. "You know he doesn't want me here."

"It doesn't matter. It's a good deal for you. And I want you here." Cole sat down on the leather couch in the center of the tasting room.

"And why is that?" She leaned against the wall opposite Cole.

"You know exactly why I want you here."

"Indulge me."

"I need someone to help run the tasting room. I'm notoriously abrupt with customers; I need advice. I know next to nothing about the wine."

"You could hire a hundred people in the valley to fill those needs."

"You're right. So you want the truth? I'd have you around every minute if I could. I figure if you're around enough, I can wear you down."

Sam smiled. "Well, not tonight. I think all the toasting has already worn me down. You think you can drive me home? Dad dropped me off this morning."

Moments later, at her door, they kissed. Their first since high school, several lifetimes ago. Cole keyed her front door and pushed it open. As they stepped inside, Sam gently placed her hand on his chest and looked into his eyes as if to ask that he stop and focus on what she was about to say.

"The first time we made love, the truth is, we were children. I thought I was in love but, the reality is, I had no idea what I was doing, or what it meant to really love someone. What it meant to give your body, and your heart, to someone wholly. I do now and I don't take it lightly."

Cole took her in his arms and kissed her hard and she met his passion fully. Then she pulled back. "Cole, I'm a little drunk."

She sat down and looked back at the man she still loved. "The next time I make love, I want to be sober... and married."

15

---◇---

L ife on the ranch slowed as the harvest passed and a warm fall lingered. The grass had long since turned. The tourist trade from LA slowed. The tasting room had fewer visitors.

Cole resolved to catch up on the tasks he least liked. He drove into Solvang to meet with his accountant Mick Woodson. For the first time in Cole's recollection, they had extended the ranch filing date and Mick had some questions he needed answered before he could finalize the return. They'd been at it about fifteen minutes when Cole's cell buzzed and the caller ID flashed "Sam." He pressed the auto response—"I can't talk right now"—and returned to the discussion with Mick.

He had known Mick since high school. Sweating in his own office, Mick insisted on wearing a sports jacket every day, a habit intended to reinforce his expertise as he waxed poetic about the intricacies of the tax code.

Cole fingered a draft two inches thick, a jumble of incomprehensible lines and numbers. "Whatever happened to that whole tax simplification thing? Didn't Trump promise you'd be able to file on a post card?"

Mick's laugh was hardy. He loved tax humor. "Every politician promises that. It'll never happen. Gets more complicated every year, thank goodness." He laughed again. Self-serving tax humor was even better. "Besides, your return this year is more complicated."

"Why's that?" Cole's phone rang again. Travis. He didn't answer. He wanted to answer Mick's questions and be done with it.

"Because you've been making new capital investments. They need to be capitalized properly."

He flipped through several pages of numbers.

"And we have to estimate your next year's taxes to make a payment against the first quarter on the off chance any of these investments actually make money."

"So what do you need to know, amigo?"

"Well, you sold the steers. You're now running…" He looked at his notes, "a cow-calf operation. You own these animals and just made a significant investment in them."

"Yeah, I used the loan from Indigo to invest in high-end Angus cows. If we are lucky, we can sell most of the offspring as replacement heifers or bulls. They are not sold by the pound for beef. It's a much more profitable deal when it works."

"Why doesn't everyone do it?" Mick said, leaning back and spinning his number two pencil like a propeller. Cole was impressed. He thought of a high school band leader twirling a baton. Too much time with a number two pencil.

"The short answer is I don't know. It's risky, I guess. You have to get the DNA of your cows and bulls right."

"So what's the useful life of these cows? We can amortize your investment against your income on sales."

"You'd have to ask my bulls. They seem happy."

Mick just stared.

"Okay, you can count on eight to ten years of calving

productively. Could be longer. I've seen them go dry after five. I don't know."

"Fine, I'm sure there are some revenue rulings I can use. Now, the winery and tasting room. You already have some income there."

"Yeah, Indigo leases the winery and the tasting room. He also makes quarterly payments on an option on some acreage he may plant."

"Is he going to exercise the option?"

"I don't know."

The third time his phone rang it was Sam again. Cole answered.

"Where are you?" She asked.

"My accountant's, why?"

"There's a fire on the ranch."

Fire was a fact of life on the Central Coast. Cole could not remember a stretch of more than two seasons without a fire somewhere on the ranch. Brush fires cleared mesquite and mustard and usually improved the following year's pasture. His voice was even when he responded.

"Okay, bad?"

"It started simultaneously in three different areas off the highway on your eastern perimeter. Santa Anas blew them up and over the hill. Yeah, it's bad."

Cole hung up and gathered his papers. "I have to go. Call me if there are other questions."

Cole blew through the front gate minutes later, ignoring the police roadblock along Highway 101. Black smoke billowed from three separate fires. The heaviest smoke came from the south, the plume moving rapidly toward the center of the ranch and the *hacienda* where most of the improvements rested. Sam was there now.

Almost simultaneously, various fire assets—Santa Barbara County Fire, Cal Fire, and a crew of "hotshots" from nearby Vandenberg Air Force Base—pulled through the ranch gate. An SUV with a Cal Fire logo slid to a stop beside Cole's truck. Cole rolled down his window.

"I'm Cole Clay, the owner. What do you need?"

"I'm Chief Malosa, Santa Barbara County Fire." He pointed to a heavy plume to the south. "How do my guys get there?"

"Follow me." Cole lurched forward and the captain followed at a quick but deliberate pace. Six minutes later Cole pulled to a stop on a high ridge line east of the burn, the fire moving rapidly toward them.

Chief Malosa got out of his truck, a little too slowly to Cole's mind. Another day at the office. "Good. This is the green/black line." They both looked west across the deep gorge that transected the ranch, the fire visibly blowing up the slope. Wind-blown embers advanced the fire's assault in a seemingly random pattern leaping over one section of brush, touching and torching the next. It reminded Cole of a malevolent schoolgirl playing hopscotch with a blowtorch. Malosa got back in his truck and spoke into the radio for several minutes as Cole waited, now anxious. This was not a brush fire.

Malosa returned.

"So can you explain the plan? What exactly is the green/black line?" Cole asked.

"We'll let everything west of here burn. We'll stop it here." He pointed west toward the mushrooming smoke. "That's black." He turned and pointed behind them. "That's green. This is the line."

"Any idea how this started?"

"No. Too early. Fact it started simultaneously in three different areas along the highway means might be some idiot dragging a loose trailer chain kicking up sparks. That or arson. If its arson, we won't know for a while. May never know."

The chief returned to his handheld radio. "No, SB has the line south central. Cal Fire should go north... bullshit. This is Santa Barbara and we're on site. We've got command here."

Cole returned to his truck with a cacophony of conflicting voices in his head. On the one hand, fire assets had arrived within minutes of the fire being reported. They were calm and deliberate. At the same time, Malosa had casually resigned a third of the ranch to burn before turning his attention to the politics of who was in charge. All in all, Cole's anxiety was not much dissipated.

He drove quickly to the *hacienda* and found Sam.

"We're under a mandatory evacuation order," she said.

"Great. Ignore it. We have to move the livestock. Get in."

When they slid to a stop at the corrals, Carlos had already saddled three horses. "Where are the other horses?" Cole asked.

"Travis took the ATV to go turn them loose. They were too close," pointing toward the smoke.

"Good. They'll fend for themselves. We have to get the herd through that gate on the east. They'll be safe there. If not, we're all screwed, anyway."

They swung into their saddles and pushed the horses to a lope, looking for a hundred cows and their calves. They were soon enveloped in a thin smoke, more like mist than carbon and ash. It lingered in the branches of the live oaks and settled in the low spots of the pasture.

As they cleared the first hill moving northeast, Cole pulled up, unsure, momentarily confused by the sight of pickup trucks and horse trailers, men on foot with shovels, riders on horseback, a flatbed offloading a bulldozer. Some he knew and some he did not. No one had called them. They had seen the smoke and they came. Neighbors.

A young man on horseback approached. Cole had never laid eyes upon him. He was about twenty. He wore a Lucero ball cap, a dirty tee shirt over jeans, and black-laced boots. Dressed more for a punk bar than a horse, he reined up and spit a line of tobacco, then smiled. "Hey, hope we did the right thing but we pushed them cows through that gate over there. They was happy to go."

"You did the right thing. We were coming to do just that. Thank you."

"Sure."

Just then a county helicopter hovered low a hundred yards to the south. Cole, Sam, and Carlos gathered their horses and rode toward the dust cloud.

A loudspeaker from the copter buzzed. "Move away from the fire. This is Santa Barbara Fire. You are not safe."

As they approached they saw the dozer that had been unloaded by a neighbor earlier. Its driver was pushing burning debris back from a wellhead and generator. The fire was closing.

The tractor operator answered the warning with a hand gesture sent skyward suggesting an indisposition to comply.

"The propane tank for that generator is in there," Cole yelled over the thump of the copter's blades. He rode into the dust plume toward the tractor. "Get out of there! Let it go!"

But it was too late. A second later the tank exploded in a flash of yellow and orange. Hot metal shrapnel shredded the brush nearby instantly igniting a dozen smaller fires.

In the end, it was not the fire department's ground crews, or even the neighbors, that put the fire out. It was air power. Two Grumman S-2T twin engine tankers had dropped retardant from on high and two water transport helicopters had repeatedly pulled water from a neighbor's reservoir to douse the flames into submission. The ground crews had held the line. Air power extinguished the threat.

Four hundred acres burned. Trees and grass, but not a single structure. No livestock lost. Cole owed that to the neighbors, working men and women, who just showed up. Farmers and heavy equipment operators; blacksmiths and cowboys. Men and women some would dismiss as "deplorables."

Cole was pondering that irony as he walked into Santa Barbara's cottage hospital and found his way to room B–1103. Unbeknownst to Cole, Hammer had joined a shovel crew trying to clear brush near the propane tank when it exploded. He had been lucky. The explosion blew him into the air but away from the flames. His burns were mostly superficial.

As Cole entered, a young man stood to the side of Hammer's bed, his hand in Hammer's. He turned abruptly as Cole entered.

"Oh, I'm sorry. I was just leaving."

"Didn't know you were coming," muttered Hammer, embarrassed.

"I didn't think I needed an appointment," Cole replied. "You're still on the clock."

There was an awkward silence, until Hammer spoke. "Well, now you know why I didn't bring a date to our little celebration the other night."

"That was a dumb thing you did, trying to save the generator," Cole said.

"Yeah, well I do a lot of dumb things. That ain't the dumbest."

"It was also gutsy and I appreciate it. "

"Then give me a raise. Talk's cheap."

Cole smiled. "Not a chance. But Sam needs a few hours at Manny's on Fridays if you want extra work. Maybe she'll give you a raise. She's a better boss."

"And better looking."

"What would you know?" Cole asked.

Hammer smiled, the ice broken.

Cole returned to the ranch by way of the post office in Los Olivos. His PO box was stuffed to the brim, mail cascading to the stone floor as his key popped open the lock. A clerk peered through the rectangular tunnel from the other side. "Hey, you need to empty this thing once in a while, Cole. Can't hardly stuff the new stuff in."

"Okay, sorry, Lex. Been busy. You can trash anything you don't have room for. I'd probably be better off." Cole bundled the paper and exited the small post office.

Back in his truck, he flipped through the enve-lopes—mostly bills and junk mail—until he saw it. A crisp white envelope with a law firm's name and return address. Jessica's lawyers. He tore it open and unfolded the letter.

Dear Mr. Clay:

As you know, the Superior Court of the county of Los Angeles has granted the uncontested petition of my client Jessica Clay for dissolution of your marriage. A copy of the court's final order is included for your records.

Pursuant to the Marital Settlement Agreement, upon entry of a final decree of divorce, my client undertook to remit to you one half of the proceeds secured from the sale of the home you jointly owned and occupied as a married couple in Santa Barbara prior to the dissolution of your marriage. A copy of the final escrow statement pertaining to the sale of this property is also attached.

One half of the proceeds from this transaction has been wired to your banking account as provided in the Marital Separation Agreement. Please contact our office at your earliest convenience to confirm receipt. It is our understanding that division of this last cash asset affects final and complete execution of my client's obligations under the MSA.

Yours,

Hemsworth Davidson, Esq.

Cole had no idea the sale of the house would bring the amount it had. He should have been elated, the divorce complete, the assets divided, more than he expected. But he wasn't. He had come to understand that his relationship with Jessica was fatally flawed, probably from the jump. But he couldn't shake the feeling that he had failed—Jessica, Dustin, and himself.

He resolved to chase the silver lining. He picked up his cell and called Jack Callson. After a brief conversation, he punched in a second number.

"We need to talk. Where are you? Okay, I will be there in ten."

Cole pulled into the gravel parking area outside the Zaca Winery and walked in. He knew at once his timing was bad. Indigo was mid-sentence, extolling the virtues of "his" new winery and describing his plans for expansion in the Santa Ynez Valley. The twenty-something journalist from *Wine Enthusiast Magazine* was sopping it up faster than dry pasture in a summer rain.

"We are very pleased with our first vintage, that Grenache Blanc you're enjoying, but it's just the start, little darlin'."

Seeing Cole, the little darlin' stood, ready to wrap it up. She extended a bird-like hand.

"Nice to meet you. Are you an investor?" she said.

Cole touched the brim of his hat. "Yes ma'am. I guess you could say that."

As she left, Cole put his hat on the table between Indigo and himself and sat. He got to the point. "I'm going to exercise the call when it matures. I thought it only fair to tell you now so you can make your plans. You'll get a letter from Jack tomorrow."

There was a long silence, the fuse running its course. Then it hit powder.

"YOU'RE SHITTIN' ME, RIGHT?" Indigo barked.

When he realized Cole was serious, he lost it.

"You have got to be fucking kidding! You can't do that! We put up exactly one vintage, after all this work? Do you know who you're dealing with here, cowboy?" He pointed a stubby index finger in Cole's face to underline his point.

"You can sue, Indigo. But the deal is pretty clear. One year in, there's a put/call. I'm going to exercise it. I will repay the loan in full, with interest. I will refund the option money you just paid on the vineyard even though I'm not legally required to do so."

"You can't exercise a call that has not matured, that's bullshit."

"Jack doesn't think so. We are giving you notice now of our intent to exercise the call when it matures in a couple of months. You can sue, of course. But know this, you haven't fully covered the costs of production, so you've breached your end of the deal. And I also have a right to stock that tasting room with anything I want as long as you have the front display cases. It could be a very unproductive arrangement."

Cole stood. "For what's it's worth, I don't like how you treat your employees, or mine, but that's all in the noise. The fact is, we agreed if either of us disliked the marriage, either could bail."

Indigo was still fuming. "Wait, you said you didn't have the money to exercise the call. You lied! That's fraud, buddy."

"I didn't have a dime at the time, Indigo. I had debt. But this partnership hasn't worked out and now I have the money to repay what I owe you. It's as simple as that."

"And where'd you get this money all of the sudden?"

Cole put on his hat and shook his head. He thought about the irony, knowing he would give anything not to have the money, to reverse all of those moments that had brought him to this place.

"I guess that's none of your damn business."

16

---◇---

The following Sunday, Cole and Sam saddled up for something Cole had long promised—a trail ride with no purpose or point, no work or mission.

Cole hated "trail rides." Sitting on a horse in a dead walk was not fun and certainly did not qualify as exercise. Maybe for the horse. Still, Sam loved it, all the more because there was no point other than absorbing the beauty of the ranch and, for once, doing nothing. Maybe even talking.

They reached the high point on the ranch and stopped to take in a wide view of the entire Santa Ynez Valley. Cole pointed east to a vista dominated by vineyards and white canopied pot farms.

"Looks like you guys are winning."

"You guys? You're one of us now."

"Hell I am. I'm not doing any vineyard. This Valley is awash in grapes. I'm not devoting an inch of pasture to it."

"Well, Indigo sure will. He has an option on a big piece of your best pasture."

"He did."

"What do you mean he 'did'?"

Cole didn't answer. He pushed Slick down the slope

and into the draw leading back to the barn. Sam followed
in silence, waiting for an answer. Cole abruptly pulled up
in the shade of a giant live oak standing in the center of a
broad pasture. Cole dismounted in the mottled light that
filtered through its canopy.

Sam followed suit, confused.

"That's what I wanted to talk about. He's out."

"What?"

"I told him I'm exercising the call. The winery is
ours."

"How? I mean, that was a lot of money," Sam said,
incredulous.

"My divorce is final. I got some money in the settlement from the house."

"Holy shit."

"I thought you didn't curse?"

"There are exceptional circumstances that justify an
occasional swear word." Sam caught her breath. "Yours,"
she said.

"What?"

"You said the winery is ours. It's yours. I just work
there sometimes."

Cole took her reins with his and tied both on a low
branch. He turned to face Sam.

"I still don't know a thing about making wine. I was
hoping you'd run it. You can make yours and resell local
vintages. So it's ours if you'll have it."

Then Cole took Sam's hand. "I love you. You know
that. I always have."

Cole laughed out loud, his joy spilling over in truth
finally spoken. "I'm not even sure where I end and you
begin. I know that's not politically correct but I also

know that you and I are connected, bound to play this out, whatever happens, together."

Cole stepped back and looked out at the rolling hills and pasture that surrounded the single oak under which they stood. "I have no idea if we can save this ranch. For Dustin, for our children if we are lucky enough to have them. But I can't imagine trying with anyone but you."

He took her hand again. "What do you say? Samantha Pastore, will you marry me?"

"Oh, my God…wait…is this too fast? Your divorce…"

"Yes, it's too fast. And long overdue."

With that, Sam burst into tears as she threw her arms around him and held him tight.

The next day, Cole found himself in the antechamber to Father Donal's office at the mission reflecting on the last forty-eight hours. In an instant, it seemed, the trajectory of his life had changed. Or had it? Was he now not on the path always intended? Predetermined. He thought back about his conversation with Marisa. Did he have a choice in his life's course? It didn't matter. He was as happy as he could recall, possessed of an abiding sense of calm, a firm confidence that the disparate bits of some digital map that defined his life had aligned, the image they formed now clear. That image carried no promise of prevailing in the battles he and Sam would fight; only a sense that he would engage those struggles properly, in an alignment that was strong, to purposes that were right. The end result did not matter. In that belief, he found comfort.

Father Donal entered with his usual flourish, the weight of his presence belying his diminutive stature.

"You've done it! Well done, my boy. A fine girl. More than you deserve!"

"No doubt."

"And now we've but to plan the ceremony! A full mass, I assume. Samantha will insist."

"Indeed."

"Then you'll need to be in a state of grace of course. First we must deal with the matter of your marriage to… Jessica?"

"Yes, Jessica."

"Tell me. You were not married in the Catholic Church as I recall."

"Correct. It was a civil ceremony."

"And was Jessica ever baptized? I know you were. I performed the joyous rite myself."

"Not to my knowledge."

"Good," came Donal's reply.

"Good?"

"A sacramental marriage cannot be set aside; our church does not recognize divorce. A sacramental marriage takes place between two baptized Christians, even if in the wrong church so to speak. If yours was a sacramental marriage, it would have to be annulled. If not, your marriage to Samantha would be adulterous."

"I have a child. I won't make him a bastard. The marriage happened. It was real."

"I understand your reservations. Let me think…. As Jessica was never baptized and your ceremony was civil, it seems yours was a natural marriage but not a sacramental marriage. You may be eligible for a Pauline or Petrine privilege, which is technically not an annulment."

"Father, with respect, this is the problem with the Catholic Church. A lot of form over substance. Trust me, I was married."

"Let me deal with that. Now, when was your last confession?"

"You'd know as well as I. You took it."

Father Donal was dumbstruck. "But you were about twelve, as I recall."

"Exactly."

"This is quite serious, my son. We best get started."

And so they did. Cole held back nothing. He willingly cataloged the transgressions. There was drunkenness and gambling, profanity and fornication; there was jealously and pride; he had taken the Lord's name in vain; he had failed his family and been selfish; he had not been a perfect father, far from it. And for all these sins he was truly contrite, save one, one he willingly confessed: He could not forgive Jessica for what she had done. He held that judgement like a cold hard stone in a clenched fist, a fist he could not release, and it was upon these shoals that his confession, and absolution, seemed to crash.

"You are not God. It is his place to judge, it is our place to love, to forgive, not the sin, but the sinner, the sinner whose mortal being is no better, no worse, than yours."

"And are we to forgive that for which the sinner is in no way contrite? Can that sin be forgiven?"

Donal hesitated. "You'll get different answers to that question among the clergy. I can only tell you what I believe. It is for God to make that call. He may well not forgive sins for which there is inadequate contrition. But it is not your place to judge—at least that is what I believe."

"And you base that on what?"

"Jesus. Moments before his earthly death, he forgave the very Roman soldiers who crucified him. I can assure you, they were not contrite. Yet he called upon the Father

to forgive them saying they know not what they do. It is
the same with the sin of which you speak. Was she a victim of our culture or a knowing actor in the sin? Probably
both. But it is not for you to judge, Cole."

"Well, Father, I'm not Jesus. I'm not sure I can meet
that standard."

"Try. Pray for the unborn child whose soul rests with
the Father at this very moment, in far less torment than
you, my son. Pray for Jessica."

Cole stood. "I can try."

Donal stood, too. "I'll be back with the acts of contrition the Lord will require of you. You'll be lucky to
complete them before the wedding."

The next few months were the best Cole had ever
known. The Zaca tasting room proved popular with the
locals and continued to attract some tourists even in the
off season. The crowd Cole used to resent he now saw in
a different light, a green light—one that suggested he
might push Zaca into the black. Sam was in her element.
She loved wine and talking about it, the endless vari-
ations from her beloved Central Coast. Somehow her
riffs on a pinot's "fruitful bouquet" were substantially
less irritating than Indigo's on the same subject. Mostly
Sam loved people and managed to find something good
in everyone she encountered. Cole's inbred skepticism
found no safe harbor in Sam's psyche.

Sam was true to her word regarding their relationship. While Cole was divorced and dutifully moving
toward the "state of grace" that would allow his reentry
into the church, he had not yet placed a ring on her finger. She occupied every corner of his heart, but not his
bed. He tried, just once, to dismiss their abstinence as

a matter of form over substance. Her answer was simple but clear. "These formalities," she said, "they come from centuries of human experience, right? Treating one another with respect; honoring a vow; saying please and thank you; wearing a tie. They must mean something. At a minimum, they distinguish us from the lesser beasts." And more, Cole thought. He knew that these "formalities" and the abstractions that attend them—ideas like "duty" and "honor," often seemingly irrational in a specific context, formed the guardrails within which a people over time defined their character and their culture.

He had to concede her point.

And so, he waited. And he loved her more, it would seem, every day. He had heard his mother say that every relationship, certainly every marriage, requires work; a constant will to communicate, to compromise. Certainly it had been true of his relationship with Jessica. But it was not true of his relationship with Sam. It was easy. It was comfortable, even fun. He had never laughed as hard, or as often, as he had since he and Sam had recommitted themselves to their relationship, to living out their ends together whatever the future held.

In the months leading up to their wedding, Cole poured himself into the task of turning the ranch's economics around. The new cattle operations had improved the ranch's prospects. The high-end heifers he had purchased had been "preg-checked" and ninety-five percent were positive. General Mattis, their prize bull, had done his job. As the price of beef "on the hoof" fell, Cole was happy to have shifted their strategy to the sale of replacement heifers and young bulls with excellent DNA. Cole hoped to double net profits within two years.

The rough stock business still struggled. Rodeos paid little to rent a bucker for the night, and transport costs were increasing with the price of fuel. The controversy surrounding the death of Wade Roy on Ragged Edge had doomed her chances of going to The Show in Vegas and, hence, her value as breeding stock. Cole had resolved to shut down the rough stock business. His work would be redirected to cattle operations and an inventory that now required greater care. They might also try to buy some green-broke two-year-olds and finish them for resale to the growing number of "civilians" in the Valley who wanted a good ranch horse.

All considered, things were looking up.

And then Jack called.

"Cole, you have a minute to come by the office? We are about ready to close probate on Elliot's estate. There are some things we need to discuss."

"What's up?"

"Let's talk."

It took Cole fifteen minutes to exit the ranch and wind his way to Jack's office. The traffic slowed on Highway 246 in downtown Solvang. It was clogged with tourists buying wooden shoes they would wear once before using them as planters. But the pastry at Olsen's was indisputably the best available. Forget the patisseries of Paris. The manifest superiority of an apricot Danish from Olsen's could not be disputed.

Cole pulled over and walked inside. The girl behind the counter smiled as if she knew him. She was all of seventeen and sported the white lace dress and red gingham apron intended to bring to mind all things Danish. Cole resisted the temptation to check for clogs.

"Hey. Eh…" he opened.

She was still smiling.

"I wanted an apricot Danish. I don't see them."

"I'm sorry. We had a run on apricot."

"Really? I can't imagine. What explains a thing like that?"

"Chinese."

"Chinese?"

"Yes, sir. They love apricot Danish."

"You don't say? Actually, come to think of it, you shouldn't say that. That's a racial generalization. I'm shocked to hear you say that actually…" looking at her name tag…"Hilvig."

"Generalizations are only bad when they're negative. If they are true and fall anywhere between good to neutral, they're okay. I mean, if I were to say cowboys generally eat cheese Danish because they are constitutionally indisposed to eat healthy and, hence, avoid fruit Danish, that might border on negative. I would never say that."

"I would hope not."

"You're not a cowboy, are you?"

"Why would you say that? Are you stereotyping again, Hilvig?"

"Most of the guys who come in with Cinch jeans, a Carhartt jacket and Roper boots are cowboys. And there's the hat. Wild guess."

So far, she owned him. He looked into the case of Danish and spoke as he pondered his choices. "Is your name really Hilvig or is that like an Olsen's stage name? I mean your mom gives birth and says, 'Oh, Sven, it's little H I L V I G!' You really expect your customers to believe that?" He looked up and smiled knowing he had reclaimed the upper hand in their impromptu contest of wits.

"What's your name?" she asked.

"Cole Clay."

"Aha!"

She had him. "My given name was Colter Wyatt Clay but even I thought that was too cowboy," Cole said, all but conceding.

"Okay, cowboy, much as I would like to chat about stereotypes all day, my manager, Johan, is in a bad mood. His clogs gave him blisters. How about that cheese Danish?"

"Nah, I feel like something fruity today. Something a little lighter. Healthy. I've been eating too much jerky out on the trail."

"Okay, then." Hilvig spun around and wrapped a Danish, then turned and handed it to Cole.

"What is it?"

"Prune"

"Prune? That's not light," he protested.

She smiled as she moved toward the next customer. "No, but it's very healthy—helps with all that jerky."

Cole arrived at Jack's office with a smile on his face.

"So what's up? We need to close this out. I have a wedding to plan."

"So I understand. Congratulations. But don't be spending your inheritance on a big party. As I said, there are a few things we need to discuss."

He had his attention.

"What's up, Jack? Spill it. I pay you by the hour as I recall. Let's not spend fifteen minutes on the prelims."

"You're a cheap bastard like your ol' man." Jack

gathered himself. "There's a problem. The trust dissolves on your thirtieth birthday. You are not yet thirty."

"Almost, and my mother always said I was an old soul."

"Like me," Jack interjected.

"No, you're just old." Cole made the "get on with it" hand gesture.

"The trust provides for an interim trustee in the event of a lapse between you and Elliot. However, it also provides that the interim trustee can abolish the trust, hand the reins to you, if he finds that, in the exercise of his fiduciary responsibilities, that serves the interests of the beneficiaries, you and Travis."

"So it obviously would. I'll talk to our banker, C.J. He's been our financial adviser forever. He'll have no problem with this."

"It's not C.J. Your banker can't be the trustee of assets he manages. That creates a conflict. It's someone in their trust department."

Jack looked at his desk and retrieved a card. He handed it to Cole.

"Richard Thomas David III."

"Who the hell is that?"

"The interim trustee manager of the ranch."

"Oh, bullshit. What does some big city banker know about a cow-calf operation in Santa Ynez?"

"Nothing. Actually, I spoke to him. Less than nothing."

"So it's in the best interests of all parties, especially the beneficiaries and their progeny, like Dustin and all the children Travis has yet to acknowledge, that the trust be dissolved."

"Calm down. There's more."

Jack pulled a pile of documents from the left corner of his too-large-by-half desk and took one off the top.

"He won't do it. He is concerned about mismanagement, specifically, the ranch's debt. He's afraid you are part of the problem."

"What are we talking about?"

"Your father was in debt up to his ass."

"I know that. It led to a boatload of trouble but it's behind us. Tommy and his buddy Yellow Sky fronted a scheme to recoup the casino debt by betting on rodeo under the table. Unfortunately, Elliot was involved. That led to the incident at Manny's."

"Yeah, I know. Elliot told me," explained Jack.

"But how would our bank know about a gambling debt?" Cole asked.

"To my knowledge, they don't. That debt was forgiven—what remained, anyway," Jack explained.

Cole took a double take. "Wait. What do you mean? How do you know?"

"I called the casino."

"Why? When?"

"Right after you spilled the beans on drugging that horse to the PRCA overlords. Your father got a subpoena; they wanted to take his deposition on the whole deal under oath," explained Jack.

"I know. We all got one."

"Elliot came to me right away, asked me to represent him and Travis. Told me the whole story. They were in deep shit. Getting sanctioned by the Rodeo Association was a given. The exposure was criminal. I figured the DA would need the cooperation of the casino, the source of the debt. I figured the casino would want to distance themselves from the whole mess, Wade Roy getting killed and all. I tried to call Vallin Ross first since he was their outside counsel of record."

"And?"

"He never returned my call. So I called the casino directly, their general counsel. Guy named Dan Motts. Just as I suspected, they didn't want any part of the mess."

"I'm sure, but they held the debt and employed the two assholes who fronted the scheme," interjected Cole.

"Well, that's just the thing. Motts told me that Elliot had paid off most of the debt months ago. They had decided to forgive the rest, about a hundred thousand. Wasn't worth the trouble. But it was more than that. This Yellow Sky. Apparently, he was your father's drinking buddy for a while. Got him into the high roller's game. That's how Elliot got so far down. About half a million. Yellow Sky had no authority to do that. Elliot should have had nowhere near that level of credit."

"So why didn't Yellow Sky get his ass canned?"

"You know why."

Cole paused. "I know what you're implying, but I knew him in high school. His name was Alavara at the time."

"Yeah, but his mother is Native. And on the council to this day."

"Did the casino ever tell Elliot they weren't pressing for the rest?"

"Not to my knowledge. They had written it off but sure weren't going to object if he sent them a check out of some sense of moral obligation."

"Did Elliot ever know any of this?"

"Of course. In the next day or two, once I knew."

Cole thought about it. Five days had elapsed between Cole's confession to the PRCA, which triggered Jack's investigation and the shootout at Manny's. That meant Elliot knew everything when he walked into that bar.

Cole felt sick.

"Did the casino's outside counsel, Ross, know the debt had been forgiven?" he asked.

"As I say, he never returned my call. I don't know."

"Tommy or Yellow Sky?"

"No idea."

Cole thought about everything he had just learned. One piece didn't fit.

"Wait. You started this meeting by saying the ranch was in debt. But you just explained there was, in effect, no remaining casino debt."

"Yeah. That was what I called you about. Jack reached for another set of papers resting beneath a miniature Charles Russell bronze. "The ranch is encumbered, about a million bucks. That's what Richard David found. He ran the title on the ranch and found a mortgage. There's a deed of trust."

"Held by whom? For what?"

"One of those reverse mortgage outfits—you borrow against equity in real estate. Appears Elliot never made a payment on it. They've started the foreclosure process, Cole."

"How would I not know that?" Cole asked.

Jack leaned back in his leather chair. "I wouldn't have known any of this. Elliot wasn't exactly forthcoming. But as executor I can order up bank records and whatnot. I saw a piece of correspondence. Had a PO box. Name of 'C. Cody.' I ran it down, right there in Los Olivos. It was stuffed with mail. Mostly past-due notices, then the foreclosure letter. You ever hear of a C. Cody?"

"Yeah. That box is about three down from mine at the post office. I should have known. His first horse: Coffee Cody. Where in hell is the money he borrowed?"

"I'm trying to piece that together. The best I can tell, the ranch owed Merchant Bank about $225,000 on a line a credit Elliot used to dig your new well and irrigation system. They were pressing him. He paid that off. He also paid back taxes of $130,000 to the county."

"And the casino?"

"He paid the casino about $400,000 dollars."

"Where's the rest of it? Two twenty-five to the bank, $130,000 to the county and $400,000 to the casino. That leaves about $245,000."

"I don't know. I asked Elliot flat out. He wouldn't say. My guess?"

"Yeah, why not?"

"I think he bet a chunk of it on the rodeo deal he was trying to fix. He knew he was a million down to this bank in New York and he was missing payments. It also balloons in five years. There's about $37,000 in an equity account at Royal Bank of Canada. That's all I could find."

Jack continued: "The bottom line is the bank won't hand the reins to you until this debt is cleaned up. You owe this outfit in New York a million dollars and it's in default. They could foreclose."

"Who is it?" Cole asked.

Jack pulled a card from his desk and handed it to Cole.

"Firston Capital Partners," a New York conglomerate. Reverse mortgages are just one of their deals. They're in cannabis, too," Jack added.

"Perfect. You have a name?"

Jack retrieved a letter from a file labeled Firston Capital. "Moss Becker."

Cole stood.

"I can try to help get you some time but you're going to have to make some big back payments to hold off these New Yorkers. You have any other assets you can borrow against?" Jack asked.

Cole shook his head. "The cash flow on the ranch is growing but we barely cover operating costs right now. Surprised Elliot got them to loan that much."

"I don't think they're too particular when they can tie into real estate worth millions." Jack paused to think. "Any other assets? Life insurance?"

"Yeah. Five million. Another gift from Jessica's family. I think they were pretty neutral on which way that would play out."

"Great. Any equity in it?"

"Nope. It's term. They paid the monthly while we were married. I pay it now. But no, no equity. Nothing there to lever."

"I'm sorry, Cole. It's a shit situation, the debt he piled up."

Cole put on his hat and stepped toward the door. "That isn't the half of it, Jack. Elliot is dead and Tommy's looking for blood."

Cole had plenty of time to piece it together on his ride back to the ranch. He found Travis in the barn stacking a new load of alfalfa.

"We need to talk, Travis, about the debt that started this whole cluster fuck."

Travis kept working. "We've talked. What's there to say?"

"How'd it start? The debt, tell me again."

Travis threw his gloves down and picked up a beer. The barn was cluttered with empties.

"Elliot didn't explain much. Best I can figure, they suckered him in, offered credit. He got in over his head with some high rollers."

"Who offered him credit?" Cole pressed.

"Yellow Sky."

"Then?" Cole pressed.

"Then nothing. That's the last I knew until the shit went down in Salinas. So what's the rest of it?"

"Elliot took out a loan. Some bank in New York. Retired most of the casino debt. But this bank loan has escalating interest payments. I think his motivation to hatch the scheme with Tommy was driven more by that than the casino debt. In fact, there was no casino debt."

"What?"

"Casino had forgiven it. Not worth the trouble or the bad press. And Yellow Sky was involved. He's got protection."

"Did Tommy know the debt was forgiven?"

"I don't know. But I'm sure he was only too happy to let Elliot believe he was still in hock. He was skimming the deal, making some money himself."

"Holy shit. Elliot ever know he got scammed?"

"Yeah. Jack told him. Few days before he walked into Manny's hell bent to shoot someone."

Travis thought about it. "Hence the 'lyin' sack of shit' opener and the reference to a bank."

"Do you have any idea how Elliot got hooked up with this New York bank?"

"No. But I know Elliot was talking to a lawyer for a while. Some guy named Vallin Ross. Made sense at the time."

"Why?"

"He's the casino's lawyer. Tommy introduced him."

PART THREE

"They grow richer and richer, the more they think of fortune, the less they think of virtue; for when riches and virtue are placed on the scales of the balance, one always rises as the other falls. And as riches and rich men are honored in the State, so virtue and the virtuous are dishonored."

—PLATO, *THE REPUBLIC*

17

---◇---

S ometimes the best follows the worse, and so it was for Cole. He married the only woman he had ever loved without reservation the next day. Aristotle's conception of love—one soul inhabiting two bodies—was entirely out of step with the times, yet exactly how Cole felt. The wedding for Cole was a public acknowledgement.

They were married under the tree where Cole had proposed. It was a small wedding attended by family and close friends, people who knew Sam and Cole and the history. There were no groomsmen and no bridesmaids. Cole and Sam stood alone, under the tree, in front of God. Father Donal did the honors. When he called for the ring, it was delivered by Dustin who handed the ring to Sam, not Cole, to the amusement of all. Cole had his son near his side as he slipped the ring on Sam's finger. And it was done.

They say there can only be one first time, but you will never convince Cole and Sam. When they finally came together that night, the long intersecting lines of their lives were finally conjoined in a burst of joy that transcended the physical, that felt wholly new and complete, as if for the first time they were home.

Cole and Sam decided to go East for their honeymoon. Neither had been to Washington, DC. Cole, born and raised in the West, was anxious to immerse himself in the East, to gauge and assess its differences, to experience the environment within which Prescott had made the family's fortune and Elliot had learned the first lessons of his troubled life. Not least, Cole planned to visit New York at the conclusion of their vacation to engage directly with Firston Capital Partners, the company holding the ranch's fate in its corporate hands. But that was later. For the next several days, he would put it out of his mind.

He took Sam's hand as their Airbus bucked and shimmied on descent through stormy weather over the nation's capital. When they banked right over the Potomac on final approach, Cole got his first glimpse of Washington. It was the grey gothic architecture of Georgetown University, a Jesuit college Cole had considered for his PhD before opting for Stanford. How different his life might have been had he come here and not chosen the familiar embrace of Palo Alto, nestled in the center of California, four hours from the ranch.

A good view of the National Mall followed, its green rectangular square capped on either side by glistening monuments—the Lincoln Memorial at one end, the Capitol Building at the other. The dome of the Capitol shone with the last light of the day.

What surprised Cole most was the water—the Potomac winding its way past Georgetown to Washington Harbor, transected by classical bridges. The Arlington Memorial Bridge stood out. Connecting Washington at the Lincoln Memorial to Virginia near the ancestral home of Robert E. Lee, the placement had been intended to symbolize the unification of North and South after the Civil War. The unity had dissolved in conflict over design details. First proposed in 1886, it was not completed till 1932. The "art of war" statues at the northeastern entrance symbolizing sacrifice and valor were not completed until 1951. As their aircraft touched down, Cole could not help but wonder if America still possessed the will to produce great monuments on the public dime, or to agree on principles to symbolize in their edifice.

Sam and Cole emerged from the Jetway with their carry-on luggage to a crowded departure lounge. They were swallowed in a sea of humans of striking similarity: aged from twenty-five to forty-five, well dressed, professional, and preoccupied by the tiny screens at which they stared and poked. Few looked up as Cole pulled Sam through the throng.

They pushed through to the exit. Sam called an Uber and a black Nissan arrived almost immediately. They climbed in.

"The Hay-Adams please. Hollis, right?" Cole said, remembering his name from the confirmation.

"That's me." He pulled into the lane exiting to the George Washington Parkway. Hollis was middle aged and slightly balding. He looked bored.

As they left the airport, Cole pointed at a bronze statue near the airport exit. The former president stood tall over block letters: "Ronald Reagan National Airport." Sam smiled. The driver noticed in the rearview mirror.

"You a fan?"

"It's just ironic. We're from Santa Barbara. We live five miles from his Rancho Cielo."

"That right? Reagan must be a hero to you Santa Barbara locals," Hollis guessed.

"Actually, he plays to mixed reviews out there," Cole said, dodging.

"What's not to like? He won the Cold War, eh?" Hollis said, driving into heavy traffic.

"He also jump-started the economy," added Cole. "So what about you? You a Reagan fan?"

The driver glanced in the rearview mirror. "Me? Long story."

"Well, Google Maps says you have nine minutes to the Hay-Adams. Let's hear it."

Hollis smiled. "Okay, well, I was what you call a 'Yellow Dog' Democrat."

"What's that?" Sam asked.

"It's a term coined in the thirties for someone who would vote for a 'yellow dog' before a Republican," answered Cole.

"Exactly. Southern Democrats mostly. I'm from Spartanburg, South Carolina, myself. Tricky thing is, lots of those Democrats in the South are conservative by nature. So Reagan comes along talking about personal liberty, getting the feds off our backs. FREEDOM!" Hollis said, imitating Mel Gibson in *Braveheart*, warming to the story. "Well that kind of talk was like throwing slop to hogs. We ate it up. Took the plunge. I voted for Reagan both times. First time I voted 'R,' my daddy spun in his grave, I'm guessin'."

Hollis laughed and shook his head. He crossed the 14th Street Bridge into downtown Washington. He pointed to his right as they passed a large office building on the corner of 14th Street and Independence.

"Hell, there he is again! He's everywhere!" Hollis said.

Cole looked up as they passed the Ronald Reagan

Building. It was a beautiful structure. But Cole was now tracking the Yellow Dog's sarcasm. "So how'd that work out for you, Hollis, voting Republican?"

"Well you know, I can't say we didn't get what he promised. Free trade, free markets, lots of personal liberties…freedom to use the ladies room if I want, watch porn all day. It's amazing."

"You can't blame Reagan for all that," Cole interjected.

"You're right. But you ask me, he won some battles and lost the war. You take free markets and free trade. You think the average worker is happier because he lives in a global economy? Because he can buy cheap Chinese crap at Walmart? Come to think of it, most my kin can't cause they lost their jobs. Jobs their fathers and grandfathers had. Why? Because those producers of cheap Chinese crap compete with us."

Cole couldn't help himself. "I guess the free trader would argue some dislocation is necessary in transitioning to an information and tech-based economy, where we have our comparative advantage."

"Ha! You sound like one of them. Say, you're not a McKinsey consultant, are you?"

"I am a rancher."

"Really?" Hollis sized Cole up in the rearview mirror. "So let me ask you this, cowboy," he went on, warming to the exchange. "If the globalists are right, if the cost of goods and services on a global basis are lower, and the products are a tad better, seeing as everyone is now doing what they do best, you think we are really better off?"

"That depends on how you define better off, on how high on the scale you place economic efficiency," Cole said, giving him the textbook answer.

"Bingo! Well, I'd rather pay a tad more for stuff and have my brother-in-law employed. Have my cousin in Cleveland kick the oxycodone. Maybe have a real community instead of Facebook cyber buddies."

Hollis was on a roll. Cole saw the Hay-Adams in the near distance. He was now curious. Hollis knew his stuff. "What'd you do in Alabama?"

"I was an executive with a furniture company. Got an MBA up here in DC but wanted to go home. So I ended up trying to make the numbers pencil on American-made tables and chairs. Well, they don't. I kept telling 'em to stop making 'em so damn good. Bastards insisted on quality! Go figure."

Cole smiled. "Retired?"

"Oh, shit, no. I *got* retired by our new global economy. We couldn't compete with Asia."

"Sorry to hear that."

"Aw, don't be crying for me. I'm heavy into Uber now. Part of the new economy!" Hollis laughed out loud as he pulled to a stop in front of the hotel.

"Been good talking to you, Hollis. Tell me, how do you describe your politics now?"

A doorman in tails and top hat opened the passenger side door, impatient.

"I call myself an independent. Supported Bernie last time but couldn't pull the lever for Hillary after she called me a deplorable. So I voted for the Orange Man twice," explained Hollis.

Cole and Sam exited the car but Cole turned back to Hollis. "Good luck, my friend."

As Cole handed their luggage to the doorman, the once and future Yellow Dog Democrat pulled out of the driveway into a sea of Ubers patrolling the hotel district of our nation's capital. Most were Nissans and Camrys.

After checking in, Cole and Sam were escorted to their room. Cole tipped the bellman and pulled the curtain back on the room's lone window. Their room overlooked Lafayette Square and, beyond it, the White House.

"Wow! That is incredible!" exclaimed Sam. She hugged Cole. "Can we afford this?"

"Absolutely not."

Cole gestured through the window again. "So what do you think?"

"It looks like the White House, only smaller," opined Sam.

Cole examined the brightly illuminated façade of Casa Blanca. "You're right. It's a wonder Trump got his really big brain through the door."

"Who says he had a really big brain?"

"He did."

Sam looked back at the White House. "More Biden-sized."

"Yeah, he seems to get smaller every day."

They fell on the king-size bed exhausted, but happy. Cole noticed the red button on the phone was blinking. A message. He ignored it as he watched Sam begin to undress.

"I'm going to take a bath before dinner." She stepped into the oversized bathroom and turned on hot water for the tub. She slipped off her clothing and stood facing Cole in the door to the bathroom. Steam from the bath behind her fell gently over her shoulders and swirled between her bare legs. Cole thought to himself she looked as much like an angel as God allows in this life.

With Sam in the bath, Cole called the front desk for this message. He wrote a name and number on the pad near the bed and made himself a drink at the mini bar. He opened a bottle of wine and poured a glass for Sam.

Sam emerged from the bathroom in a thick white terrycloth robe, her hair wet and shiny at her shoulders. "I'm exhausted. Let's crawl into bed, order room service, and watch a movie. We'll conquer Washington tomorrow."

Cole handed her the wine. "Perfect."

"What was the message?"

"One of Prescott's buddies. His roommate at Princeton. Still works here in Washington. Prescott let him know we were in town. He wants to have breakfast."

Sam was no longer paying attention. She had dropped the robe and slipped between crisp sheets. "Go take a shower, cowboy." She pulled the room service menu from the bureau. "I'll order."

The next morning Sam and Cole entered the main dining room of the Hay-Adams at the appointed hour of 8:00 a.m. The maître d' approached. He was a tad rotund, all rosy pink and white, like he'd been scrubbed too hard. A polished brass plate on his lapel read "Fabron."

"Good morning, sir, madam."

"Morning," Cole replied, not risking an attempt at Fabron.

"Do you have a reservation?"

"No, I didn't think to get one. Didn't know you needed one for breakfast."

The rotund maître d' looked down at his book, now quite concerned.

"Tell me, are you guests of the hotel?"

"Yes. Room four hundred and ten."

Fabron smiled. "Well, that helps. I will find something. Just the two of you?"

"No. We are here to meet someone. Sanford Coleman is his name. Maybe he made a reservation."

"Oh! We have no problem! Mr. Coleman needs no reservation. We hold one of our best tables for our…well, for people like Mr. Sanford," Fabron said, now visibly relieved.

He escorted them to a table for four at the window. It held a perfect view of the White House. Sam examined the sterling silver cutlery and bone china plates over the white tablecloth. Fabron gestured to a waiter and departed.

Cole smiled. "What do you think?"

"It ain't Santa Ynez."

"I'm sorry, sweetie. We'll be back soon," Cole offered.

Sam leaned forward. "Screw that. I could get used to this. Maybe you should…"

"What?"

"I don't know, get appointed Secretary of Education? Commissioner of Irrelevant Ancient Knowledge?"

Cole smiled. "What are you going to have?"

"Not sure. I was looking for a breakfast burrito," she said.

Just then a gentleman entered the dining room with an energy that pulled almost every eye to the entrance. Fabron shook his hand a tad too enthusiastically, turning, mid-shake, to point in the direction of Sam and Cole.

"Must be him. Maybe pass on that burrito," Cole commented under his breath. He plucked a small biscuit from the crystal bowl that sat at the center of their table.

"Good call. Let's go with eggs Florentine and a croissant," she said, overemphasizing the French pronunciation.

"What's that?" he deadpanned.

"You'd call it a crescent roll. You know, they come in a can that pops on the edge of the sink."

The man they suspected was Prescott's Princeton roommate reached their table. "You MUST be Cole. The learned grandson of whom I have heard so much." He shook Cole's hand and turned to Sam. "And you, Samantha, no doubt. You are so much more beautiful than I had imagined."

Cole wondered why he had been imagining Sam's beauty. Then he had a Woody Allen moment. His initial impression—"what an asshole"—floated in a bubble just over his head as he heard himself say: "You must be Sanford. So great to meet you!"

They sat. Sanford snapped the cloth napkin to attention and floated it onto his lap. "First, I must apologize for being late. Believe it or not, this is my second breakfast meeting this morning."

"Really?" Sam offered, unsure if he sought condolence or congratulation.

"Well, Washington is different, I guess. There are only so many hours in a day and much to be done. It requires personal contact. Breakfast, lunch, and drinks. Whatever it takes."

"Wow. Sounds crazy. How do you ever keep up?"

Sanford took a sip of his coffee, as if it had been a serious question. "It's hard. Just this morning, as I was saying, I had breakfast at six thirty at the Four Seasons. Senator Clobar. She needed some advice on repositioning her positions. She'd love to make another run at the presidency, but I'm afraid the moderate wing she represents is, well, let's just say out of vogue."

Sam was fascinated, her first exposure to Washington double speak. "That must be tough. How does one 'reposition' one's positions…I mean, assuming they are one's positions?"

Sanford laughed and patted Sam's hand. "Oh, dear, you are new to Washington!" he said.

Cole dove in. "I know you went to Princeton with Granddad, then law school?"

"Harvard Law," he specified.

"I know you've been in DC awhile but I'm not sure Prescott ever mentioned in what capacities."

The waiter appeared and used a silver scoop to remove a crumb from the table. Cole had apparently blown the biscuit grab.

"Many, really. I graduated from Harvard in 1970. I was recruited to work at the Justice Department, the Antitrust Division. Apparently, someone at Justice had read my law review article regarding misapplications of the Sherman Act. After the unfortunate business with the president—"

"You mean Watergate?" Cole asked.

"Yes. Anyway, after the president resigned, I stayed on with Ford. There was so much dislocation, they really couldn't afford to lose me. You might say I knew where the bodies were buried and how to keep them there."

"And then, when Ford lost to Carter? Did you stay on?"

"Oh, heavens, no. There was no way I could work for that peanut farmer. Those were dark years in DC. Those Georgians just didn't get it."

"What?" Sam asked.

Sanford paused for emphasis. He sipped his coffee. "Washington. Its culture. Carter thought a dinner party at Katherine Graham's was a burden, a distraction! Ha! Why parties like that…and others, the Kennedy Center Honors, the Alfalfa Club dinner…. They ARE the business of Washington! Where the elite of this city mingle, where we can put aside petty policy differences and get things done. It's the process. It's how the nation's business is conducted."

Cole paused. If he had to endure breakfast, why not some fun? "Wouldn't the populists say that's the problem: too much mingling of elites indisposed to fight for their policy differences? Favoring, instead, a process that produces similar policies across Republican and Democratic administrations alike?"

Sanford looked up at Cole, not used to interruptions. His eyes narrowed, which, at his age, meant they disappeared. But only for a second. He was apparently attempting to ascertain whether Cole was serious.

"Who knows what they think! Or if they do. All I know is they're lucky we so called 'elites' do the work to take care of their interests and the nation's."

Sam wanted to lighten things up. "You mentioned an Alfalfa Club. I'm curious. We have an Alfalfa and Hay Alliance out West. It lobbies for policies that allow farmers to profitably grow these crops. I wonder if they are similar."

"Oh, dear me. No, the Alfalfa Club is probably the most prestigious club in Washington and I can assure you it, has nothing to do with ag issues," Sanford said.

"Oh, my mistake. Why is it called the Alfalfa Club?"

"It's an inside joke. The alfalfa plant, as you doubtless know, consumes more water than any other. Our club is a drinking club. Get it?"

"No, not really."

Cole explained. "Alfalfa consumes a lot of liquid; these guys drink a lot."

Sam shook her head. "Oh. Yeah. How clever. So what do you Alfalfans do, I mean, besides drink?"

"Well, we have a dinner once a year. It is attended by members and their guests, principals only…"

"Meaning?" Sam asked.

"You can't just bring your wife unless, you know, she is somebody," Sanford explained.

"Oh. Well, presumably she is *somebody* in the sense that just about everyone is," Sam baited.

Cole threw Sanford a rope. "So who does attend? Give us the lineup."

"The titans of business and politics: Rupert Murdoch, Warren Buffet, Jeff Bezos, former senators and former presidents. I am proud to say I expect to receive my medallion this year, I will be a 'sprout' come February."

"A sprout?"

"Yes, an inductee."

"And the medallion?" Sam asked.

Sanford beamed. "Every Alfalfan wears a beautiful medallion suspended around the neck by a red, white, and blue ribbon."

"So tell me, with all those powerful and wealthy members, I would think that group could do a lot of good. Charities, bipartisan policy recommendations?"

"Do?" Sanford was confused.

"Yeah, besides drink and sport those medals?"

Sanford hesitated. "Alfalfa is primarily a social club. The annual dinner is our only event. It allows for networking at a very high level. I am not sure you can fully appreciate how important that is."

Cole braced. Sam was okay with chauvinism. She grew up with cowboys. But she wasn't so good with condescension.

"Well, I'm sure I can't," Sam said. "It's just that, from what you've said, it seems like Alfalfa is a sort of self-congratulatory social club for older white guys. Isn't that what golf is for?"

Sanford keyed on the "white guys," missing the wider indictment.

"I will have you know we have several Black members."

"Really? I stand corrected then," Sam concluded smiling broadly.

Cole couldn't stand watching Sanford twist at the end of his medallion anymore. He pushed back to the timeline. "So during the peanut years, what did you do?"

"Oh, yes, well I joined a firm—Gibson Dale and Koosher—running their DC office.

"Of course."

Breakfast arrived, which came as a surprise since no one had ordered.

"Oh, forgive me. I have my usual and I thought you might enjoy it. If not, order away, of course!" Sanford explained.

Cole examined the egg-white omelet and baked tomato. It came with a side of gluten-free bread. "No, this looks great. Sam, you okay?"

"Absolutely" she lied, knowing that any new order would prolong breakfast.

"And during the Reagan-Bush years?" Cole asked.

"I transitioned to lobbying. The National Association of Broadcasters."

"What did you know about broadcasting?"

Sanford literally waved the question aside. "Nothing! But I knew a lot of congressmen." He laughed as if the answer had been obvious.

"So that was it for government service?"

"Oh, no. I worked for Obama. A presidential appointment in fact, Deputy Director of the National Telecommunications and Information Agency. NTIA."

"Really? I thought you were a Republican?"

"I am."

"Didn't that present some ideological conflicts?"

Sanford buttered a piece of gluten-free bread. "No. That is why we have elections. They have consequences. Policy changes. A professional adapts."

"Wow. That's so..." Cole struggled to find the word. The word that occurred, 'gutless,' wouldn't do...."Flexible."

Cole took a bite of his baked tomato. He was reconsidering the breakfast burrito idea.

Sanford turned to Sam. "Enough about me. Tell me about you, young lady."

"Oh, there's not much to tell, really. I'm in the wine business back home. We also run a small bar—"

"I love wine!" Sanford interrupted. "French whites are my favorite. In the United States 'Chablis' is a pejorative; hell, I'd take a good Montrachet over the best California chardonnay any day of the week. Twice on Friday."

Sanford abruptly reached into his pocket and retrieved a pulsating iPhone. He covered the phone and whispered at Cole: "I'm sorry. I have to take this, it's Steny." He stood and left the table, the phone glued to his left ear.

Cole looked at Sam, a moment to themselves. They both smiled.

"So you'd rather be eating at the Longhorn and talking beef prices?" Sam asked.

"Absolutely."

Sanford returned. "I so apologize. Steny wants to talk." He turned to explain things to Sam. "Steny Hoyer is house majority leader."

"Of course, Maryland's fifth district. Elected in 1981 during your Republican phase," Sam said.

Sanford was surprised, but let it pass, not wanting to turn the attention away from his meeting. "Exactly. But it has been so delightful to get to know you. Hopefully our paths will cross again. And give Preston my fondest regards."

"We sure will. 'Preston' will be happy we met."

Sanford was off, swooping through the double-glass doors of the dining room and into his black, chauffeured SUV.

Cole turned to Sam and smiled. "Impressive guy."

"Yes, and flexible," she said. "Are you sure he was Prescott's roommate at Princeton? Apparently, he roomed with some guy named Preston."

"Details…. At least now we can put a face on it," Cole said.

"What?"

"The deep state."

Sam shook her head. "The not-so-deep state, I'd say."

Cole dabbed the remains of his tomato with the last biscuit. "Got me there, young lady."

Fabron arrived with the check. "Shall we put this on the room?"

"Sure," Cole said, a little surprised he was getting stuck with the bill.

"Great. Just sign your name. We do hope you enjoyed your breakfast," Fabron added, making his retreat.

Cole glanced at the bill. "Wow. Turns out it costs money to extract the yolks and the gluten…and the flavor."

Sam stood, ready to go. "Stop complaining. This is Washington. A professional adapts."

The afternoon was spent touring the National Mall. They started in the east with the Capitol Building and worked their way west. The National Air and Space Museum, the National Gallery, and the Natural History Museum. Cole insisted they dwell, a full two hours, when they reached the National Archives.

"There it is." Cole pointed at one of the original hand-penned copies of the Magna Carta.

"What?"

"The original source. First inklings of this idea of individual liberty, innate rights. Everything else—Locke, Hume, Jefferson—all derivative."

Sam leaned in to see the date. 1215. "Pretty prescient of ol' King John."

"Not really. He signed it to avoid a revolt of his nobles, to keep his head. We've been trying to perfect the deal he cut ever since."

They ate lunch on the run—bratwurst served up hot by an acerbic proprietor with a heavy Russian accent. Cole and Sam sat on a bench near his steaming push cart.

"These are great. What's your name, my friend?" Cole said, wiping mustard from the corner of his mouth.

"Anatoly."

"Russian?"

"American."

"Fair enough. So what do you think of Putin?" Cole persisted.

"A thug."

"What did you think of Trump?"

Anatoly laughed. "A good thug!"

"What's a good thug?" asked Sam.

"One who lets you call him 'thug' and does not poison your tea," Anatoly laughed, turning to serve a group of Pakistani tourists.

"Strikes me as a pretty low threshold," Cole said, taking his last bite of bratwurst.

"This is the problem. You Americans. You expect too much."

Cole and Sam reached the Lincoln Memorial at the opposite end of the Mall at dusk. They ascended the eighty-seven marble steps from the reflecting pool to the memorial itself and entered the vestibule. A group of Chinese tourists moved about taking selfies with Abe. After a few minutes, their tour guide issued an indecipherable command and they were gone without another word.

Cole and Sam found themselves in rare waters, alone and staring up at the somber resemblance of our sixteenth president in the shadows of early evening. They stood beneath the statue for several moments in silence. Neither could escape the feeling that Lincoln was looking down, not at the Mall to the east, but at them.

"He looks sad," Sam said.

"He was. He had profound bouts of depression. His

victory came at a huge cost. He never fully reconciled himself to the price that was paid."

"But he was right," Sam added.

"He was right on slavery. He held the nation together against the odds, with a divided cabinet, incompetent generals, an unhappy marriage, the melancholia. He was probably the smartest president in our history." Cole gestured toward the Gettysburg Address etched into the marble walls of the monument.

Sam read the two-hundred-and-seventy-two words Lincoln believed the world would "little note nor long remember."

"Wow."

Cole nodded. "Yeah. A self-educated farmer from a flyover state. There aren't five Ivy Leaguers in America today who could have written that."

"Too busy perfecting their tweet style," Sam said.

Cole and Sam turned to leave and descended the steps of the monument. Cole was quiet.

"What?"

"Nothing. Just thinking about Lincoln. That period of our history. It wasn't just about slavery. It was about industrialization versus agrarianism, a republic versus centralized government."

"And?" asked Sam.

"We lost on that one."

The next morning, they caught the Amtrak Acela Express from Washington's Union Station. They would arrive in New York City's Penn Station in two hours and thirty-five minutes, just in time for Cole's afternoon appointment with Firston Capital. Cole had an appointment with the executive responsible for their loan, Moss

Becker. But he tried to put it out of his mind. Right now, he pushed down the aisle looking for two empty seats. The train was crowded with creatures of the 'Acela corridor'—dark suits, short hair, and earbuds—scurrying between NYC and DC in hot pursuit of money, or power, or both. Most had buried the adjacent empty seat in documents, a briefcase, and a coat. They were careful not to make eye contact as Sam and Cole passed for fear they'd have to clear the space. Cole found two seats in the rear of the last car. They stowed their bags in the overhead and settled into the ride up the eastern corridor of the United States.

They watched as the outskirts of DC sped past the window, the train gaining speed.

"What'd you think?" Cole asked.

"Ugly as hell," Sam said and she was not wrong. The view that flew past their window transitioned from suburban to rural and back in a cascade of muted greys and browns, the structures old, the foliage thin. The grey light didn't help, muted and dull, as if the sun was wrapped in a thin wet cloth. Cole missed the crisp clarity of California's light, the light that had driven a generation of artists to Laguna Beach and Santa Barbara to establish a new school of impressionism.

"You're spoiled by the Central Coast," Cole said.

"Damn right. No wonder everybody pushed West."

"Your people pushed north."

"Whatever. We reached the light."

The Acela sped through the tunnel in Baltimore on its way to Philadelphia. By the time they reached New Jersey, Sam was asleep and Cole had retreated to his notes in preparation for the meeting. Income expected from the new cow-calf operation and winery had not yet pushed operations into the black. He wondered how he was going to convince Firston to extend the loan and forgive Elliot's defaults. He closed his notebook. He had scant insight into the niceties of money lending.

Cole followed the illuminated sign to Café Acela. A portly Amtrak employee manned the small counter. Cole surveyed the offerings.

"Can I get a roast beef sandwich?"

"You could if we had one. All out. North of Philly we run out of most everything."

"So what's left?"

"TracPacks."

"What's in a TracPack?"

"Oh, lots of stuff. Think of it as a surprise."

"Great. Give me two."

Cole returned to their seats, Sam now awake. She smiled when she saw he had returned with food and two "single serve" bottles of wine.

"Great! I'm starving."

"Don't get too excited."

Sam opened her plastic box. "Cool. Four crackers and some cheese. I always love a small ball of Gouda. Especially when its flavor has been preserved by a red wax skin."

"And don't forget the wine. You've wanted to sample…" Cole examined the tiny bottle… "Sunset Vineyard Chablis."

Sam unscrewed her bottle and poured some into her plastic cup. "I have. Isn't that a Screaming Eagle estate wine?"

"No. It's a subsidiary of Amtrak."

"Makes sense."

Cole ate his crackers and sipped the wine. He passed on the Gouda. Watching Sam slice the wax skin with her plastic knife brought back memories of the frog in high school science. He retreated to a dark place and Sam sensed it, as if she read the energy in the air between them.

"What's the matter?"

"I have to think of something. They could foreclose."

Sam leaned into Cole, her head on his shoulder, but she could think of nothing to offer. Nothing that would help. "You'll think of something. It could be worse. Think about Lincoln. We might lose the ranch; he stood to lose the country. Few are likely to die in our deal."

Cole finally smiled. "Unless Manny's was our Fort Sumter."

The conductor passed through the aisle repeating the same message every few feet: "New York's Penn Station, ten minutes. Everybody exits."

Upon departing the train, Sam and Cole found themselves in a cavernous underground station packed with travelers, vendors, and others, seemingly aimless, content only to escape the more purposeful demands of the streets above. Cole took Sam's arm and pushed to a tunnel angled upward, determined, like a rodent on the ranch, to follow its line to the light. They surfaced on 31st Street and jumped into a long cab line, where they waited.

Manhattan was every bit as depressing as Cole had imagined, maybe more. It was, so far as he knew, a bright and sunny day. Somewhere. But all Cole could see was shadow cast by the nondescript, high-rise structures. Honeycombed stacks of small office cubicles within which, Cole imagined, money was made and lost and stolen. It was like traversing a cold canyon of steel, all cement and ill intent. He couldn't wait to leave.

They had chosen the least expensive hotel within walking distance of Firston Capital. Checked in, Cole traded his jeans and sweater for a suit and tie and readied to leave.

"I never see you in a suit and tie. You look great."

"Only if you value form over substance. The jacket is too thin to offer protection; the shirt collar pinches; and the tie? What in hell does a tie do?"

"It finishes the ensemble. It looks nice."

"That's how people in the eighteenth century felt about powdered wigs."

"Well, you'll fit in, anyway. Good luck."

"Thanks. What're you going to do? This shouldn't take long, one way or the other."

"Shop Fifth Avenue, then Madison."

"You might want to wait to hear how the meeting goes."

"No matter. If you save the ranch, we'll need to celebrate. If you don't, we'll have more disposable income. Won't have to carry that shitty ranch."

Cole smiled and kissed her goodbye.

The building at 592 Madison Avenue stood near the corner of 57th. Forty floors of black glass and steel. Cole's first thought was of the Death Star. He walked into the lobby and reached into his pocket for the card Jack had given him. He couldn't remember Emperor Palpatine's suite number.

"May I help you?" The receptionist at the lobby desk, a mature woman in her fifties, all business, was apparently tired of waiting for Cole to retrieve the card.

"Yes, I am here to see an Moss Becker of Firston Capital."

"Do you have an appointment?"

"Yes."

She called a number and turned her head to speak, apparently confirming appointments involved sensitive exchanges.

"Mr. Becker's assistant will be down to escort you."

Cole stepped to the side and waited. The assistant arrived shortly as predicted. Late twenties, navy skirt and jacket, cream-colored blouse. All business, except for the diamond stud earrings and the black, stiletto high heels.

"Mr. Clay?"

And they were off, into the elevator and up forty floors. The elevator doors parted and Cole found himself in the lobby of Firston Capital. By any measure, the lobby was stunning. Panoramic views of the Upper East Side with a good cut of Central Park. Cole stepped out of the elevator and onto a plush Persian rug over inlaid wood floors. Cole's escort handed the ball to the lobby receptionist, a gay man in his thirties.

"Mr. Clay?"

"Yes."

"Welcome. Have a seat. Mr. Becker's assistant will be here shortly. May I get you some water?"

"That would be great."

"Sparkling or still?"

"Still is fine."

"Oh! Too late."

A man Cole presumed to be Becker burst into the lobby from a hallway to Cole's left. He extended his hand.

"Mr. Clay, Moss Becker. Nice to meet you. Please follow me."

They were seated in an office, which, if anything, was more impressive than the lobby. Corner office, big view of the park, antique furniture. Becker sat in a wing chair near the couch where he indicated Cole should sit. Cole looked up at the painting on the wall behind his desk.

"Is that…"

"Good eye. Yes, an original Leroy Neiman," Becker volunteered.

"Actually, I was going to ask whom it depicted."

"No one in particular. A sort of symbolic Olympic athlete, an archetype of athleticism and grit. What matters is the identity of the artist," Becker informed.

"I guess so. An original Neiman must be expensive."

"Very. I don't own it personally. The firm does."

"How do your shareholders feel about that?" Cole asked.

"They feel great about it. Our art collection has been a good investment for the company and, therefore, for our shareholders."

"Can we talk about why I'm here?" Cole said.

"Of course. I have reviewed the file." Becker pulled a manila folder open.

"Then you know that several payments on the loan are delinquent; that you have declared the loan in default and initiated foreclosure."

"Yes, sadly I am quite aware, Mr. Clay."

"What you may not know is that, as result of circumstances I won't bore you with, we—that is, my brother and I, the equity owners of the ranch—were unaware of the default on this loan. Indeed, we were unaware of its existence until quite recently."

Becker listened passively but offered no comment. Cole pushed forward. "We can meet the amount in arrears if given a short extension. We've turned things around—"

Becker raised his hands, interrupting. "Mr. Clay, I'm afraid it's not that easy. I have examined the P & L you forwarded. The 'cash flow' you have, and I use that term loosely since, as far as I can tell, you have no real 'profits' as yet, is grossly inadequate to cover future installments even if the amount in arrears is paid. We have a formula we must apply here. The income-to-debt ratio is way outside our perimeters."

"Well, I don't know about the 'income to debt ratios' you like to see in Manhattan, but I can assure you in ranching—small family farms—we have to stretch a bit. But what I'm saying is that I can make this loan good, and soon."

"And what about the next time? As you know, your father signed a variable interest rate instrument. Your monthly debt obligation will increase. It already exceeds your expected capacity to cover."

"You might be surprised what you can cover when the alternative is losing your ranch. If I can explain—"

Becker jumped in: "Mr. Clay, we are not in the business of extending loans we expect to default."

"Well, that's curious."

"Meaning?"

"When you made this loan to my father, the ranch was in far worse shape. Looks to me like the only recoupment you might have expected was in foreclosure."

Becker bristled. "We make our money in interest and fees, not by incurring the legal costs and delay occasioned by default."

"That's good to hear. I was concerned you might find a foreclosure attractive in this case."

"And why might that be?"

It wasn't going well so Cole went for broke.

"Because our ranch might be valuable to your fastest growing subsidiary?" Cole asserted.

"What are you talking about?"

"Your cannabis business."

"We're not in the cannabis business."

"Really. I'm confused then. From your SEC filings, it looks like you're holding a lot of real estate. Ag land, most of it leased out to cannabis farmers. They pay twice the going rate to lease prime ag land. In cash."

Becker leaned back in his chair. "Well, I see you have done your homework. Yes, we hold some agricultural land. In many cases, such as this one, we come into land on loans that default. We lease the land for cash flow and hold for the real estate appreciation. What our tenants farm is up to them."

"Okay, just a coincidence I guess," Cole said.

"Not coincidence. It's called the market. If you're trying to make money, and that's what we do for our shareholders, Mr. Clay, the market is rarely wrong."

Cole gazed out at Central Park, the only green in NYC as far as he could tell. "My guess is, the eight hundred and forty acres I'm looking at would be more profitably devoted to luxury condominiums."

Becker smiled. "Maybe. Our city planners had other values they had to balance."

"Exactly. And so do I. We're not going to default. My father never should have secured this loan and I didn't know a damn thing about it. Had I, there would be no late payments. We've already improved cash flow by transitioning to more profitable replacement heifers and bulls. We have amped up our wine business. We can meet this payment schedule."

Cole hesitated. He knew this was the moment it would all be decided. "Mr. Becker this ranch has been in my family for generations. And, you're right, ranching is a tough business. The margins are thin. But I can assure you, that ranch is worth a lot more to me and my brother, my grandmother, all of us, than that balance sheet suggests. And we sure in hell won't lose it for want of interest on money we never should have borrowed in the first place. We will meet the payment schedule and pay it off within two years."

Becker looked at his watch. His expression changed. "Mr. Clay. I couldn't care less how long your ranch has been in the family. And I wouldn't know a 'heifer' from a pot hole on Seventh Avenue. We have one objective around here: making money. We lend money to make money, not to preserve an anachronistic way of life. Maybe you should cash out and find something that makes sense in this century."

Becker stood signaling the meeting was over. "Frankly, this is your problem. Once you defaulted and ignored the notices, your rights to cure delinquencies lapsed. We are going to settle this loan out. It won't be extended. You now have two options: Pay the whole loan off now or let someone else do it at foreclosure."

Cole stood. "Your call, but good luck with the local press when you turn out a family that acquired the ranch from the Mexican government a hundred and eighty years ago on a loan we can make good. Won't be a great backdrop for your IPO."

Becker smiled. "We don't pay too much attention to local press. We are a national concern. Indeed, we open an office in Paris next month. So global, I guess. Good day, Mr. Clay."

Becker's assistant had entered. Cole was escorted from the office.

18

---◇---

Cole and Sam returned to California the next day. The only good news: Sam had not done a lot of damage on Madison Avenue. She'd been bluffing. Cole judged that Becker wasn't.

The next morning back in Santa Ynez, Cole parked in front of a white craftsman-style building. Its signage read: "Vallin L. Ross, Attorney at Law." Cole had known Ross for years. Born in the Valley to a dairy farming family, Ross left the farm for college and then law school. He failed the bar on his first attempt, passed on the second, and hung his shingle in Santa Ynez. His first client was the tribal council that ran the reservation. They had come to him mostly because the more established lawyers in town wouldn't represent them. They wanted to expand the casino and add a tribal residential development. They intended to utilize every exception allowed by their special status as a Native nation. The locals, without such special status, resented both the development and the manner in which it was done. Controversy and litigation followed and Ross's practice thrived. It was widely rumored that Ross was dishonest, but it had never been clear to Cole whether that rumor was grounded in resentment at Native development projects or actual corruption on the part of Ross.

Cole was sure Ross was involved in his family's recent troubles but wasn't sure how. As he walked through the door, he only knew that it was a conversation he had to have. He had nothing to lose.

Ross looked up as Cole entered. "Cole Clay. What a surprise."

"I'm sure it is. I apologize for not making an appointment."

"No problem. Have a seat. I have a hearing in Santa Barbara at eleven, but—"

"This shouldn't take long."

"Coffee?"

"No, I'm good."

"I'm sure sorry about your dad. I haven't seen you since he passed. I always liked Elliot," Ross lied. He poured himself a cup of coffee. Cole noticed a slight tremor in his hand.

"Thank you. Elliot, in a way, is why I'm here."

"Really? An estate issue?"

"No. Jack Callson has that covered. In fact, it was his review of the estate that brought this matter to my attention."

"What matter?"

"The debt to the casino and what followed from that."

Cole had been intentionally ambiguous. Much followed from the debt, some perfectly legal.

"I understand you represented the casino in their efforts to recoup," Cole opened.

"Yes,"

"Most of it was repaid, I guess."

"Correct."

"About $400,000. That sound about right?" Cole asked.

"Yeah, I think so," Ross said.

"And what was the remainder? What he still owed?"

"I forget exactly. It was never repaid."

Cole let his next question hang.

Ross looked at his watch. "You know Cole, I do have to run soon."

"I understand. I'm just curious about the rest. Since you represented the casino, I assume you would press for the rest."

"Well, yes, but there is only so much you can do in a situation like that," Ross said. "I'm confused. What does all this have to do with me or this 'matter' that was brought to your attention? What matter?"

Cole sat back and waited for the moment. He wanted to watch Ross's face.

"Tommy Kyel and Tony Alavara, goes by Yellow Sky, they shook Elliot down for the remainder of what he thought he owed the casino. No one told him the casino had forgiven it. They strong-armed him into a conspiracy to fix some rodeo events, improve the odds, make some money under the table. A young cowboy died as a result. So did Elliot."

Ross had stiffened in his chair. "I'm sorry, of course. But again, what does this have to do with me?"

"I never understood why Elliot would assume someone like Tommy, a bouncer, could hatch a scheme to retire legitimate casino debt. But then I learned Elliot was in touch with you. If you laid hands on the arrangement, Elliot might bite."

"That's preposterous. Why would I involve myself in a two-bit scheme to fix rodeo? I represented the casino. We secured some repayment and the casino chose to forgive the rest. That's the extent of my involvement."

Cole took his measure, then gave it a push. "But you never told Elliot they had forgiven the remainder."

"And why should I? He owed the money. The casino had written it off, but I'm sure they would not have objected to being paid the remainder."

"You also referred Elliot to Firston. And it was that loan that had him by the balls," Cole said.

"You're fishing here, Cole. And you are conflating two different transactions. Yes, of course your father and I discussed monies owed the casino. I represented the casino. And I tried to help him, and my client, by facilitating the loan from Firston. I had no involvement in any rodeo scheme. I resent any implication to the contrary."

"What's your relationship to Firston?"

"Well, not that it's any of your business, but it's simple. They lend on agricultural land. Naturally that is of interest to my practice from time to time."

"That's it?"

"Yes."

Ross stood. "Tell me, Mr. Clay, why come to me with these vague allegations and wild speculation? What is it you want?"

Cole thought about it. He stared out the window of Ross's office, the small town of Santa Ynez now coming to life. Young cowboys buying Skoal, old ones drinking coffee and telling each other lies.

"I want Wade Roy at home on his shitty little ranch in Oklahoma with his young bride. I want Elliot to be back at Zaca raising hell. I want someone to lend me the money to avoid foreclosure on the usurious loan you arranged."

Ross's demeanor softened. "Well, maybe we can talk.

I represent a number of players in the cannabis market always looking for long-term leases."

"Thank you, Mr. Ross. I'm sorry I wasted your time." Cole stood and left.

19

---◇---

"**H**ow'd you do?"

Jack Callson sat opposite Cole in Solvang's Hans Christian Andersen Park a block from his office. Jack had brought them sack lunches.

"Not well," Cole replied. He tossed a kettle-cooked potato chip to a squirrel. The squirrel passed.

"See, even he prefers Lay's. Can't beat the original. You've gone all New Wave on me, Jack."

"What happened?"

"Firston won't budge. They seem intent to foreclose." Cole took a bite of his turkey and brie and dried cranberry sandwich. "Tell me again, how does foreclosure work relative to what we owe? Could we pay what we owe and be done with it? I mean, if I could scrap it together?"

"Technically, no, unless they agree to it. You had to cure the delinquencies before the date set in the notice of default," explained Jack.

"And what's Firston's role in that sale?"

"If the lender chooses to bid, it does so in the capacity of a purchaser. The only distinction between a lender and any other bidder is that the lender is entitled to a credit up to the amount of the indebtedness," Jack explained.

"So our only option now is to go to foreclosure and

buy back our own ranch by offering the full amount of the debt?" Cole asked.

"It's worse than that," Jack added.

"Why?"

"Because you can be outbid. The ranch is worth more than your debt to Firston," Jack explained. "Depends on who shows up at the auction besides Firston. I'm not sure it's worth more to them. They know the ranch loses money."

Cole shook his head. "As a cattle ranch. But that's not why they may want it."

"Firston's not your only problem," added Jack.

"What else?"

"There's another bidder."

"Who?"

"Indigo."

"Perfect. A heavy hitter seeking revenge."

"And your superior *terroir*," Jack smiled. "What about your visit with Ross?"

Cole shook his head. "I wanted somehow to tie him to the scam Tommy pulled, use that as leverage. He denied any knowledge."

"You believe him?"

"Yeah, unfortunately. He represents the casino. I doubt he'd jeopardize that relationship for an off-the-books scam. I think Tommy was just skimming off Elliot's misfortune, bottom feeding. Too small and too messy for a serious crook like Ross."

Cole watched as the squirrel climbed an adjacent trash barrel. He emerged with a piece of giant pretzel.

Jack stood. "I have to go. Let me know what you want to do."

"Wait. Sit a minute," Cole insisted.

Jack sat and pulled out an electronic cigarette.

Cole shook his head. "I knew it. You should move your office to Venice Beach."

Jack waited, impatient.

"I think we're looking at this all wrong. Elliot got scammed. He got levered by Tommy on debt he no longer owed. But why would Elliot do it? Why would he risk everything with that lowlife; trust him to retire casino debt?" Cole stood, thinking it through. "He didn't. He was using Tommy—to meet his Firston debt. That was his bigger problem, the one that might cost him the ranch."

"Makes sense. But how does it change things now?"

"We're focused on the wrong scam. When I met with Ross, he dismissed the whole deal, like he was swatting away flies. But when I said what I really wanted was money to retire Firston, he went immediately to a lease. To pot. His contacts there. And when Travis was strong-armed by Tommy at Manny's? It wasn't cash he wanted. It was a lease. Becker made no bones about it. Their business plan is to default loans and hold ag land if they can. And they love pot farmers as tenants. That's why they might bid more than the debt."

"Sit down. You're making me nervous."

Cole sat. "And how did Elliot get connected to Firston Capital?"

"I don't know," Jack said. His e-cig glowed. He was nervous, or warming to the argument.

"Tommy. Tommy referred him to Ross. Ross sent Elliot to Firston. And I'm thinking they got exactly what they wanted. A default."

"Maybe. But there's nothing illegal there. And nothing that gets you off the hook of foreclosure."

"Not yet," Cole said. He looked at the finicky squirrel, his cheeks bulging with pretzel. "So these pot farms—the conversion from grazing to cannabis—it requires a public hearing, right?"

"It has. It's been very controversial. Gone all the way to the Board of Supervisors," explained Jack.

"So there is a public record? I want you to look at every application, every conversion approved or pending. All the applicants. Everything about who they are, who owns them."

"Bueno." Jack stood to leave. "Gotta run."

As Jack retreated in the direction of his office, Cole called out, "And their counsel. I need to know who represented the applicants."

Jack waved without turning.

For the next several days, Cole heard nothing. He used the time to canvass lenders who might advance money to Zaca. As expected, they declined, none willing to take a second position to Firston Capital.

Finally, Jack called. He had secured a postponement of the foreclosure sale with a stay request strategically filed with a friendly judge, a *ranchero* buddy of Jack's partial to keeping local land in local hands. Jack warned the postponement was temporary but it would give him more time to review the pot farming applications. Ownership of the applicants in some cases was, as Jack described it, "a bit opaque."

Cole tried to put it all out of his mind for the next two weeks. He focused his efforts on Sam and improving cash flows on the ranch. Indigo had pulled his product and operations from the winery within days of Cole telling him he would exercise the call. He also sued Cole and Arroyo de Zaca, alleging fraud and breach of contract. He sought compensatory and punitive damages in numbers that reflected less the strength of his allegations than the size of his injured ego. Jack gave the suit minimal chances of success: There is no express or implied breach in announcing the intent to exercise a call when it matures. It was Indigo's decision to pull the plug upon hearing the news.

With Indigo's product removed, Sam had taken out a Small Business Administration loan, expanded her family's nascent vineyard, and began to utilize the now-excess capacity of the Zaca winery. Together, Sam and Cole negotiated resale deals with a handful of local vintners. The winery and tasting room became a "one-stop shopping" destination for wine enthusiasts up from LA. Sam had even rehired the young singer-songwriter from Manny's to entertain guests on Saturday and Sunday afternoons. Sam and her father resolved to sell Manny's. With their efforts focused on Zaca, it had become a distraction.

The Angus herd continued to thrive, their superior DNA manifest in ninety some calves they would produce each year. With Cole's concurrence, Travis was easing them out of the rodeo stock business and made frequent trips to Texas. He returned with two-year-old "prospects" they would break and resell to the Valley's weekend warriors. He even found a dead-broke strawberry roan gelding for Dustin. Flynn would be Dustin's horse until the colt sired by Slick was ready. Dustin had named the colt Slickster and vowed to be "ready when he is."

With Manny's for sale, business tapered off and Sam

lost her manager to another bar. Sam and Cole traded nights watching the store for its final week in business. Cole and Hammer were closing down on a Tuesday night when Tommy and Yellow Sky shuffled through the front door. They threw themselves down at their usual table in the corner near the back of the bar.

"We're closing, guys," announced Cole.

"Not what the sign on the door says," Tommy replied.

"We were just about to flip it," Cole said. "Hammer, go turn it and start locking up." He turned back to Tommy. "With the place for sale, we pretty much close now whenever we want. Like, for instance, when there is no business."

Tommy feigned incredulity. "So what'a we look like? You best not refuse us service; might get your ass sued for discrimination."

"Last time I checked, being an asshole is not a protected class," Cole said.

Tommy just stared, then looked at Yellow Sky and laughed. "Come on, Cole. We've had a tough day. Just wanna take a little of the edge off. Tell you what, you don't have time to serve a beer, maybe your twinkie there can just give us a blowjob."

Tommy and Yellow Sky shared a laugh. Tommy directed his next comment at Hammer. "That was big news to my brother when he got sprung. You batting for the other team."

Tommy lit a cigarette. "Surprised you'd work with a homo, Cole, you being a born-again Catholic and all."

"No surprise in it. Maybe if you attended mass once in a while you'd understand. Sin lies in what we do, not in who we are."

He approached their table and looked directly at Tommy.

"Take you, for instance. I suspect that you can't help your innate disposition to be a bully. It's not really your fault. You were born with bad instincts. You sin only when you give in to those instincts. So let me save you from the *actus reus* of sin. Get the fuck out of here."

"What? You and your homo-home boy goin' toss us?" sneered Yellow Sky.

Maybe it was the comment, or the history. Maybe it was just the waiting; waiting for it to come to a head. But Cole charged their table and grabbed Yellow Sky by the collar of his canvas jacket. He jerked him out of his chair then abruptly released him, turning his rage to his true target—Tommy. But he never had the chance. Yellow Sky collapsed instantly, toppling the table and two chairs as he did. Yellow Sky's leg would not support his weight, not without the cane he had placed behind his chair, the one he had used ever since Cole had removed his knee cap with one blast of a sawed-off shotgun several months before.

Cole immediately reached down and offered Yellow Sky his hand. "I'm sorry, but—"

"*Jódete!*" Yellow Sky screamed, his face an unnatural shade of red. He slapped Cole's hand away. He tried to stand but slipped again, his humiliation complete. Tommy leaned down to help him up.

They retrieved Yellow Sky's cane and hobbled toward the door. Tommy turned as they reached it. "This is not over, motherfucker. Not by a long shot."

As they left, Hammer straightened the chairs and said nothing.

"I didn't know your dad was out," Cole said in a low tone.

"He just showed up. Got paroled. He conned 'em, I guarantee you that. Hasn't changed a bit."

"How was the reunion?" Cole asked.

"Like old times. Beat the shit out of me."

Hammer flipped the "CLOSED" sign. "Least he had a reason this time—in his mind, anyway."

"There's a room above the winery. You need it, it's yours."

"May take you up on it."

Hammer picked up his backpack behind the bar and pulled it over his shoulder. "Can I bring my dog? Actually, it's Frank's dog but he beats it near as much as me."

"Then by all means."

The next morning, as Cole walked to the winery, his cell rang. It was Jack Callson.

"Got some information on the pot farmers."

"Shoot."

"Four different applications to convert ag land to pot have been processed by the county. Three approved. Of those, two are local. I know one of them personally. Look legit, couple a dirt farmers looking for higher margin crops."

"Yeah, and the third?"

"Little more interesting. Outfit called Decker D Farms. An LLC formed in Texas. The Articles of Formation list two owners: guy named Franklin Wolder, another one by the name of William Gatner. Wolder is listed as president. They leased fifty acres in Lompoc. At the county hearing, they laid out plans to acquire or lease up to three hundred additional acres."

"Yeah, so what's interesting about that?"

"Well hold on, pard. I did some research on Decker D. It was formed by three guys originally. The third, guy named Dennis Fonton, left the company about six months before they leased this ground in Santa Barbara. He sold his shares to the other two for a dollar. That didn't look right seeing as Decker D already had businesses in Texas with significant cash flow. So I did some digging. Turns out Fonton is an ex con, did time in Texas for drug trafficking a few years back."

"Okay. So Decker D may be a little shaky. They didn't want someone with a rap sheet involved. Makes sense. Anything else?"

"Yeah. Two things. The land in Lompoc? It's owned by a company called Aplon Acres. Aplon is a partnership. One of the limited partners is Firston Capital."

"Well, what a coincidence."

"It gets better. Firston held their equity below twenty percent, which is a disclosure threshold for a lot of state and federal filings. But from the board composition, I'm guessing they have control. All have ties to Firston."

"Ties?"

"Former employees or joint venture partners."

"Why would they try to hide it if they owned that land? Becker made no bones about their business plans—foreclose and lease to the highest bidder."

"I don't know. Maybe they know more about Decker D than we do and didn't want to be too close."

"You said there were two things."

"Oh, yeah. Decker D? Vallin Ross is their attorney."

There was a long silence as Cole absorbed the news.

"Thanks, Jack. One more question: Frank Kyel, Tommy's brother. Did you know he got paroled?"

"No. I'm surprised. Figured they'd hold his ass as long as they could."

"Why?"

"The background on his case."

"Which was?"

"Kyel owns a trucking company. Does a lot of business trucking heavy machinery between the US and Mexico. We do forty billion a year with Mexico in that bucket, so it's big business. The feds made Kyel for transporting more than machines across the border...cocaine, heroin, illegals, and teenage girls—sex trafficking. But they couldn't make it stick. So they got him on the usual tax rap. They proved he had a shitload of money he never declared but never proved its source."

"Holy shit."

"Yeah. He's a first-class thug."

"How do you know all this?"

"You forget. When I'm not doing dinky stuff for you, I do some criminal defense. Kyel came to me when he was charged. You know, use the homie lawyer who may know the local judge? I politely declined once I got read-in."

"Thanks, Jack."

"No problem."

"By the way, I think you just violated the attorney client privilege."

"Yeah, well screw him. He deserves it. Besides, the indictment was mostly public record. Where're you going with this, Cole? I don't see the connection. Firston, Ross...and Kyel?

"I don't either, yet."

"Well, tread lightly my friend. Frank Kyel would dump his mother in a shredder if he thought the mulch would sell."

"Thanks, Jack, I'll keep that in mind."

As Cole entered the winery, he found Hammer prepping the common areas for the arrival of wine-tasting tours later that day. A small black-and-white dog trailed him.

"I take it this is the other orphan."

"Yeah, that's him. Name's Bosko."

"What is he?"

"Pretty much a rat terrier."

"Pretty much?"

"Technically, he's what you call a Decker terrier. Some guy in Texas crossed rat terriers with basenji to get a more aggressive hunting dog. Called a Decker—that was the guy's name. Frank is obsessed with them. But hates Bosko cause he ain't too aggressive. Frank thinks if he beats him enough he'll get meaner."

Cole shook his head, always surprised by the depravity of the human mind. He tried to lighten it up. "Didn't work with you."

Hammer had to smile. "Oh, I can be plenty mean. Why just the other day—"

"Wait," Cole interrupted. "Decker?"

"Yeah, it's a Decker terrier. Why?"

"Decker D," Cole said. He pulled out his notes from Jack's call. "You ever hear of this guy, Franklin Wolder?"

"Nope."

"How about Bill Gatner?"

"Don't think so."

"Dennis Fonton?"

Hammer's expression changed. "Hell, yeah. One of my dad's asshole buddies. Real douche."

Cole shook his head. "Well, I'll be damned."

"Why? Haven't seen him since we left Texas."

"Nothing. Don't mention I asked."

Cole left the winery and walked back toward the house. He found Travis watering his horse near the barn.

"Little brother, we have to talk."

"What'd I do now?"

"Calm down," Cole said. "Here's where we are: In about two weeks, this outfit in New York is going to foreclose and we are going to lose this ranch. I think we got played here and, it turns out, it has very little to do with the stunt Tommy pulled. Some of the same players, but it's a lot heavier. I think Frank Kyel is behind this."

"Frank? Tommy's brother? Thought he was in prison," Travis said.

"He's out now. No matter. He did most of the damage behind bars. The way I figure it, we can sit back and watch it happen, or we can get in their face. There's a chance if we do, they'll back off. Not a big chance, but maybe our only shot."

"What we got to lose?" Travis asked.

Cole thought about it, knowing they were about to cross a line. "You remember when we were kids and we found that den of badgers?"

"Yeah, I remember."

"And you decided to shoot one—with a pellet rifle? How'd that work out for us?"

"Not good. So bring some heavier ordinance."

"I'll bring what we have but you need to watch our

backs. The ranch...Hammer, anything that makes us vulnerable." Cole stood. "You up for this?"

Travis popped open another beer can and smiled broadly. "Saddle up, big brother."

The next day was Tuesday, "law and motion" day at Santa Barbara Superior Court. Cole ambushed Vallin Ross just inside the lobby of the courthouse. Jack had tipped him to Ross's next appearance.

"Vallin. What a surprise."

"Mr. Clay."

"Happy to see you. Curious about something," Cole said.

"And what is that?"

"How it is you can feed on both sides of the trough?"

Ross moved them out of earshot in the hallway. "What in hell does that mean, Clay?"

"Did some research after our talk. Surprised to find you represented Decker D in that cannabis app before the county."

"Why? I told you I represent cannabis applicants."

"Just seems a bit cozy, seeing as Firston owns the land they leased."

"What are you talking about? They do not. That parcel is owned by Aplon Acres."

"Yep. A company in which Firston holds twenty percent and board control. With your help, they leased it to Decker D, a company founded by an asshole buddy of Frank who mysteriously disappeared from the paperwork about the time you filed with the county. Wouldn't want a convicted money launderer tied up in a cash business like that. Wouldn't look right."

"I don't know what you're talking about, Clay."

"Sure you do, Vallin. You're playing both sides of the fence. Refer debt-ridden farmers to Firston; they lock in a deal that drives inevitably to default; then you rep the pot mavens who lock up the land. Big issue is, to what end?"

Ross was rattled. "You're a lunatic, just like your drunk of a father."

"Maybe. But if Firston forecloses, I'm driving to the bottom of this pile of shit. I just hope Frank is not up to his old tricks and looking to wash some ill-begotten gains. Be a tad embarrassing for all concerned, starting with Firston and you."

"What in hell does Frank Kyel have to do with this?"

Cole just stared, his suspicion—and worst fear—confirmed by Ross's question.

"I didn't say 'Frank Kyel.' I said Frank. There are a lot of Franks around, including the guy that fronts Decker D as president. But thanks for clarifying which Frank we're talking about."

Cole turned to leave, Vallin Ross visibly shaken.

"Tell Frank I like his dog. May get myself a Decker."

The next day, Cole briefed Jack on his conversation with Ross, everything he knew, and suspected, about the hole into which Elliot had fallen. And then he waited.

It didn't take long for the badger to crawl out of his hole. Three days after his conversation with Ross, Cole walked into the winery to check on inventory. It was 9:00 p.m., the tasting room long since closed.

The first one he saw was Hammer, his face freshly bruised. He nodded to a table in the back.

Frank Kyel occupied the table with a bottle of Sam's best cab and two glasses.

"Thought we might have a drink."

Cole walked to the table and sat down. "Then you should have called. Didn't have to slap your son around to see me."

Frank poured wine into each glass and took a sip. "That's a nice cab. Your Mexican girlfriend make this?"

"Surprised you'd know anything about wine, Frank. They serve a lot of it in the federal pen?"

Frank shook his head. "You got brass balls, Cole, I'll give you that. Sorry you got short changed on brains."

"Get to the point, Kyel. I assume you didn't come to sip wine."

"The point is you're making a lot of wild accusations that might jeopardize my tenuous position with the state of California. I need that kind of talk to stop."

"Yeah, well if there's no truth to it, I'd say you've got nothing to worry about."

Frank stared at Cole. He had small dark eyes that did not blink. They looked like the eyes of a man who could beat a son, or a dog; like the eyes of a man who could transport young girls in the belly of a Peterbilt, their bodies to be sold for his gain.

"What do you want?"

"I want people like you to be locked in a dark hole somewhere. I want everyone you have ever victimized to stare into that hole and know you'll never crawl out. That they are safe. But I'll leave that to God in his good time. What I want now is for Firston to back down. To allow me and my brother to pay off that loan and keep this ranch and the distance it allows from a world that lets vermin like you fester."

"I got no control over them."

"No, but you have a deep understanding of the shit they will be linked to if they foreclose and I blow the cover on Ross, on Decker D and its founders, on plans to use cannabis to hide the fact you're back in business, if you ever left it. My guess is they won't want the press."

Kyel finished his wine and wiped his mouth with the back of his small corpulent hand.

And then he left.

The week ended with no word, not from Kyel, Ross, or Firston. Cole awakened early Saturday morning, poured himself coffee in a Styrofoam cup and walked to the barn. The sun was just cresting the Figueroa Mountains to the east. Slick snorted when he saw Cole and moved to the rear of his turn out. But Cole followed, haltered him, and led him to the tie down. He brushed him out, thinking of nothing as he did. The blanket, the saddle, the bridle. He pulled into the saddle and nudged Slick into a trot.

Cole always rode on Saturday mornings through the canyon. It rarely failed to restore his mood, to remind him of things that were abiding, things immutable.

He had ridden about a mile along a trail on the western perimeter of the ranch when he saw two heifers outside the fence line grazing peacefully on the meridian of Highway 101. He dismounted and eased the heifers back in. He pulled the strains of barbed wire and twisted them together. It would have to do for now. He pulled out his cell phone. Travis did not pick up. He left a voicemail.

"Hey. There's fence down on the west side just short of the canyon along the 101. Looks more like a cut then a break. We may have a poacher. Send Hammer down here and fix it right."

Of all the spectacular mornings Cole had seen on the ranch, this one, he thought, might be the best. It was cool, crisp, and clear. The sun was a pure yellow, almost brittle, as if you could crack it with a hammer. Slick knew the way to the canyon. Cole loved to ride through the broken shadows of its oak canopy toward the light. They would ride between two steep canyon walls until they emerged at the southwest corner of the ranch, then climb the steep rocky trail to the highest point on the ranch; the plateau from which one could see everything there was to see.

Travis heard the message and tried to call Cole. He didn't pick up. There was no cell coverage in the canyon, exactly what Cole preferred on his Saturday morning rides. Travis felt a cold shudder run up his spine. It carried a message he didn't want to receive.

"Hammer. Get in that truck now and go to the section of fence on 101 between here and the canyon mouth. Stay there. You see anyone coming that way, stop them. Any way you have to. But don't fuckin' lose 'em."

Hammer looked up. "Okay, why?"

"You have that pistol?"

"In the truck but I never used it. What in hell's goin' on?"

Travis quickly threw his saddle over the back of his horse and mounted. "You speak to your father or uncle lately?"

Hammer looked sick. "Yeah, Tommy."

"When?"

"About an hour ago. He called looking for Cole."

"What'd you say?"

"That he wasn't around. Out riding…"

Travis spurred his horse and was gone, his worst fears aligning like the disparate elements of a nightmare you know is coming. It wasn't deer season. Poachers don't cut fence line, they slip under. You cut a fence when you need to get an ATV in or out. When you need to leave fast. And everybody in Santa Ynez knows where the Clays ride for pleasure.

Cole walked Slick through the canyon until they could see the light at the end of the canopy, the place where the morning sun had already warmed the dirt and the rocks and sent their warm scent into the air. Cole smiled as Slick slowed his gait, as if to enjoy it himself. Slick would walk, as he had been trained, up the steep canyon trail that lay before them.

Cole heard it clearly and knew in an instant that it was the report of a rifle, sharp and clear. It had come from his right, high above them, from the canyon wall.

He thought of everything that was important and some things that were not, some which did not seem so, but were. He thought of Dustin and understood, in that instant, that he would be the only permanent mark Cole would leave, the only piece of eternity he had touched and he hoped that he had told him enough, and he prayed that he had and he longed to talk to him in that very moment; to tell him all that he now finally knew but had not seen for so very long; he thought also of the child he had never seen or known but whom he might see and know much sooner than he had imagined, and he wondered what he would say; he thought of Sam and her eyes, mostly her eyes, and their light and the joy that shone through them as if a window to a perfect heart, which was good beyond all measure, and better than he deserved;

he thought about her body and how he loved always its touch and its smell and its shape and its warmth and how it fit against and on and over his own, always, as if they had been created by God together, as a pair, only to be separated at birth and then allowed to conjoin for a short moment in time before they would be united for good; and he thought about Zaca, the land, its wholeness and its integrity, its timelessness and generosity, the time it had allowed within its crevices and folds, privy to its secrets, to its own special joy and pain, its perennial rebirth, its struggle; finally, he thought of Slick who had always been honest as the best horses are; Slick who was steady in that very moment as Cole flinched and buckled and dropped the reins and then fell as Slick side-stepped gently to avoid him and then stopped and became still and lowered his head to pull grass from between two stones, not because he didn't care, but because he had done for his friend all that God had given him command to do and so it was left to him to return to his nature, as it is with all things.

Travis reined back hard and slid to a stop from a full gallop. He knew immediately. The wound and volume of blood seeping through rocks beneath Cole's head left no doubt. He covered his face with his shirt and remounted and rode hard up the canyon trail, then to the north, toward the broken fence line.

He reined up when he saw the ATV on its side, the handlebars twisted, the fuel tank broken and leaking. He dismounted and walked around a stand of oak. Tommy Kyel held his nephew in a headlock as he drove his face into the fender of Hammer's truck.

"You little bitch! Coulda killed me runnin' into me like that. Damn it to hell!"

"Wish he had. Save me the trouble." Travis stepped from behind the oaks.

Tommy startled and lifted Hammer's pistol. He pointed it at Travis briefly, then lowered it to Hammer's temple.

"You take one step and I'm going to blow his brain pan all over the hood of this truck."

"Your call. But either way you're going down, Tommy. I just left my brother. You're going to burn, just a question of how."

"Bullshit. I'm driving this piece of shit off the ranch and ain't nothing you can do."

"Then what? You think you're going to skate on this? Your brother might. I'm sure he put you up to this. He may skate. Him, Ross. All of 'em. But you? No way. Might as well take them down with you."

Travis saw that Tommy's left pant leg was soaked in blood, his leg fractured. His speech was now slurred and uneven.

"What in hell you thinking? You think you can threaten Frank? He's goin' just stand down?" He dragged Hammer closer to the truck's door. "I know what you're doin'. I ain't say'n another word. I'm driving off this ranch now. You follow, you do shit, he's dead."

He pushed Hammer into the truck, pistol to his head.

Travis watched as Tommy started the truck and slowly bounced over uneven terrain toward his escape.

There are moments, moments of stress and mayhem and violence, when choices are literally ones of life and death, when the pulse slows and clarity comes; as if, in those moments, God gives the will and the calm to act. For Travis, this was one such moment.

He walked deliberately back to the ATV and pulled the rifle from a canvas sheath strapped to the rear roll bar; the one Tommy had used to kill Cole, the one he had, in his haste, forgotten to remove. Travis stepped to the high ground above the wreckage of the ATV and sighted the truck through the rifle's high-powered scope.

A .223 cartridge fired from a Remington 700 takes less than a tenth of a second to carry a hundred yards. But to Travis it felt like an eternity; a lifetime between the moment he felt the trigger give way to the even pull of his index finger to the moment the back window of Hammer's truck exploded in a plume of shattered glass and final resolution.

"That's for you, big brother."

He lowered the rifle and watched as the truck rolled slowly to the left and into the barbed wire fence. It came to rest thirty feet from the section that had been cut. Travis walked to the truck and helped Hammer out, then retrieved the pistol from the cab and used his gloved hand to discharge three bullets from its chamber.

Epilogue.
One Year After Cole's Death

———————◇———————

The FBI had taken great interest in the briefing Jack Callson provided after Cole's death. The Bureau, along with law enforcement in Santa Barbara County, had been frustrated by the slap on the wrist Frank Kyel had received in the first prosecution—even more so by his early parole for "good behavior." With the information Jack had provided, they relaunched their investigation and confirmed that Frank Kyel had an undeclared controlling interest in Decker D farms, which, it turns out, had already leased hundreds of acres across the country. As Cole had suspected, it was not about pot: It was about laundering profits from his trade in contraband.

The key witness proved to be Frank's longtime friend Dennis Fonton. The feds quickly made a case against Fonton for securities fraud and tax evasion based on his undeclared interests in Decker D and a number of other companies, one of which was publicly traded. Looking at a return to prison on a second bounce, he turned on Frank. Unfortunately for Frank, Fonton was intimately familiar with Frank's ongoing enterprises having been, in effect, his "chief operating officer" while Frank was in prison. As Cole had suspected, Frank had never left the business. In exchange for his cooperation, Fonton got a reduced sentence in a minimum-security prison. Frank didn't. He was sentenced to thirty-five years in maximum security on charges ranging from drug and human trafficking to money laundering and fraud.

Frank Kyel was never charged with Cole's murder. The case for Frank's involvement in Tommy's crime was strong, but circumstantial. Prosecutors believed that Tommy's own motive to kill Cole might well be enough for "reasonable doubt" about Frank ordering the hit. Travis told the family it didn't matter. "If Frank Kyel ever draws a breath of free air, he'll be dead before he exhales."

Firston Capital withdrew the notice of foreclosure to avoid any linkage with a controversy that might jeopardize the initial public offering of their stock and severed their relationship with Vallin Ross. Their IPO went off without a hitch and valued the company at over three billion dollars. It didn't hurt that the stock was rated a "strong buy" by the New York financial elite. Cable news even helped with a well-timed puff piece on "Moss Becker: Real Estate's Rising Star." Prescott severed any connection to Firston by paying off its loan to Arroyo de Zaca with proceeds from Cole's life insurance policy.

The Santa Barbara County DA declined to prosecute Travis for the death of Tommy Kyel. The fact that the pistol in Tommy's possession at the time of his death had been fired buttressed Travis's claim of self-defense.

Cole's murder burned a painful hole into the hearts of all who remained behind. But they moved on. And they did so, at least in part, on the strength of the edifice Cole had created by word and deed.

Cole had revised his will shortly after he and Sam married. His directives were simple: The liquid assets of his estate were to be used to retire any debt then owed by the ranch. He left the remainder of his cash assets to Sam in trust for her maintenance and support and for the maintenance, support, and education of his "direct descendants." At the time, that meant Dustin, though he and Sam had hoped to add a child of their own. He left his half interest in Zaca to those same descendants in a trust administered by Travis; that trust would expire, as had Cole's, on Dustin's thirtieth birthday. Sam would enjoy a life estate on the ranch with a perpetual lease for her wine operations.

His final directive concerned Slick. He was to be turned out in his favorite pasture, with his favorite mare, and never saddled again.

Cole left a handwritten letter to Dustin.

When you read this I will be, in the words of another, "in a far, far better place." Not that I didn't enjoy the ride on Zaca during the time I had. And with you. Indeed, there is no question that you were, and are, the most important and treasured piece of the time I was allotted. The only permanent mark we make is through our progeny—you and the children and grandchildren you will someday leave behind.

Would that I were smart enough to say all the things I should have said already, that need to be said now. I am not. Suffice it to say that I believe in you, in your essential goodness and strength, and pray that you will call upon both as you ride the trail God lays before you. I cannot tell you it will be easy. Indeed, I can tell you it won't. As the modern world spins farther and farther away from its true center, the challenges will only intensify. God does not promise us a life that is easy or fair. But remember that in every challenge you face, God gives you an opportunity to make of your life what you would have it be. The ancients, whom I am fond of quoting, believed that it is in adversity that we find the opportunity to seek virtue and to live it.

I know that this is easier said than done. I struggled. I did not always get it right. Nor will you. But we are defined by the struggle, by the journey, by how close we come, by perseverance. By faith.

And what are the loadstars, the guardrails by which we stay the course? That is, at the end of it all, the most important question. If I knew "the" answer, I would have told you long ago. I can only give you now my best guess. It seems, as I write this, far simpler than ever I imagined: your faith in God and your understanding of His word, your family, your neighbors, and friends; your innate sense of the right—the right answer, the right course. The Greek word is 'logos'—the word, the center of things; order in a way that works and pleases Him.

And then there is the ranch. The world will tell you that ranching is an anachronism, that it is out of step with the times, a grossly inefficient allocation of resources, time and energy; that you would be better off selling and investing the proceeds. They may be right. You would live easier if you sell. But I'm not sure you'd live better. You will have to decide for yourself. I can only tell you that I came to a different conclusion. In a world in which the values we hold seem destined to collapse, I found in our land something permanent and real, something I could hold on to with a sort of metaphysical certitude, as if, as Richard Weaver once wrote, "a bulwark against a culture spinning out of control."

I hope this makes some sense to you or will someday in the future. I loved you unconditionally. I still do. Dad.

On a sunny morning in June, the grass on Zaca had largely turned. A light breeze lifted it in checkered patterns of fading green and gold. Marisa and Prescott, now in the twilight of their own lives, sat on the *hacienda*'s porch with Travis and Sam.

Sam held a baby fast asleep. She had given birth eight months and three days after Cole's death. Neither had known she was pregnant. She named him Colter Wyatt Clay but refused to let anyone call him junior. He would, like his father, be his own man. She lived in the main house and managed the burgeoning wine business, which now eclipsed the ranch's cattle revenue. But she never planted vineyard. She purchased her grapes from the many vineyards that now dominated the Santa Ynez Valley. They held the prime pasture for cattle grazing. She was sure Cole would have preferred it that way.

Dustin spent the school year in Los Angeles and his summers on the ranch with Sam. Jessica had long since resigned herself to the fact that Dustin was "his father's son" and raised no objections to the arrangement. She had even come to see some value in the "cowboy" culture he had so wholly absorbed. She and Sam, so very different in their natures, had found common purpose in Dustin.

Travis, now married, managed the ranch. Cole's shift to breeding replacement heifers and bulls had proved prescient. Their superior DNA brought a ready market and a steady income to the ranch. Travis and his wife also opened a coffee shop in Los Alamos called Fat Pedros. Rumor had it, they served the best coffee in the Valley.

It was the first day of Dustin's summer vacation on the ranch. He had saddled Flynn and now walked him from the barn.

"Where you off to, cowboy?" Travis asked.

"Checking fences on the south end. Carlos saw some mavericks down near a break in the fence," Dustin said as he pulled himself into the saddle.

"Don't be chasing the profits off the ranch now, *jefe*," Travis smiled.

Carlos emerged from the barn and mounted his buckskin. Now in his mid-sixties, he moved a bit slower but still carried his weight. After Cole passed, Sam had asked him when he expected to quit the ranch. His answer had pleased her: "*Justo despues de plantarme debajo.*"

"You need some help?" Sam asked Dustin.

"Nah, we got this," he said.

Dustin waved and they turned and walked out down a sandy trail that had been carved by cattle walking south. As they did, a grey SUV pulled in and stopped near the porch.

Clive Westgate rolled down his window. "I thought I'd come by and give you this myself."

Travis stepped off the porch as Clive handed him an envelope through his open window. It had a Professional Rodeo Cowboy Association return.

"Committee finally concluded their investigation. Found neither you nor Cole at fault in that wreck. Your father sent in a sworn statement before he died. Said you guys didn't know a damn thing. So well, that's it I guess. Your eligibility's restored if you still want to compete."

Travis looked at the envelope. "I'd have to think on that."

He looked to the south pasture. He could just make out Dustin and Carlos cresting the high point that drops to the south end.

Clive followed his eyes across the pasture. "I thought you guys were doing vineyard."

Travis turned back to Clive and shook his head. "No, sir. Clays run cattle. Five generations." He watched as Dustin and Carlos disappeared from view. "Six, I guess."

When they reached the sandy knoll overlooking the entire Valley to the east, Dustin reined up and dismounted. Carlos stayed in the saddle and watched.

The headstone Prescott had commissioned now stood next to Elliot's in the same grey limestone.

COLTER WYATT CLAY
1992—2021

Lord, give us an unconquered and upright heart, which no unworthy purpose may tempt aside.

—THOMAS AQUINAS

After a moment, Dustin remounted and pushed his horse down the steep slope to the southeast fence line, Carlos following. The fence had been broken by a fallen oak. Three calves grazed lazily on the Zaca side.

Dustin watched.

"What'd you think?" Carlos said finally.

"Too much ear," Dustin replied.

He walked his horse to the mavericks and gently pushed them back through the opening in the broken fence and dismounted. He pulled a pair of wire cutters from his saddle bag and looked back to Carlos.

"You gonna help?"

Carlos shook his head. "You got this, *jefe*."

THE END

Author's Note

————————— ◇ —————————

The story at the heart of *Santa Ynez* occurred to me on a bumpy transatlantic flight from New York City to Budapest, Hungary, in 1990. I was working for Time Warner at the time doing cable deals in newly opened Eastern European countries. Secretly, I would have preferred to be working for Warner Brothers. I have always loved stories and the creative processes that fuel their telling in film or fiction. The idea for *Santa Ynez* gestated in the back of my mind for the next thirty years. In the interceding years I moved to Santa Ynez, California, took up cattle ranching, and got to know the cowboys and farmers who live along California's Central Coast. I was struck immediately by the anomaly of men and women living much as they have for the last two hundred years while sandwiched between two of America's most "modern" cities, Los Angeles and San Francisco. What started as a simple tale of contemporary cowboys became a broader exploration of the conflict between traditional lifestyles and the various forces of modernity. While the story and its characters are entirely fictional, both are informed by the ranchers and farmers I have come to know in Santa Ynez. While by no means homogeneous in their politics or perspectives, more often than not, they are united by the core set of values I attempt to elucidate in this novel. Of course, not every reader will share the views of characters in this story. Enough that we should better understand and respect that such perspectives exist, and that they are sincerely and thoughtfully held.

Acknowledgments

◇

My first and most important acknowledgment is to the good citizens of Santa Ynez (and to today's cowboys and farmers everywhere) whose character, strength and values form an important foundation for the increasingly unstable edifice of twenty-first century America. Where the book falls short, I take full responsibility; where it works, I must share the credit with them and many more.

My wife Hayley Firestone suffered through every draft of this work offering patient and always insightful advice. My friend Peter McBreen offered less patient but equally insightful advice to an early draft (wholly rewritten). Peter Quinn was an early writing mentor who set the bar high with his own monumental works of fiction. Many thanks also to my editor and publishing partner Gail Kearns, whose team had to reteach me the arcane rules of English grammar and more.

Last, I must acknowledge my sons, Conor and Austin, who remain the inspiration for all that I do and who, in their own lives, model the intelligence, wit, and moral strength I attempted to capture in the book's "sons"—Cole and Travis Clay.

D ennis Roy Patrick served on the White House staff of President Ronald Reagan and later as Chairman of the Federal Communications Commission in Washington D.C. After government service, he served as a senior executive with Time Warner, AOL and National Geographic. He now lives on the family's cattle ranch in Santa Ynez, California, with his wife Hayley Firestone.